MARBLE RANGE

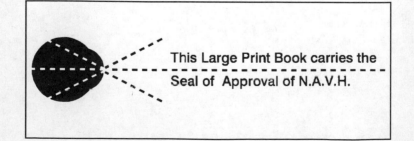

This Large Print Book carries the
Seal of Approval of N.A.V.H.

MARBLE RANGE

A WESTERN STORY

ROBERT J. HORTON

THORNDIKE PRESS
A part of Gale, Cengage Learning

GALE
CENGAGE Learning®

Detroit • New York • San Francisco • New Haven, Conn • Waterville, Maine • London

GALE
CENGAGE Learning®

LIBRARY OF CONGRESS CATALOGING-IN-PUBLICATION DATA

Horton, Robert J., 1881-1934.
  Marble ranch : a western story / by Robert J. Horton.
    pages ; cm. — (Thorndike Press large print western)
  ISBN-13: 978-1-4104-5133-0 (hardcover)
  ISBN-10: 1-4104-5133-X (hardcover)
  1. Large type books. I. Title.
PS3515.O745M37 2012
813'.52—dc23   2012021850

Published in 2012 by arrangement with Golden West Literary Agency

MARBLE RANGE

CHAPTER ONE

Spring had flung her mantle of green over Marble range. The trees along the river in the south were in full leaf. The colors lay in broad stripes against the sides of Marble Dome. Cattle by the thousands grazed peacefully in this vast domain. The sun, climbing steadily in the east, shed a golden glory over the land.

Yet all was not serene on the range. Midway between the butte and the river a strange scene was being enacted. A lone rider was coming westward at a fast pace, and some distance behind him several other riders were pushing their horses, evidently in a strenuous effort to overtake him. Now the first rider would spurt and widen the distance between himself and the others; again he would slacken his pace as if to encourage them, only to spurt again and leave them farther behind.

All this was being observed by a man who

sat his horse at the edge of the trees some distance ahead of the oncoming horsemen. His face wore a puzzled expression as he watched the drama being enacted before him. He was a middle-aged man, gray at the temples, keen-eyed, who sat his mount with something of a soldierly bearing. At first glance he would give one an impression of suppressed authority. A little exclamation escaped his lips as a puff of smoke drifted above the pursuers. Even as the echo of the gun's report reached his ears, he saw the man ahead lean low over his horse's neck and spurt so that it seemed as if the animal flew over the ground. There was no need for more shots for in a twinkling the pursuers were left hopelessly behind.

The man murmured aloud in admiration, drew his gun, and spurred his horse out as the rider approached. The rider saw him immediately and eased his pace. Shortly he came up to the other and drew rein. After a quizzical inspection he spoke: "I wonder what that outfit back there think they're doing . . . playing a game?"

"It looked to me as if you were playing the game," was the reply. "And no wonder, with *that* horse."

"I was experimenting," said the stranger. "I wanted to see if they'd fire at me. Well, they did. Now shooting at a man you don't know who he might be, and shooting at him you don't know what for is right ornery, uncertain business."

"They are members of my outfit," the other observed, noting that this rider was dark, young — about twenty-eight, he surmised — well set up, good-looking, and dressed more or less elegantly and expensively for the range country. Silver shone from his bridle and saddle; the butt plates of his gun were pearl.

"And what outfit is this?" the rider asked.

"This is the Half Diamond M," was the answer, "commonly called the Half Diamond."

At this point the pursuing cavalcade arrived, led by a burly, glowering, red-faced individual with a stubble of red beard and small beady eyes of a mean brown.

"What was your play in pullin' that stunt back there?" he demanded of the stranger. "What you doin' on this range?"

"I was just taking my morning exercise," was the tantalizing reply.

"You mean you was runnin' away because you was sizin' up the cattle down there," the leader accused harshly.

At this point the man who had met the stranger broke in. "I'll attend to this,

Hayes," he said sharply. "Go back up where you belong."

The man called Hayes frowned darkly, made as if to reply, met the other's eyes, whirled his horse, and led his men away, leaving a string of curses in his wake.

"Nice amiable disposition," the stranger observed. "You'd think he'd be better natured on a fresh, spring morning like this, even if he does look like a train robber."

"That was Big Bill Hayes, foreman of this ranch," said the other sternly, "and he had a right to ask you what you're doing on this range. Now I'm asking it."

The stranger nodded and his eyes narrowed slightly. "What right you got to ask it?" he inquired coolly.

"I'm Henry Manley, manager of this ranch, and who are you?"

"I'm Bannister, manager of this horse."

"Yes?" Manley was surveying the new arrival closely and was frowning. "That's a smart answer. As long as you're on the Half Diamond, I've a right to ask you questions, and I want to know where you're from and what you're doing here."

"I don't aim to be smart," Bannister drawled. "It's just the way you ask your questions that I don't exactly take to. And just because I happen to be here is no

10

reason why I should tell you where I'm from, is it? And I've the right to refuse to answer your questions, for that matter, but just to be sociable I'll answer one of 'em. I'm here because I want to find out the way to the next or nearest town."

"Well, then, why did you run away from Hayes and his men?"

"I didn't like the way they came racing down there," was Bannister's reply. "They acted plumb hostile. How'd I know but what something had been pulled off around here and I might be mistaken for somebody else? Caution isn't a bad thing to carry up your sleeve."

Manley considered this and slowly his frown faded. "You crossed the river at the upper ford, I suppose," he conjectured.

"I crossed it up by that butte," said Bannister, pointing toward Marble Dome.

"Are you a cowhand?" Manley asked curiously.

"Well . . . ," — Bannister eyed the other speculatively — "I suppose yes," he conceded. "I was born on the range."

"You don't exactly talk like a cowhand," Manley observed. "And you're sure and certain not dressed like one. Maybe you're one of Cromer's men."

Bannister shook his head. "I don't know

11

who Cromer is, and I'm not one of his men. And I had just enough schooling when I was younger to learn how to talk halfway decent, and I've kept at it. I've got tougher clothes than these in the pack on the back of my saddle."

Manley appeared impressed. "Maybe you're looking for a job," he ventured. "I'll confess you look capable."

"I am that," Bannister agreed.

"Well, we need men on the Half Diamond," said Manley in a very civil tone. "If you want a job, I'll give it to you."

"I can't take you up this morning," said Bannister. "You see day after tomorrow is Decoration Day and I just have to be in town on holidays. Sometimes I edge in when it isn't a holiday. I suppose there's a town around here somewhere?"

"Twenty miles west," Manley grumbled. "Come along and I'll put you on the road."

They proceeded westward along the river, Bannister looking straight ahead and maintaining a silence that Manley, for some reason he could not determine, did not feel inclined to break. The Half Diamond manager studied him with a puzzled frown on his face. There was something about the man's personality that stirred his interest. He didn't believe the holiday story for a minute. He doubted that Bannister was a cowhand, yet he wasn't sure. He had caught a peculiar flash in the man's eyes two or three times that belied his age. And he was certainly unacquainted with the country. Why had he flirted with Hayes and his men? Why?

"Would you mind telling me who owns this ranch?" Bannister asked suddenly. "It's just curiosity on my part."

"The Half Diamond is owned by Florence Marble," Manley replied tartly. "This is the famous Marble property. Maybe you've heard of it?" He paused, but Bannister shook his head. "Well, it's the greatest ranch on the north range," Manley went on, somewhat nettled. "And it's a mighty good outfit to work for," he added hopefully. He needed men badly, and, if Bannister knew anything at all about working cattle, he could use him. Anyway, stockmen didn't usually ask for recommendations when hiring men.

"I reckon so," was Bannister's comment.

Manley shrugged. "I was wondering," he said, "since you got up here rather early and spick-and-span . . . I was wondering where you were last night."

"I was down at the Macy ranch," Bannister volunteered. "And old man Macy

13

didn't ask any questions, either. I just rode in and he said . . . 'Howdy, stranger. Put up your horse and I'll tell the cook to slap down an extra plate in the bunkhouse.' He was plumb hospitable."

"Oh, Macy's all right," said Manley in a patronizing tone. "He's one of the old school of stockmen. Big place, too. Didn't he tell you the way to town?"

"Said to ride north and get the road, which is how I got in here," Bannister replied crisply.

They came to some bottom lands where there were hay fields, then pastures where thoroughbred horses grazed, then grain fields, a garden, and finally a windbreak of towering cottonwoods. Bannister glimpsed some of the ranch buildings through the trees, and by their size and number realized that this was truly a big outfit.

Manley led him around the windbreak, thus avoiding the buildings, and up a road to a high bench. He pointed westward.

"Prairie City is twenty miles west on this road," he said.

"Fair enough," said Bannister with a flashing smile. "I'll push along. Much obliged."

Manley stared after him both irritated and puzzled. That remark about Macy not asking questions and his hospitality had been a dig at him. Moreover Manley was a man who didn't like mysteries, and Bannister was a mystery. *I bet he's one of Cromer's men just the same,* he mused as Bannister disappeared in a racing cloud of dust. He turned back toward the ranch buildings.

Two hours later Bannister rode into Prairie City. He walked his horse down the dusty street, looking for the livery. A man in shirt sleeves with a gleaming star on his vest saw him from the doorway of a resort, looked after him, stepped out into the street, and walked after him.

Bannister found the livery behind the hotel, put up his horse, and went into the hotel to engage a room. While he was at the desk, the man of the star strolled in, observing him closely. When Bannister had gone upstairs with the clerk to be shown his room, the deputy stepped quickly to the desk and scanned the name inscribed upon the register.

Then he went out hurriedly.

CHAPTER TWO

Prairie City was the terminus of a branch railroad from the transcontinental line in the south. It was also the county seat and as such was naturally the headquarters of the sheriff. On this noonday, Sheriff Campbell sat in the front office of the jail with a pipe in his mouth, leaning back in his swivel chair with his feet on his desk. Business was slack.

The door opened and the deputy, a large, round-faced man, came in.

"Chief," he said with some excitement, "a man rode in town just now who is a dead ringer for The Maverick."

The sheriff was unperturbed. He was a short, stout man who looked like anything but an officer of the law. He removed the pipe from his mouth slowly.

"Van Note," he drawled, "if I was to follow up all your hunches about men who look like The Maverick, I wouldn't have time to do anything else. You get a suspect on an average of once a week."

"But this is the best hunch I've had," Deputy Van Note protested. "He's got the height, he's got the build, he's got the eyes, the cleft in the chin, the dark complexion, and packs a pearl-handled gun."

"Yes," drawled Campbell, "and you've suspected every man with a pearl-handled gun that's shown up here in the last two years."

"I wish you'd take a look at him," said Van Note desperately. "I bet he'll start you guessing, anyway. And it's natural he'd show up here now if he's planning a job in this section. There'll be money floating like water here the next few days, for they're coming in from all directions to celebrate. The bank will be loaded with cash, the safe of every resort in town will be crammed, why, it's as good a time for a clean-up as the Fourth of July."

"No doubt," said the sheriff. "But we've had a lot of holidays here and there's never been a clean-up yet. What's more, I'm going to swear in half a dozen special deputies or more. I'll have a man stationed in every place in town where big amounts of cash are handled."

"All right," said the deputy, "but I'm going to keep an eye on this fellow who signs himself as Bob Bannister."

"I'm going over to the hotel to eat," said Campbell. "Do you suppose he'll get his dinner there?"

"He's registered there, so I suppose he will," Van Note grumbled.

"Then I'll take a look at him," the sheriff announced, rising. "I reckon I'll be able to pick him out."

It so happened that Bannister did go into the hotel dining room for his dinner. He didn't for a moment suspect the identity of the short, stout man who sat down at his table and, after ordering, engaged him in casual conversation. He, in turn, made some inquiries — where were the squarest games run, and the like. The sheriff went back to his office with a satisfied look on his face.

"Listen, Van Note," he said pleasantly. "I sat across from your man at dinner. I talked with him. The fellow is a gambler for he asked me about games and such. Another thing, he talks good. His eyes haven't got the hard look that the eyes of a man like The Maverick would have. A man who's a killer and a bandit shows it in his eyes first off. What's more, he's neat. Do you think an outlaw like The Maverick would take the trouble to keep his fingernails clean? He

18

doesn't wear the kind of clothes this Maverick would have on. A man like The Maverick is tough, and he shows it in his look, his talk, his actions, and his clothes. I've seen enough of that stamp to know."

Although the holiday was two days away, Prairie City was already making carnival. Festoons and streamers of bunting were everywhere; flags fluttered in the breeze. The town was rapidly filling with celebrants. Dust spirals on the roads and on the plain signaled the coming of men from the ranches, stockmen with their families in buckboards and spring wagons, cowpunchers on their ponies. Morning and evening incoming trains were crowded. For Prairie City was the only town of any size within a radius of nearly a hundred miles.

Bannister looked the town over in the afternoon and brought up at The Three Feathers, the largest resort in the place. It was a large room with bar, gaming tables, dance floor, and lunch counter combined. It was here that he chose to try his luck, first at the roulette wheel, and then at stud poker. His winnings were negligible, for he did not indulge in high play. The high play, as he knew, would be in the private rooms in the rear. At midnight he went to the hotel.

As he idled about the lobby, smoking a

cigarette before going to bed, a poster on the wall caught his eye. It read:

BUY NOW BEFORE IT IS TOO LATE!
Only a Limited Amount of Stock in the
MARBLE DOME
LAND AND IRRIGATION CO.
Will be offered to the Public
$10.00 a Share at Par.
REMEMBER!
A soon as the stock issue is sold —
which will be soon — it is certain to
increase in value.
A dollar invested NOW in this great
enterprise, which means so much to this
community, will be worth TWO within six
months!
INVEST NOW AND YOU WON'T
REPENT!
Send subscriptions to or call at the office
of
MARBLE DOME LAND AND
IRRIGATION CO.,
PRAIRIE CITY, OR
ON THE PROPERTY
AT MARBLE DOME.

SYDNEY CROMER, President

Bannister studied this notice with a

puzzled frown on his face. Cromer? Where had he heard that name before? After a time he had it. Manley of the Half Diamond had asked him that morning if he was one of Cromer's men. He turned to the sleepy clerk.

"Where is this irrigation project?" he asked.

The clerk roused himself. "Up north of the Half Diamond," he answered, yawning. "Named after the big butte on the Marble range. Lots of work up there if you're looking for work." Then he again relaxed in his chair.

The information did not particularly interest Bannister. It was merely the name that caused him to put the query. He threw away his cigarette and went upstairs to bed.

In the morning after breakfast he strolled to the livery to take a look at his horse. As he reached the barn door, he heard the thunder of hoofs. He turned and saw a magnificent bay come dashing around from the street. He had to leap aside to avoid the animal as it came to a rearing stop at the very door of the barn. The rider was out of the saddle in a twinkling, laughing joyously, his eyes shining as he flung up a hand in greeting. He was young, this rider, not more than eighteen, tall, well-built, good-looking.

21

Bannister frowned. "You came near running me down," he accused. He could hardly keep his eyes off the horse.

The youth laughed again as the liveryman came hurrying for his mount. "Mike wouldn't run anybody down," he said. "You needn't have moved." Then to the liveryman: "Take good care of him. I'll be in till day after tomorrow."

With a wave of his hand to Bannister, he was off.

"Who's that kid?" Bannister asked the liveryman.

"That's Howard Marble," the man drawled. "He's pretty wild now, but he'll get tamed in time."

"Marble?" said Bannister. "Any relation to the Half Diamond outfit?"

"He's Florence Marble's cousin. Lives out there. She thinks he's the candy, sugarcoated, an' lets him run. That's what the matter with him. But he's a good kid at that."

Bannister had been struck by the boy's riding, his free and easy manner, his sparkling eyes and display of exuberant youth. Perhaps in Howard Marble he saw the reflection of what he had been himself at eighteen. "He'll break his neck or kill his horse one of these days," he muttered to himself.

The premature celebration got under way full blast early in the morning. And this day Bannister played for high stakes. Deputy Van Note followed him from resort to resort, still suspicious. As he had no regular assignment, but was simply ordered to keep looking around, he could do this. He saw Bannister go into several games and emerge a substantial winner.

About 10:00 that night Bannister saw Howard Marble again. It was in The Three Feathers. The youth was at the bar and it was all too evident that he had been imbibing freely of the vile liquor that was being served. His face was flushed, his voice loud but lacking the wholesome ring that had characterized it that morning. Also hc was engaged in some sort of argument with a short, dark-faced man, beady-eyed, thin, who spoke with a queer accent.

"If you haven't got enough room at this bar, go somewhere else," the boy was saying.

Bannister moved down toward them.

"Where would you say I go?" the little man purred.

"You can go to blazes for all of me!" Howard cried.

Bannister could see the bartender shaking his head vigorously at the youth. He moved closer.

"You are the brave little boy," the dark-faced man said. "But you need go home now. You no talk good. Maybe you go somewhere else."

His eyes had narrowed, and Bannister saw that several wanted to interfere, but something held them back. What was this? Were they going to stand around and see the youth get into trouble because they were afraid of the small man? And Bannister's experienced eye showed him that this man had been drinking, too. But he was holding his liquor well, so far as outward appearances indicated.

"Why, you confounded little shrimp, if you don't move, I'll pick you up an' carry you out!" sang the boy, rising to his full height of six feet.

"Ah!" The little man's tone might have signified delight. "The bold little baby-face." Quick as a cat he leaped and struck Howard across the mouth. His laugh was like a cold wind suddenly sweeping into the place.

Howard's face went red, then white. His hand darted to his gun. But instantly it was grasped in a grip of iron as Bannister

24

leaped. In that moment — the wink of an eye — Bannister's gun was at his hip, leveled at the little man whose eyes darted fire into his own.

"Take your hand off that gun!" Bannister's words rang like a clash of steel through that room of silence.

The beady, black eyes narrowed to slits through which blue fire gleamed. "It is good," came the soft, purring voice. "You save the life of the baby-face and I save yours." His hand came away from his weapon and he turned to the bar with another laugh.

"You come with me," said Bannister sternly to the boy. And still gripping him with his left hand he led him out of the place.

Howard went willingly enough. He was sobered by the swift-moving drama in which he had participated. He realized that the man at his side had probably saved his life. For the little man's move had been lightning fast. He hadn't seen this new-found friend draw at all. His gun had appeared in his hand as if by magic. He looked at Bannister respectfully.

"Listen, kid," said Bannister, "drunk or sober, I take it that you've got more nerve than brains. That fellow in there is a gunman. I can tell the breed a mile away. You missed a slug of hot lead by a hair."

"I'm sure much obliged to you, old-timer," said the boy contritely.

"In that case I wish you'd show it by going to the hotel, or wherever you're stopping, and stay there till tomorrow," said Bannister. "And tomorrow I'd like to have a talk with you."

"Well . . . all right," said Howard reluctantly. "I'll go up to the hotel."

Bannister walked with him up the street to see that he kept his word.

Five minutes later Deputy Van Note was pounding his fist on the sheriff's desk. "What'd I tell you!" he cried. "That fellow who calls himself Bannister may be a gambler, which I happen to know he is. But he's a whole lot more than that. I came into The Three Feathers a few minutes back just in time to see it. He threw his gun on Le Beck . . . on Le Beck, understand . . . and he beat him to the draw."

CHAPTER THREE

In a town such as Prairie City, where horses furnish the common means of transportation, the liveryman is pretty apt to know just about everything as to what's going on and who's who. Therefore, on this occasion, Bannister turned to this source of information. He described the appearance of the small man in The Three Feathers with whom Howard Marble had clashed, but before he had finished the liveryman interrupted him: "That's Le Beck," he said with conviction. "He's bad medicine. Gunfighter. Sure-fire shot. Killer, too. Comes from up north somewhere an' don't get in here often or stay long. But he's been here over a week this time."

"Where does he get that accent from?" asked Bannister.

"French-Canadian, I guess," was the reply. "People don't know much about him, except that he's dynamite an' a good *hom-*

27

bre to stay away from."

Bannister walked out of the barn with a thoughtful look on his face. From what little he had heard, when he entered the resort, he surmised that the trouble between Howard and the gunman had arisen over crowding at the bar. He didn't doubt at all but that Le Beck would have shot down the youth. He would have permitted the boy to draw first and then claimed self-defense. Plain as a mule's ears. The thought in Bannister's mind now was whether Le Beck would go gunning for him. He smiled grimly and walked down to The Three Feathers.

Le Beck still was in the place. He was playing cards. He paid no attention whatsoever to Bannister, although almost everyone else in the place did. Bannister resumed his play. Only once during the rest of the night did their glances clash. And on this occasion Bannister read the message in Le Beck's eyes and caught its significance. But he shot a message back. Men of the lightning draw talk with their eyes.

Bannister played until dawn, and as a result he didn't get up until noon. When he went downstairs, he found Howard Marble in the dining room. The boy smiled and beckoned to him to come to his table. Bannister hung his hat on a hook and sat down.

"You look better this morning, or noon, than you did last night," Bannister observed.

"Had a good sleep," said Howard. "The stuff they peddle out around here is great stuff to sleep on."

"Well, that's all it's good for then," Bannister grunted. He gave his order and leaned his elbows on the table. "I'm no veteran now," he said slowly, "but when I was your age I was just as big a fool as you are . . . almost. I guess that's why I took a fancy to you. But you're playing the wrong end of the game."

Howard appeared to resent this. "I was a little excited," he said with a slight frown. "The white stuff hits me quick."

"Then quit it," said Bannister sharply. "Oh, don't worry, I'm not going to lecture you, although I have the right. Do you know who it was you ran up against last night?" The boy nodded. "Well, then, I reckon you know he'd have bored you quick as light. Did you know who he was when you got tangled up with him?"

"I . . . I found out who he was this morning," replied the youth sheepishly.

"Then you know the chance you took, and every man in there was scared to interfere or even say a word out loud, so. . . ."

29

"But you wasn't," Howard interrupted with a look of admiration. "Everybody's talking about you, Mister Bannister."

Bannister shook his head impatiently. "No, I wasn't," he said with some irritation. "I can throw a gun and make no bones about it. But if I'd been drinking, you'd be in Kingdom Come this minute. I started out when I was a kid the same way you've been going. I was hitting up the hard stuff and every time I slipped a few under my belt I thought I had the world by the ears. Then one night I got mixed up just about the same as you did last night, only not with so fast a man. It ended in gun play. He missed me, but I didn't miss him. Call it luck, for that's what it was. But it left me so cold sober that I was like a cake of ice. It's mighty serious business, Howard, killing a man. I've been through a lot since then and I've never taken a drink."

The boy was listening, wide-eyed, impressed.

"Now, Marble," Bannister went on, "you owe me something. You. . . ."

"I know I do!" Howard exclaimed.

"Don't interrupt me," said Bannister crisply. "As I say, you owe me something, and I want you to pay it. It's a promise. I want you to promise me that you'll never

30

take another drink."

The youth sat silently, fingering his fork and looking at the tablecloth, while Bannister watched him keenly. Then he looked up and smiled. "All right, Mister Bannister," he said in a clear, sincere voice, "I give you my promise."

Bannister held out a hand. "A mighty good night's work for you and for me," he said earnestly.

"I wish we had somebody like you out at the ranch," said Howard as Bannister turned to his meal.

Bannister made no reply to this. Howard remained until the meal was finished and then they went into the lobby. Deputy Van Note was there waiting. He approached Bannister, and Howard moved away.

"Ah, Bannister," said Van Note, "the sheriff wants to see you a minute."

Instantly Bannister's expression changed. His eyes became hard and cold, his jaw squared. He looked at Van Note almost insolently. "I suppose it's that business last night," he said icily. "I reckon you know if I hadn't butted in that kid would be ready to plant. Has he had Le Beck on the carpet, too?" Bannister sneered openly.

"I . . . I don't think it's that business last night," the deputy said, appearing ill at ease.

"I don't know exactly. . . ."

"Does this sheriff know where I'm stopping?" Bannister interrupted sharply.

"Why, yes . . . of course. He sent me here."

"Then tell him if he wants to see me, I'll be here in the lobby for half an hour," said Bannister. And he deliberately turned his back on the deputy.

Van Note hesitated, wet his lips, and then hurried out. Bannister rolled a cigarette and went into the little sitting room, telling Howard he had an appointment.

Sheriff Campbell came, somewhat flustered, his face red, but with eyes that snapped angrily. He was not accustomed to going to see people; people came to see him. In this case, well, it was a delicate and perhaps extraordinarily important matter. If this man should indeed prove to be The Maverick, he was the most dangerous man who ever came to Prairie City. In which case it would be well to humor him — until he was safely behind bars.

Bannister rose, stepped to the doorway leading into the lobby. He beckoned to Campbell, who came in, looking at him queerly. Now Campbell might not look like a sheriff, but he had all the qualifications just the same. He was not a coward; he was fearless; moreover, he had brains and tact

— the latter characteristic being lacking in most officers of the law.

"You wanted to see me, Sheriff?" said Bannister coldly. "I suppose it's something about that business last night. I don't reckon it's against the law in this town to pull a gun to save a life." His tone swam in sarcasm.

"Well, sit down," said the sheriff. And, when they were seated: "This has nothing to do with last night. I want to know who you are, and what you are, and where you're from." In his hand he held a folded paper.

"My name is Bob Bannister," replied Bannister evenly. "I'm whatever I want to be . . . a free lance, free to gamble, to punch cattle, and a number of other things. I'm from parts south of here. I've been wandering since I was eighteen."

"It's the number of other things I'm interested in," said the sheriff, looking at him closely. "Your answer is vague. Where did you work last?"

"Down in Big Falls," said Bannister easily. "I played every joint in town."

"And where were you before that?" the sheriff demanded.

Bannister's gaze hardened. "I don't see any reason why I should answer a lot of questions unless I know why. Or, are you questioning all visitors today? If you are, you've got some job on your hands."

The sheriff held out the paper. "Read that," he said sharply.

Bannister read:

WANTED!
$5000 REWARD
This sum is offered for the apprehension
of the man who calls himself
THE MAVERICK
He is six foot one or two; dark complexion; black eyes and hair; cleft in chin; about 28 to 30 years; packs a pearl-handled gun; always works alone; very fast with his gun. Wanted for MURDER and ROBBERY, by Big Falls county authorities. Communicate with JOHN WILLS, Sheriff, Big Falls, Mont.

Bannister handed the paper back to the sheriff. His eyes narrowed and he turned them fully on the official.

"So that's the reason you are so interested in me," he said sarcastically. "How does it come, Sheriff, that you bother with a mere suspect when there is a man with a record a mile long right here in town who you know . . . I mean Le Beck?"

"Le Beck is covered," the sheriff snapped out. "I have nothing on him."

"Have you anything on me?" asked Bannister sharply.

The sheriff frowned and bit his lip. It was a hard question to answer. "You refuse to tell me your history," he said finally. His questioning was getting nowhere and he realized it to his great discomfiture.

"Do I have to tell you my history just because you've got some kind of a hazy idea that I might be this Maverick person?" Bannister demanded harshly.

The sheriff's frown deepened and his eyes flashed.

"Listen!" The word fairly cracked in the little room. Bannister leaned over and tapped the sheriff on the knee. "You think maybe I might be The Maverick," he said in a low, vibrant voice, "but before you go any further, you make sure."

Sheriff Campbell went back to his office, baffled.

Bannister found his way back to the tables. There was an abandon about Bannister's method of play that bewildered old-time professionals. They couldn't put their finger on him, so to speak. He played stud poker exclusively. At times he discarded the science of the game and tried to draw out

— and almost invariably his luck would bring him a needed card. He was caught bluffing just enough that when one was sure he was bluffing he wasn't. Always it cost plenty of money to see his hole card. He won steadily.

He did not see Howard Marble again that day. He sauntered about after supper among the throngs and late in the evening looked in at a dance. A great pavilion had been erected for the rodeo the preceding fall and this was being used. The dance was in full swing, the floor crowded with couples. As the music stopped, people everywhere turned to look at him. The incident of the night before — a small matter in his own eyes — had assumed great magnitude in the eyes of the male celebrants, who had enlarged on the story and passed it along to the women. This attention irritated him and he turned to go, but at that moment Howard Marble pushed through the crowd and grasped his arm.

"Come on, Mister Bannister, I want you to meet my cousin," said the youth eagerly.

"What!" Bannister exclaimed. "Me to go into that mob. Not on your life! No, son, it can't be done . . . no use urging me."

"All right, come along," said Howard.

They went out and Howard started

around the pavilion. Bannister objected.

"We're just going back to this refreshment place," pleaded Howard. "Wouldn't you do me that much of a favor?"

Bannister knew that by his cousin Howard meant Florence Marble, owner of the Half Diamond. He finally gave way to his curiosity and consented. Howard left him at a corner table and hurried away. When he returned, Bannister stood up, drawing a long breath.

"This is my cousin, Florence Marble," said Howard.

Bannister didn't hear the rest. He took the girl's hand, hardly knowing he did so, and mumbled something — he couldn't afterward remember what. For Florence Marble was a girl of the type he most admired. She wasn't slim or short; she came up to his shoulder and more; beautifully formed; hazel eyes; cheeks where roses bloomed; red lips and full; and a mass of hair the color of burnished copper. Yet there was something about her that suggested she could ride and shoot and was well able to take care of herself. She was Western with a slight veneer of Eastern manner, obtained at some distant school likely. In which surmise he was correct.

"Howard's been telling me some wonderful things about you, Mister Bannister," she said in a voice that fell pleasantly on the ear as the boy moved away. "He says you're a terror with your gun and saved his life. Anyway, I want to thank you for what you did last night. I think a lot of Howard. He's all I've got." She kept looking at him searchingly as she said this.

Bannister was not embarrassed; he was merely surprised that the owner of the great Half Diamond should turn out to be so young and so good to look at. He shook his head and laughed. "I'm not a terror of any kind, Miss Marble . . . unless they prod me," he returned, smiling. "I just stepped in because the business looked too one-sided. I don't know as this Le Beck would have gone the limit."

"From what I hear, I believe he would," said Florence Marble seriously. "I'm always worried when Howard's in town. He's wild, and all that, but he's good at heart. But the thing I want to thank you most for is the promise you got from him. I've been trying to get such a promise for two years and he's always talked me out of it. If he'll only keep it."

"I think he will," said Bannister. "There's good stuff in that boy. It's sticking out all over him. He's just got to get his bearings,

38

that's all. From the way he hesitated before he promised me, and the way he looked at me when he did, I'd be willing to bet my horse and saddle that he'll keep it."

"I hope so," said Florence, brightening. "Mister Bannister. . . ."

"Please leave off that mister," he said with another smile. "I'm not used to it. I'm just plain Bannister."

"All right, Bannister. I was wondering if you maybe were not the man who rode through our place the other morning. Manley was telling me of a rider and you seem to fit the description. You act like a man who would sass him back."

"I'm that same *hombre.*" Bannister chuckled.

"Manley said you were a cowman, that he offered you a job, and you turned him down flat," she said, smiling.

"I told him I had to have my holiday," Bannister explained. "Well, I'm having it."

"So I see." She nodded. "I need men on the ranch, Bannister. I need one particular kind of a man for a . . . well, a special job. No, I know what you're thinking about. I don't want a gunman, although I was born in the West and I don't object to a man being handy with his gun. The kind of man I want is hard to find. I depend on Manley to hire my men . . . him and Hayes . . . but Manley's brains are, well, so much machinery. Would you take a special job with the Half Diamond at good pay without knowing what it is going to be? For I haven't time to tell you now."

Bannister's smile flashed instantly. "Now you've got me, Miss Marble. All my life I've been taking chances. I've gone out of my way to take a chance. If you'd said you wanted to hire me as a cowhand, or a horse breaker, or anything else, I'd have said no. But you've got me in the dark and guessing. I'll take the chance."

"It may be more of a chance than you think," she warned. "And I'm taking a chance, too, because I know nothing about you except your name. We'll go out to the ranch in the morning. Oh, here comes Mister Cromer. He'll want me to dance."

Bannister saw a man of medium height, muscular, square-jawed, thin-lipped, with a close-clipped, bristly tan mustache. He was moving rapidly toward them, a slight frown on his face. Then Bannister saw his eyes at close range. He didn't like them.

So this is the irrigation man, he said to himself.

"All right, Miss Marble, let's go," said

Cromer in a proprietary voice as he came up.

Bannister did not like the voice, either.

"Just a minute, Mister Cromer," said Florence, "meet Mister Bannister."

"Howdy," said Cromer with a jerky nod. He did not extend his hand.

Bannister saw a slight frown on Florence Marble's face, as if she resented Cromer's slight, and he was gratified. "How's the ditch digging?" he said pleasantly to Cromer. There was no reply, and Florence smiled back as they moved away.

As Bannister went down the outside steps from the refreshment stall, a figure stole away into the shadows behind the pavilion.

CHAPTER FOUR

When Florence Marble asked Bannister to take a special job without knowing what it was to be, she really had him guessing as he had said. And when she hinted that he might be taking more chances than he thought, it clinched his acceptance. Now, as he strolled down the street toward The Three Feathers, he pondered the matter in an effort to come to some conclusion. But the more he thought about the matter, the more mysterious it became. He finally decided that she was worried about something, that she wanted him to find out something for her. Well, he was sure of one thing; he was ready and willing to do anything she might ask of him. He let it go at that.

The Three Feathers resort, of course, was thronged. The tables, wheels, and other gaming layouts were going full blast. The bar was lined three deep. Bannister had an eye out for Le Beck, but his gaze was arrested, not by the notorious gunman, but by Howard Marble, who was playing at one of the poker tables. So here was another form of dissipation that the boy had learned.

Bannister moved over near his table in time to see Howard lose a large pot after having shoved in a tall stack of chips. It was plain that the youth was not a piker. And, as Bannister watched the game, it was also plain that Howard had to have good cards to win. The finer, scientific points of stud were not within his ken apparently. Then, too, it was evident that the game was plentifully supplied with house boosters.

Howard's stack of checks steadily dwindled until but a few reds remained. He spoke to the dealer. "Can you put somebody in this chair to hold it until I go get some more money?" he asked.

The man in the slot nodded to a man behind Howard. The boy got up and the man slipped into the chair to hold it against his return. The dealer passed him a moderate stack of checks.

Howard pushed past Bannister without seeing him and picked his way out of the place with Bannister following. Up the street they went until the dance pavilion was reached. Bannister was of the opinion that

Howard was going to get money from Florence Marble. But this did not prove to be the case. He saw the youth coming out of the hall again with Cromer behind him. He barely had time to step into the shadows when they were down the steps.

"Here's two hundred," he heard Cromer say. "You can give me the slip tomorrow."

Bannister followed Howard down the street, thinking rapidly. Cromer was getting a hold on the boy by lending him money. Why? Because, indirectly, he might be getting a hold on Florence, also, or, at least he was cementing the boy on his side in any project he might have in mind. He remembered the look the man had given him and scowled darkly. He increased his pace and overtook the youth in front of the hotel.

"Wait a minute, Howard."

The youth whirled, startled, but when he saw who it was, he smiled and greeted Bannister cheerfully enough.

"Come in the hotel. I want to ask you something," said Bannister, taking him by the arm. He led him through the lobby into the deserted parlor, where a lamp burned on the table.

They sat in chairs, facing each other, and the boy was frowning. Evidently he suspected something unpleasant and did not

44

relish the interview.

"Howard, how much do you owe Cromer?" Bannister asked pointblank.

The boy's eyes widened and the red gathered in his cheeks. Then his eyes flashed. "What do you know about it?" he demanded hotly. "Are you spying on me?"

"No, I'm not spying on you," said Bannister, shaking his head. "Or, you can call it spying if you want. But I saw him give you that two hundred you've got in your pocket now, and I've got a good reason for asking you how much you owe him. Don't you think you can trust me? How much?"

"Eleven hundred dollars," said Howard slowly, as if he were awed at the size of the amount for the first time. Bannister reached into a pocket and drew forth a roll of yellowbacks. He counted out eleven of the bills and put them in Howard's hand.

"Now go pay him and get your slips," he said as he put the roll back in his pocket. "And that two hundred in your pocket is from me."

The red returned to Howard's cheeks. "Why, I can't do that, Bannister. I can't take your money. Cromer understands it's just a loan. I've a small herd, and, when I ship in the fall, I can pay him back."

"Well, you can pay me back, can't you?"

45

demanded Bannister.

"I know, but . . . it's different. And you mightn't be around, or something."

"Don't worry, I'll be around," Bannister assured him. "Your cousin offered me a job out at the Half Diamond tonight and I took it. That's why I want you to pay off Cromer. I don't think it's a good idea to be borrowing big money outside the outfit."

"You're coming out?" exclaimed Howard, his eyes sparkling.

"I won't come if you don't pay off Cromer," said Bannister. "And I'm going to hang around up there and hear what he's got to say. I reckon, Howard, he just wants you to keep on owing him that money for some reason or other. Did you ever think of that?"

The boy's brows gathered in a frown. "Might be," he muttered. "He started it by offering me a stake in the first place."

"Well, pay him off," said Bannister, rising, "and then you're not under obligation to him. And don't think you're cutting me short any, for I've got more juicy kale than you could throw a rope around."

"Maybe I hadn't better take this two hundred," said Howard in indecision. "I'll only go back into the game."

"Try the wheel a while," Bannister suggested. "Maybe it'll change your luck."

Bannister was again in the shadows at the side of the pavilion when Howard came out with Cromer.

"You're a fast worker," Cromer was saying. "You must be betting them high to lose that two hundred so quick. Don't go too swift. Well, how much do you want now?"

"I'm settling," replied Howard. "Here's eleven hundred. Give me the slips."

There was a pause of several moments. Then came an easy laugh from Cromer. Bannister, listening in the shadows, didn't like the laugh any more than he liked the voice.

"Oh, a winning, eh?" said Cromer. "You must have bet the works. Well, that's all right, boy. There's no hurry about paying that money back. Don't worry. Everything's all right and you can have more if you need it. Go back and play some more. Play your luck while you've got it."

"No," said Howard stoutly. "I want to settle and I want to settle now. Here's the money, and give me my slips, and we're even."

The boy's tone evidently convinced Cromer, for he took out his wallet and handed over the I.O.U. slips, accepting the bills in return. "Remember," he said artfully, "any time you're short, you know." His tone was as good as a hint and a promise.

When Cromer had gone, Howard found Bannister and pressed the $200 in his hand. "I'm going in to dance," he announced. "Maybe I'll have better luck on the Fourth of July."

Bannister went back down the street and for the second time that night a figure darted from the shadows behind him.

That's number one, Cromer, he mused to himself.

There was no more gambling for Bannister this night. Having accepted a post with Florence Marble, he decided that his holiday was over. He had had enough of the smoke-laden air, the smell of kerosene lamps, the curses and shouts and ribald laughter, the clink of glasses, the crowding, the tense moments of card play. He looked up at the stars and breathed deeply, for Bannister was essentially a man of the open.

There were groups of men in the street indulging in drunken arguments, groups of stockmen talking cattle, groups of cowpunchers from different outfits renewing acquaintanceships. Bannister wondered, idly, if any of the Half Diamond outfit were in town. But if there were, he would not know them.

He walked on down the street, past the flaming resorts and cafés, past the improvised hot dog stands, past the darkened blacksmith shop to the edge of town. Here the street became a road that pierced the cottonwoods along the stream and led eastward toward Marble Dome and the Half Diamond. He paused, breathing in the pure, cool air, baring his head to the whispering prairie breeze. Suddenly his sixth sense of the open, that subtle instinct that is the heritage of those who are range-born and reared, caused him to whirl about.

Four figures had stolen from the shadows. He had just time to whip out his gun when they were upon him. He swung the heavy barrel about and felt it crack upon a head or jaw. One of the figures went down. He reeled from a blow on the head from behind, but in staggering forward he struck out with all his strength with his left and another of the attackers sank to the ground.

He turned on the two behind, swinging his gun viciously. They stepped back and he leaped after them. Recovered from the blow he had received, he was quick as a cat, fighting like a tiger there in the semidarkness. His gun found its mark again. There was a cry of pain, a curse, and a man sank to his knees. But the other two men on the ground had recovered.

Bannister edged away, trying to keep them in front of him. Two of them dashed at him from either side. He met the one on the right with his left and a smash of his gun. It settled him. The other ducked and kicked.

"You dog!" gritted Bannister through his teeth. He was on the man in an instant like a fury, beating him down, laying him out cold.

He whirled, and there was a burst of flame almost in his face. Then his own gun spurted fire, and his assailant tumbled backward, fell, and lay still. The other two were on their feet, and the trio, apparently not knowing who had been shot, took to their heels, with Bannister dashing after them.

They dodged behind the buildings up the street, with Bannister keeping well in the shadow behind them. He saw them pause and enter a small building by the rear door. When he reached it, the door was closed and locked.

He stood for some moments, breathing hard. Then he sheathed his weapon and walked around through a narrow space between the buildings to the front of the building the trio had entered. Emblazoned on the wide window in gilt letters was the sign:

MARBLE DOME LAND AND
IRRIGATION COMPANY

Bannister smiled grimly. *A hunch is as good as a mile,* he mused, *and I had the best of them by a mile at the start.*

There was no light in the front office. The men were in a back room. *I'll take a look at that fellow up the road,* he decided.

He hurried back down the street to its end and reached the scene of the encounter. There he lighted matches and looked about. But he could find no trace of the man who had gone down at the flash of his gun. He had either walked or crawled away.

"Just nicked him," said Bannister aloud in disgust.

CHAPTER FIVE

Bannister walked hurriedly up the street, proceeding straight to The Three Feathers. He strolled about the tables until he caught sight of the man he was looking for — Le Beck. Then he left the place. He hadn't believed anyway that the gunman had been one of the four who had attacked him. Le Beck would do his fighting with his six-shooter, and, being a gunfighter of caliber, Bannister doubted if he would attack a man in the dark from behind.

Having satisfied himself that Le Beck had not been involved, he strolled back to the hotel. He had no interest in the trio secreted in the rear of Cromer's irrigation office. They were merely tools; he might never see any of them again. It was what their attack signified that interested Bannister. That they had acted under orders from Cromer was all too apparent by the fact that they sought refuge in his office. It was plain that Cromer didn't want him around. He had doubtless instructed the quartet to beat him up and tell him to clear out. The man who had fired the shot had either been frightened or had deliberately disobeyed orders.

Bannister decided that Cromer had learned — from Florence Marble, or from some other source — that he was taking a job with the Half Diamond. It was possible that he suspected that Howard Marble had obtained the $1,100 from Bannister. He must have learned of Bannister's championing Howard's cause the night before. In any event, Cromer didn't want him around, and that was enough to cause Bannister to stay, even if it were raining bullets.

After a quiet smoke in the lobby, Bannister went upstairs to bed. The strains of the pavilion orchestra came to him on the cool breeze that stirred his window curtains. He dropped off to sleep, thinking of Florence Marble and a pair of hazel eyes under a wealth of copper-colored hair. A whim, perhaps — for Bannister had never considered himself romantic.

Everyone, it seemed, except himself, slept late the next morning. The dance hadn't broken up until dawn; the games had run all night, and some of them might keep on running all day. He ate breakfast in a deserted dining room. Then he looked in on his horse and strolled down the street. There was a chance Cromer might be about. It was after 8:00.

When he reached the office of the Marble Dome Land and Irrigation Company, he found his surmise well-founded. Cromer was inside at his desk. Bannister opened the door and entered.

"Good-morning, Mister Cromer," he said cheerfully. Cromer looked up quickly and his customary expectant look immediately changed to a frown.

" 'Morning," he said. "Was there . . . something?"

"Why, yes," said Bannister amiably, settling himself in a chair across the desk. "I wanted to see you about something."

"I'm very busy," said Cromer gruffly. "I've got to get up to the project."

"Just so." Bannister nodded. "Up and doing. You have to be, I reckon."

Cromer compressed his lips, shook his head impatiently, and then looked at Bannister keenly. "What do you want to see me about?"

"Well, this irrigation business," said Bannister, taking out tobacco and papers. "I made some money at the tables yesterday

54

and they tell me your stock is a good proposition."

Cromer's face was a kaleidoscope of conflicting emotions. Surprise and suspicion vied for the most prominent expression. "Where'd you hear that?" he asked, though the question sounded foolish.

"Oh, here and there," Bannister replied easily. "You know how you hear things . . . bits of conversation, comments, and one thing and another when you're playing cards and there's a crowd around. As I say, I made a little money yesterday, and . . . it's ten dollars a share, isn't it?"

Cromer nodded without speaking.

"Well," said Bannister, wrinkling his brows as if he had just made up his mind, "I'll take a hundred shares."

He drew a roll of bills from a pocket and took off ten $100 notes while Cromer sat and stared, wet his lips, looked out of the window, back at the bills on his desk, and then at Bannister. His expression had changed to one of commingled perplexity and uncertainty. Was Bannister really investing, or . . . ?

"There's the thousand, Mister Cromer," said Bannister in a pleasant voice. "Just make out the certificate and I'll be going so you can attend to your work."

55

Cromer hesitated a few moments, frowning, and then he jerked open a drawer and took out a pad of ornate certificates adorned with a big red seal. He wrote rapidly on the top certificate, impressed the seal with the company die, and pushed it across to Bannister, who, in turn, pushed across the bills.

Bannister then folded the certificate, placed it in the inside pocket of his coat, rose, and went to the door.

"Good morning, Mister Cromer," he said with a slight bow, and went out the door, leaving Cromer staring after him. This time Cromer's expression was blank.

It was 11:00 A.M. when Bannister saw Howard and Florence Marble in the hotel lobby. The girl was dressed in a natty riding habit and wore the regulation stockman's hat. In this attire she appeared even more attractive than the night before. Her face lit up with pleasure as she saw Bannister.

"We've just had breakfast," she said with a light laugh. "Isn't this wild dissipation, Bannister? We'll start for the ranch right away, if you're ready."

"All set," said Bannister. "C'mon, Howard, we'll get the horses."

In a few minutes they were in the saddle. They rode down the street, past the spot at its end where Bannister had been attacked the night before, crossed the creek, and emerged from the trees upon the broad plain that stretched eastward, flat as a billiard table, to the purple bulwarks of Marble Dome.

Howard led, setting the pace at an easy lope, and Florence and Bannister rode side-by-side. It was a world of gold. Golden grasses waving in the light breeze, golden sunshine flooding all, dust spirals spun golden pinwheels on the road ahead. And the air was scented with that elusive, intangible aroma of the prairie in late spring.

Bannister lost no time in putting a query to Florence that had been in his mind since the night before. "Cromer must have a big job on his hands up there?"

When she looked at him, he saw a slight cloud flit across her face. "It's a big project," she said.

"I was wondering," he continued, "if you told Cromer that I was going to work for you."

Her glance now was one of surprise. "Of course not," she said emphatically. "I never discuss ranch business with outsiders. I was rather piqued at the way Mister Cromer acknowledged the introduction to you last night, Bannister. I told him so, too."

Bannister laughed. That was enough to

set Cromer against him even if he didn't know about the job. "I don't think the irrigation king likes me," he said. "He didn't look too pleasant when he saw us talking together out there in that refreshment place."

"He has a great deal on his mind," said Florence. "He's the head, heart, and soul of the irrigation company, and he works night and day. Sometimes he forgets his manners when he's trying to think of two or three things at once."

Bannister was silent after this. He saw that whatever Florence Marble might think of Cromer personally, she had respect for the work he was doing and his ability. He must not tread on treacherous ground.

"I bought a thousand dollars' worth of his stock this morning," he vouchsafed.

"You did?" Her eyes brightened. "Well, I believe you made a good investment, Bannister. I'm in for fifty thousand."

Bannister whistled softly. "If it doubles in value in six months, as he says it will in his notices, I'd say you've made a good investment, Miss Marble," he told her with one of his flashing smiles. But he was thinking just the same.

"I hope so," she returned with a suggestion of that same cloud flitting across her face.

"Will you put me in my place if I say something you don't like, Miss Florence?" he asked in mock seriousness.

"Why . . . what . . . ?"

"I just wanted to say that you sure look like ready money in that riding habit under that big hat," he declared firmly.

The roses in her cheeks bloomed a bit more violently. "Your duties with the Half Diamond do not include flattering its mistress," she reproved.

"Why, that isn't flattery," he objected. "That's just making an . . . an observation. You can't blame a man for observing when you put up such a good appearance. You see, it's your own fault."

She looked at him in surprise. Here was a man supposed to be a cowhand who dealt in logic, who evidently was skilled in repartee. He looked mighty good himself this morning, she reflected. But she had no desire to engage in a friendly argument or banter when she wasn't altogether sure of her ground.

"Bannister," she said seriously, "you may be running into more or less danger out here. I'm giving you a hard job. I expect there will be men on the ranch who will resent your being there. My foreman is a tough *hombre* and he won't like it at all."

Bannister's face was all but beaming. "Dear lady," he said cheerfully, "danger and I are old bosom friends. We've ridden together, slept together, and played together for years. We go hand in hand, like babes in the woods." He leaned toward her as they loped along the dusty road, and his eyes lost their smile. "When I go into danger, Miss Florence," he said slowly, "I carry danger with me."

She turned her gaze away. She had seen something in the eyes of this man of mystery that almost frightened her. Perhaps she had gone too far in engaging him. He might prove to be more of a thunderbolt than she wished. At this point, Howard turned in his saddle and beckoned to them. Then he let out his bay.

Florence and Bannister spurred their horses and they raced along the road at tremendous speed. All three were magnificently mounted. Bannister could not keep the admiration out of his eyes as he noted how well Florence Marble rode. She had been a girl of the cities the night before, but here was a girl of the West — riding as one born to the saddle, wisps of hair flying from under her stockman's hat, her cheeks flushed, her eyes sparkling like diamonds with joyous excitement.

After the spurt she looked at Bannister with a flashing smile. "You ride well," she bantered.

A pained look came to his face. "That isn't fair, Miss Florence," he complained. "You took those very same words right out of my mouth, although I was going to make it stronger. And I want to say that your duties as employer do not include flattery."

She laughed merrily at this. No dub, this new hand of hers, she thought to herself. Well, all the better. If there was one thing she needed, it was a man with brains as well as a gun. The thought of the gun sobered her. She had told him she didn't want to hire a gunman but she realized, with a thrill, that she had done so, just the same.

There was little more said as they raced along toward Marble Dome and the Half Diamond. They gradually increased their pace until, when they reached the river, crossed at the main ford, and rode down the bottom lands — a different route than that taken by Bannister on his way to town — they were pushing their horses for all they were worth.

They brought up in the courtyard, hemmed in by ranch buildings, in a cloud of dust. Bannister was off his horse in a twinkling to help Florence down. But he was not quick enough. She slipped out of her saddle even as her mount was coming to a rearing halt.

"Howard will look after you," she said as she started for the house.

As they started for the barn with the horses, a small, weazened man with drooping black mustaches, his hat pulled low over his right eye, came out of the bunkhouse and looked intently at Bannister — so intently, in fact, that it drew Bannister's attention.

"Who's that fellow out there?" he asked Howard when they were in the barn.

The boy scowled. "That's Link," he replied. "One of Big Bill Hayes's pets. I don't know what he's doing in here today."

"Probably in to see that everybody got back from town all right," Bannister observed dryly. "You know, Howard, I've got a funny mind. I should have been a fortune-teller or something. That's the first man I'm going to have trouble with on this ranch."

CHAPTER SIX

The Half Diamond was bounded on the west and partly on the south by Indian River. This river flowed down from the mountains in the north, picking its course due south some sixty-odd miles, then curving gracefully and hurrying eastward to a point below Marble Dome, where it turned again and continued southward. The main ranch buildings were located in the bottoms, under the lee of the bench land, midway between the western and the eastern bends of the river. Thousands of Half Diamond cattle ranged northward and eastward about the Dome.

Florence Marble's father, Will Marble, and his young wife had been the first settlers in this north range country. They had come in the 'Eighties and prosperity had smiled upon them with the sanction of favorable winters. Their small herd increased rapidly. They built slowly, but sturdily. They acquired thousands of acres of land and controlled a vast domain of range. They saw others come; Macy and Berlinger were the first south of the river and their nearest neighbors. They saw Prairie City born and watched it grow. Will Marble waxed rich — richer than many suspected — and his thoroughbred herds became the talk of the north range.

When Florence, their only child, was sixteen years old the mother died. This loss had a depressing effect on Will Marble. He became listless, careless. Four years later, when Florence was away to school in the East, he was thrown from a horse and suffered injuries that resulted in his death before she could get back to the ranch. He left his vast property to his daughter. Almost at the same time, the widow of Will Marble's brother died, leaving Howard alone, and at Florence's insistence he came to live on the Half Diamond. With keen foresight, Florence made the foreman, Henry Manley, manager. He was not like the ordinary ranch foreman, for he was quieter and accustomed to think well before acting. She then made the range boss, big, burly Bill Hayes — known as Big Bill — foreman. Hayes was the direct opposite of Manley. But he knew men and cows and could run both. Also, he was the one choice left to her. She undertook the supervision of the accounting and financing herself, with the assistance of George French, who virtually owned the First State Bank of Prairie City, an old friend of her father's. But French had died the year before, throwing her more than ever upon her own resources. But the Half Diamond continued to prosper and was prospering when Bannister rode up from the south and into the tangle of adventure.

When Bannister and Howard had finished attending to their horses, they repaired to the bunkhouse, Bannister carrying his slicker pack, which had been tied on the rear of his saddle. There he changed into light corduroy trousers, dark sateen shirt, a large, dark-blue handkerchief, knotted behind in the cowboy fashion, but retained his splendid boots and the fine hat he had worn in town. He buckled on his gun belt with the man Link looking on, his beady, black eyes glistening curiously, and, Bannister thought, suspiciously.

"How come you're in today?" Howard demanded of Link.

"Message to Manley from Big Bill," was the reply — short, almost insolent.

"What about?" Howard asked.

"Didn't open the envelope," Link answered, his eyes on Bannister.

"Well, when are you going back?" Howard queried sharply.

Link looked at him then. "After supper," he snapped.

"Well, it's two hours an' more before supper," said Howard, his brows knitting angrily at the other's tone, "so I guess you can make the cook wagon up by the Dome by then. You might as well trail along."

"I missed dinner," said Link. This time his words fairly dripped insolence. "I reckon I'll wait for grub."

"Why, you. . . ." Howard hurled himself toward the smaller man on the bunk. But Link's right hand winked at his side and the heavy barrel of his gun knocked Howard's blow aside. The youth winced with pain as Link leaped, cat-like, from the bunk.

"Put that gun away!"

It was Bannister, and Link whirled to find himself covered. He looked steadfastly at Bannister for some ten seconds and then slipped his weapon into its holster. Howard was standing, white-faced, his eyes snapping with hot anger.

"You'd . . . pull a gun on me?" he said slowly. "Get off this ranch! Get off this ranch, you hear me?"

"I'm workin' under Big Bill," said Link in

a smooth voice. He was cool, unruffled. His manner was almost that of a man who was pleased. "Big Bill hired me an' Big Bill fires me . . . if I'm fired."

"That's right," said Bannister, to Howard's amazement. "Link has it right. He's working for this Big Bill, after all. Did Big Bill tell you to stay in for supper?"

Link's eyes glinted coldly. "What's it to you?" he demanded.

"Just this much," Bannister replied sternly. "If you are going to stay in to supper, you're going to take that gun belt off and hang it with your saddle."

"Yes?" purred Link. "Your orders?"

"Sure as tootin'," said Bannister with a nod. "And prepared to see that they're carried out. Your tongue is too slippery and your right hand too well greased for safety." He shook his head at Howard as the boy made as if to speak.

"Maybe you're right," said Link, endowing his words with a double meaning. "Maybe I better go back to the Dome. When the boy made his rush, I happened to remember that I ain't a fist fighter."

He turned on his heel and went out. Howard bent his puzzled gaze at Bannister. But Bannister merely frowned and put up his gun. Before there could be any talk, a

67

Chinese cook appeared in the open doorway of the bunkhouse.

"Lunch leady," he announced.

"Let's go," said Howard. He led the way to the wash bench on the little back porch of the ranch house.

When they were using the roller towels, Bannister spoke in a low tone. "You know I told you I've got a funny mind, Howard. Now this Link person. Whatever he brought in didn't amount to much, I reckon. I've got a dead-sure feeling that Big Bill knows everything that went on in town, and knew this morning that I was coming out here. A man would have had plenty of time to ride back after midnight and tell him. He sent Link down to keep his eyes and ears open. Now why should Big Bill be so interested in me?"

"That's no question to ask a man with an empty stomach," said Howard. "But there may be some sense in what you say."

"If you get my point," said Bannister dryly, "you'll understand why I didn't want you to run Link off the ranch."

Florence Marble had a dainty, but sustaining lunch ready for them, and they sat down at table in the big dining room with its heavy beams and dark-stained wainscoting. They talked but little, and their conversation hung on the celebration in town. As they rose after the meal, Henry Manley, the ranch manager, appeared in the doorway leading to the huge living room and the office in the front of the house.

He nodded to Florence and looked at Bannister. "So you changed your mind, I hear," he said, his gaze shifting from Bannister to Florence and back again. "Well, we can use you. I think I'll send you up north of the Dome to try you out."

"Bannister won't be taking any definite place until I've talked with him," Florence told the manager. "And that'll be after supper."

Manley made a poor show of concealing his surprise, but acquiesced gracefully. His bearing was so soldierly that Bannister would not have blinked an eye if he had saluted. "Of course, Miss Florence," he said in precise tones, "you hired him . . . not me. I couldn't get him."

"That was before the holiday," Bannister drawled, smiling comfortably.

"So it was," said Manley soberly. "And now, I suppose, you're good until the Fourth of July." With this he left them to go into the office. Florence followed him and Bannister went out with Howard into the courtyard. Link was nowhere in sight, nor was he in the bunkhouse or barn. They assumed he had gone.

They spent the balance of the afternoon and early evening looking over the fields in the bottoms, the breeded horses in the pasture, and the buildings. It was nearly dusk when the ranch bell struck for supper.

Manley ate with them, and now the talk was of range matters. Bannister learned that Big Bill's message had been to the effect that the beef tally had showed ten steers missing.

"I sent a man down to look over the fence along the breaks," he told Florence. "He said the fence was tight as a drum."

Neither of the cousins spoke, but Bannister saw a significant look pass between them. Manley did not refer to the matter again. They finished supper, and Manley and Howard went out, while Florence invited Bannister into the living room.

The girl sat down in an easy chair by the table. The subdued rays from the shaded lamp shone upon her hair, touching it with a darker, smoldering fire and casting highlights of shadow upon her face. Bannister was not unaware of her beauty and its changing moods. She was plainly troubled, and the look in her eyes, the slight pout of her lips, only served to enhance her loveliness.

Bannister took a chair between the table and a window. The room had been kept closed against the heat of the day and was cool.

"Bannister," said Florence slowly, "I hired you, as Manley said." She looked at him soberly.

"And now that you've hired me, Miss Florence," he said, "I'm ready to take your orders."

The troubled look deepened. "That's just it," she said. "I don't know what orders to give you."

If he was astonished, he failed to show it. "Is it something about the cattle?" he asked casually. "Too many strays, or something like that?"

"We've been losing cattle," she confessed.

"And you naturally want to know how and why," he supplemented.

"It's very strange," she said. "Up to last fall and this spring our losses were confined to hardships during the winters. Manley thinks they are being stolen. He's told me as much, but has found out nothing."

This information brought a thoughtful look to Bannister's face.

"And then. . . ." Florence hesitated. "An-

71

other . . . or one of the reasons I was anxious to have you out here is because Howard seems to have taken to you as he has never taken to any man on the ranch. He's just at the age when he needs looking after. I mean when he needs advice and companionship. He appears to have a great deal of respect for what you say. Oh, I didn't hire you to be a nurse" — she smiled in friendly fashion — "but if you can do something for Howard without it bothering you, I'd appreciate it."

"I reckon that won't be hard," Bannister assured her. He was not looking at her, but had turned his head a bit to the right. A slight rasping sound had reached his ears as she was talking. Now he felt a breath of air from the window behind him.

"And also, there's another matter on my mind. . . ."

"Just a moment, Miss Florence," he interrupted in a louder voice than he had used before. "Please excuse me for breaking in, but before we go any further there is a letter in my pack that I think you should see." While speaking, he was signaling her with his eyes and, with a hand held closely in front of him, indicating the window behind. He saw by her single alert glance at the curtained window that she understood.

72

"Do you mind if I go get it?" he asked with the slightest of nods.

"Of course not," she replied. "I'll wait for you here."

Bannister rose quickly, hurried through the dining room, and out the kitchen door. He stole to the farther end of the porch and dropped lightly to the ground. He peered around the corner of the house just in time to see a figure dart into the deep shadow of the lilac bushes near the window, which had been raised while he and Florence were talking. He drew back, and ran lightly to the courtyard. There was light shining from the bunkhouse windows. He sped on to the barn, where he saddled and bridled his horse. Then he led the animal out the rear door and left it, with reins dangling, in the cottonwoods. He hastened back to the house and entered the way he had left.

From the dining room he again signaled Florence. He put a finger to his lips, shook his head, and pointed toward the window that was being used by the eavesdropper. Then he entered the living room briskly.

"I'm sorry, Miss Florence, but I couldn't find it," he said in a tone of disappointment. "Anyway, it was a letter from the outfit I worked with last down on the Gallatin. It was a recommendation, sort of, and I thought you ought to see it. It says I'm a top hand at working cows."

The significance of his speech was not lost on the girl. "Then I guess Manley's proposal to put you on the north range is a good idea," she said, sighing as if she was glad the matter was settled. "I suppose Howard would like to go up there with you."

"I'll talk it over with him," said Bannister, who had not returned to his chair. "I think he'll go."

Florence rose. "We'll see in the morning," she said, and followed him into the dining room.

There, where they couldn't be seen, he turned quickly. "Someone was listening at the window behind me," he said in low, guarded tones. "Made the letter excuse to get out and make sure. What was the other matter? Tell me quickly. I don't think you'll have to give me any orders."

"It's the irrigation project," she whispered excitedly. "I may invest another fifty thousand. It means everything to our land here. But the other stock raisers are against it. They're planning something. I want to know what it is . . . and I want you to find out."

He looked into her eyes; serious and troubled eyes they were. "Miss Florence,

74

you've come to headquarters for help," he said. He grasped her hand for a moment and hurried out the back door, closing it softly behind him.

In a trice he was over the rail at the end of the porch and looking around the corner of the house. There was no figure beneath the window. From the lower end of the yard came the muffled sounds of a horse's hoofs. He ran for the cottonwoods behind the barn where he had left his own mount. In a space of minutes he was threading his way through the trees along the bottoms, following the trail by which he had first come to Marble range.

CHAPTER SEVEN

Bannister's ruse had worked perfectly. When he had told Florence Marble he was going for a letter, the eavesdropper had waited to make sure she remained in the room and had slipped into the bushes until he again heard Bannister's voice. He had returned to the window and then gone for his horse when they left the living room, thinking that the interview was over. Thus he had missed what Bannister considered the most important piece of work outlined by the Half Diamond owner. He had known from the start that Cromer's irrigation project was somehow to be mixed up with his activities on behalf of Florence Marble.

A hundred thousand dollars, Bannister thought as he sped out of the trees and past the horse pasture. No wonder Florence Marble was interested in any plan the other stock raisers might have that would hamper the development of the project. As yet he could not see just what benefits would accrue to the Half Diamond, save a profit on the investment. As he rounded the horse pasture, he saw a flying shadow far ahead, some distance out from the trees along the river. He put spurs to his horse and took advantage of the shadow of the trees, spurting to lessen the distance between himself and the rider ahead. It was not long before he could make out the forms of horse and rider in the starlight and he found his suspicions were correct. The man ahead was undoubtedly Link.

This explained, as he had suspected, Link's sudden decision to return to Marble Dome. He had tried to mislead them into thinking he had gone, whereas he had been hiding along the river for the purpose of spying on them after dark. Now he was going to report to Big Bill Hayes. Bannister was following him to make sure, to learn anything he could. Link's actions convinced him that Big Bill was aware that he had been hired by Florence Marble. Undoubtedly someone in town had spied on them and had taken the word to Hayes. Then Hayes had sent Link with the note about the cattle and instructions to find out what he could. This last thought brought to Bannister's mind Florence Marble's statement about the loss of cattle. It also brought to mind Big Bill Hayes's accusation the day he had arrived on Marble range, to the effect that Bannister had been looking over the cattle south of the Dome. This was not true, but it served Big Bill with an excuse for chasing him. It was quite evident that the Half Diamond foreman didn't relish the knowledge that a stranger was about, and didn't like the idea of a man coming to work on the ranch about whom he knew nothing.

At the point where the river turned southward below Marble Dome, Link swung north for the cow camp. There was a trickle of stream flowing down from the Dome bordered with willows. Link kept on the west side of this little stream, but Bannister crossed and swept up the east side, thus putting the willows between himself and Link as a partial screen.

There was still a fire near the cook wagon, and its yellowish eye gleamed steadily as the goal of the two riders. Cattle were bedded down on the plain about the Dome. Bannister saw the dark mass of the big herd that was being held east of the Dome, and, when he was a scant two hundred yards from the camp on the other side of the stream, he checked his horse and dismounted. On the ground he was well concealed by the willows. He hurried upstream afoot until he was directly opposite the fire. Here he found the willows cut away and a wide, worn trail leading across the brook. It had been dammed just below the trail to provide water for horses and the other stock.

Bannister crossed on the upper side and peered through the willows. Most of the men were already in their bedrolls, asleep on the plain after the long, strenuous hours of work. The small, bowlegged figure of Link was silhouetted against the dying flare of the flames. He had evidently turned his horse over to the night hawk and now was drinking coffee out of a huge tin cup and eating a fat sandwich. Big Bill Hayes towered over him. The cook was moving about and a trio of cowpunchers were squatting near the fire.

As he looked upon this familiar scene, Bannister saw Link and Hayes leave the fire and walk toward him. They paused halfway between the brook and the cook wagon and began to talk in low tones. Bannister strained his ears but could catch nothing but a faint mumble of their voices, except once or twice when one or the other of the two men swore. Unable to make out a word of their serious conversation he thrust his head and shoulders through the screen of willows and cupped his hands to his ears. The bank of the little stream was still soft from the overflow from the spring rains. The smooth soles of Bannister's riding boots slipped as he leaned forward more and more, and he went down on his knees, crashing among the willows, his boots rattling against pebbles and splashing in the water.

He didn't wait for what he knew would follow. As he got to his feet and leaped across the brook, he heard a startled exclamation and the jingle of spurs as Link and his companion ran toward the stream. He dashed down behind the willows on the opposite side toward where he had left his horse. He knew the pair behind him would soon find that there was no horse or steer there and dark suspicion would arise. He wanted no clash this night.

He found his horse readily enough, caught up the reins, and vaulted into the leather. Then, leaning low in the saddle, he raced down the line of willows with the speed of the wind, crossed the stream near its junction with the river, and streaked westward in the shadow of the trees for the ranch. But, even though he had been unable to make out what Link and Hayes had talked about, Bannister was satisfied that he knew.

He had discovered Link's presence at the window in time to avoid saying too much, and to prevent Florence Marble from saying too much. Therefore he knew just how much Link knew and what the henchman had to tell Big Bill. He knew, too, that this was the pair he would have trouble with on the Half Diamond. And with this conviction in mind he came to a daring decision. As Bannister had told Florence, when he went into danger, he carried danger with him. This time he intended to push the danger on ahead.

The bunkhouse was dark when he reached the ranch and put up his horse. Light shone in the house, but he didn't go in. He lighted the lamp in the bunkhouse, chose a bunk, prepared for bed, and, after blowing out the light once more, was sound asleep in a matter of minutes.

Bannister was busy at the wash bench at the lower end of the bunkhouse at dawn when he heard a querulous, thin voice, high-pitched, behind him. "Wal, I reckon you're the new hand the kid mentioned."

Bannister turned and looked out from the towel to see a slight figure, a leathery, thin face, wrinkled and lined, pale blue eyes, sparse and tawny mustaches over a wide,

81

thin-lipped mouth. Here was a typical old-timer, if he'd ever seen one. Such a character as is found on every big ranch — good hearted, brimming with reminiscences, proud, aching to show someone his innate generosity. "You hit it first time," said Bannister with a smile.

"Well, you're in luck," said the old man. "I'm Jeb White. I've been with the Half Diamond since Will Marble drove in his first herd of longhorns. That was some spell back. Nobody knows how old I am, because I don't tell 'em, an' it's none of their danged business."

"Why, you're spry as a kid, Jeb," said Bannister, grinning. "My name's Bannister. Why am I in luck?"

"What's your first name?" Jeb asked, his eyes blinking in the early sunshine.

"Bob," was the answer. "Bob Bannister."

"Wal, thet's a good name," old Jeb decided. "You bet I'm spry. You're sure goin' to find out how spry I am right *pronto.* I've got 'em ready for the fire. You an' me'll eat 'em. Nobody else is in to the home ranch just now. Trout! Thet's why you're lucky. Fresh mountain trout. I rode up an' catched 'em. Clear to the foothills, walked up- an' downstream. Thet's how spry I am. I jest got in, too. Rode 'most all night. Say, you're

82

a right well set-up young feller, you sure as shootin' are."

"Thanks," laughed Bannister. "Did you get many trout?"

"Wal, I got about all I could carry," Jeb boasted. "The water went down a foot with me haulin' 'em out. I wish the river'd dried up so's Cromer couldn't fill his prairie soup dish up there."

Bannister looked around from the cracked mirror, holding a comb in his hand. These old ones were often great sources of information. "Prairie soup dish?" he said. "What's that?"

"Wal, Cromer calls it a lake, an' I suppose thet's what it is," grumbled the old man. "Goin' to fill it up an' irrigate. All fiddlesticks. He's hooked Miss Flo an' a lot of 'em in town an' around as well as some danged Easterners . . . wal, it's all right to hook the Easterners. But I'm ag'in' the whole proposition. This is stock country. If the Lord had intended it for farms, He'd have stuck in more streams an' springs an' saw to it that there was some rain shed when it was needed. Thet's what. Now Cromer figures he's goin' to make the whole thing over. Sufferin', slimy, spittin' snakes! He'd never got those water rights an' done his dastardly promotin' if Will Marble had been alive."

"You don't like Cromer, I take it," Bannister ventured, finishing with the comb.

"No, none a-tall, an' he's right well aware of it," said Jeb with a fierce scowl. "I'm tendin' the barn here now, but when Cromer comes sneakin' around, he puts up his own hoss. I've taught him thet much. An' if he gets gay with old Uncle Jeb, I'll just naterchally fill him fuller of holes than a hunk of Swiss cheese." His bony right hand dropped to the butt of the ancient weapon at his right.

Bannister laughed again, but sobered quickly. "Can you keep a secret, Jeb?" he asked.

"I kin thet," declared the old man. "I've got a few tolerable secrets of my own, an' a lot of other people's in my head, an' none of 'em has ever leaked out yet."

"Well, Jeb, I don't take none to this Cromer, either," Bannister confessed.

"You've met him, eh? Wal, one look's enough for them as knows men." Jeb shook his head ominously. "There's something wrong with that feller. But he's tough, they say."

They had started for the cook shack around the bunkhouse when Howard came out on the back porch and called to Bannister. The youth walked briskly across the courtyard.

"Better come on in," he said, "breakfast is about ready."

Bannister saw Jeb's face cloud with disappointment. "I'm going to take breakfast with Jeb here," he told the boy. "He's got some trout and he's invited me."

"They're all ready for the fire," said Jeb in a pleading tone. Then, bristling: "I reckon you know I kin cook, Howard, an' I detest eatin' alone."

"Oh, all right," said Howard, catching Bannister's eye. "Was you out ridin' last night? I missed you?"

"I went out to make sure that Link had left," Bannister evaded. "He went back to Marble Dome all right."

"An' he'd better stay there," Howard growled. "Well, I'll see you after breakfast."

"Was Link down here last night?" Jeb asked as he and his guest entered the cook shack.

"Yes," Bannister replied. "Snooping around, clear as I could see."

"Wal, thet's him every time," said Jeb, busying himself at the stove. "He was born a snooper an' he's cultivated snoopin' ever since. Snake-Eye is what I call him. He lays off me, too. An' Big Bill does the same. If

85

they get gay around me, I'd just as lief bury a few hot slugs in their gizzards as look at 'em. Snake-Eye's doin' some travelin' lately. I met him ridin' like a prairie fire for up north toward the soup dish come daylight this mornin'."

This casual bit of information was seized upon by Bannister as important. Why should Link be hurrying up to Cromer's irrigation project?

"Say, Jeb," he said suddenly, "is there any kind of a town up there by the soup dish?"

"They're buildin' one," was the answer. "Got a bunch of shacks up, a lot of tents, an' some frame buildings. Oh, thet Cromer's makin' it look like something, far as it goes. Says he's goin' to get a spur from the railroad in an' sech. Goin to make farmers outta us. Huh! I'd chop both my hands off before I'd take hold of a pair of plow handles."

"How far is it up there?" Bannister asked.

" 'Bout twenty miles," Jeb answered. "Too close. Too danged close. Don't go near that outfit or you'll get polluted."

Bannister smiled as he sat down at the table to await the breakfast of trout, biscuits, potatoes, and coffee that was nearly ready. A trip up to the project would be his next move, he decided. "Have they named this town?" he queried curiously.

Old Jeb looked at him fiercely and swore. "Thet's the worst part of it," he declared shrilly. "He had the gall to call it Marble!"

CHAPTER EIGHT

Florence Marble sent for Bannister an hour after breakfast. He went around to the front porch at Howard's suggestion and she invited him into the living room.

"You rode away last night," she said without preliminaries. "Did you learn who was listening at the window?"

"It was that man Link," he said shortly. "I followed him to make sure he went back to the Dome. He had a private talk with Big Bill Hayes up there. Miss Florence, Hayes doesn't like the idea of my being on this ranch a little bit. I'd like to know more about him."

"Very well, sit down," she said, taking a chair herself. "I know that Hayes has worked for us a long time. Father kept him on the north range mostly. We call the range north to the irrigation project line the north range, and refer to the range about the Dome and east of it merely as the Dome. Hayes is a rough character . . . a hard man. But when Father died, he was the only choice I had left for foreman after I made Manley manager. As for Link . . . I don't like him. He's a gunfighter, but not as bad as that man Le Beck whom Howard had trouble with. I've been on the point of telling Manley to discharge Link, but I know it would cause a clash between Manley and Hayes, and I want to avoid that."

Bannister nodded. "That's where I'll come in," he said.

She gave him a quick glance. "Bannister," she said in a serious voice, "I don't want gun play on this ranch if there is any possible way to avoid it. I know something is wrong here, but I don't know just what it is. It is like the wind whispering in the trees. You can imagine words but you cannot connect them. And, what is more serious, the Half Diamond threatens to become a buffer between the irrigation project north of here and the other ranches to the south and east."

"You think there is going to be fighting?" asked Bannister.

"Neither faction can cross Marble range," said Florence firmly. "No, I don't think that. But the Cattlemen's Association held a meeting a week ago. I didn't attend and it is one of the rules that a member cannot send a representative except in event of serious illness. Therefore, I couldn't send Manley. Now I received word that two members, John Macy and Herman Berlinger, who have ranches just south of the Half Diamond, are coming to see me today. I expect them around noon. I want you to hear what they have to say without being seen. So keep out of sight when they come and slip into the dining room when I invite them in here."

"I don't like to eavesdrop, Miss Marble, but I'll do it for you."

"It isn't that," said the girl. "It's just that I don't want you to be seen at the meeting. It would bring questions, you understand? Yet I want you to hear them talk. Men of your caliber can tell much by a man's voice. Perhaps you may be able to sense what's in the wind."

"Miss Florence, don't get me wrong, for I'm here to take orders," Bannister declared. "I guess I know how to take 'em . . . from you."

"Then that's settled," said Florence, rising quickly to signify that the conversation was at an end. "You'll be able to tell when they come quick enough, for John Macy rides a very fine iron gray horse . . . one of the largest on the whole range."

"I know him already," Bannister told her. "I stopped at his place on the way up. Reckon that's another reason why he shouldn't see me, for I take it you don't want him to know I'm working here."

"No, I don't," she confessed. "And it won't be necessary to repeat anything that's said to the men."

"If there's one thing I'm able to do," drawled Bannister, "it's keep my mouth shut."

Florence Marble laughed lightly in appreciation as he went out the door.

It lacked an hour of noon when Macy and Berlinger rode up from the bottoms. Bannister, who had taken a point of vantage in the yard, talking idly with Howard, saw them coming in time to slip around to the rear of the house. He heard Macy's booming voice as Florence went out on the porch.

"Well, Miss Flo, howdy. Berlinger, here, an' I heard how you was outsteppin' 'em over at the dance."

"News travels fast, Mister Macy," was the girl's comment. "Jeb will take your horses. Get down and come in."

This was Bannister's clue to slip into the house by the rear door and take up his station out of sight in the dining room. He heard the voices of the two visitors greeting

Manley and Howard.

"Didn't see you over at the stock meetin', Miss Flo," Macy opened casually.

"No, I thought there would be enough men there to attend to what business might come up," replied Florence.

"Well, there was," John Macy said, maintaining a casual approach. "But we had some mighty important business, an' since the Half Diamond is the biggest ranch hereabouts, an' the farthest north, we would have liked to have had you there."

"I understand the talk didn't run entirely to stock," Manley ventured.

"No, it didn't," Macy agreed. "But I reckon we better take this matter up direct with Miss Flo, since she owns the Half Diamond." He paused to permit Manley to get it thoroughly through his head that it wasn't necessary for him to take part in the discussion. Then he spoke again to Florence. "You see, Miss Flo, it's this irrigation business. I don't know such a heap about what they're doin' up there, but I do know what they're doin' down here. That's what we talked most about at the association meeting the other day."

"Down here?" said Florence in a tone of surprise. "Why, they're not operating down this way."

92

"Well, now, if you'll excuse me, they are," Macy drawled. "They're operating to kill off our crops in the bottoms and kill off our cattle. An' in doin' that they're ruining us without giving us anything in return."

"But that can't be, Mister Macy," Florence protested. "It will benefit us . . . this project. Mister Cromer says so."

"Cromer be hanged!" Macy blurted. "An' that's just it, that's why we've come over here today representing the association. We figured you didn't quite savvy the situation. They're operating down here by taking our water. They've tapped the river up there an' are fillin' a pond which they say they're goin' to make into a storage lake. Then they're goin' to steal our water for their fool ditches an' laterals until the river will be dry as a bone. Haven't you noticed that the river's down already? What'll it be later in the summer when we need the water?"

"Oh, they can only take so much," Florence pointed out.

"Don't you ever think it," said Macy convincingly. "They've played some dirty politics and passed out some dirty money an' are gettin' just about what they want. What's more, we believe they have hoodwinked some of the higher-ups. The government sure is on the square, but these fel-

93

lows ain't. They've only got a dinky project of ten thousand acres an' they don't need all that water. An' they're figurin' on two hundred an' fifty or so small farms, as they call 'em, of forty acres each. That'll take a lot of laterals from the main ditches. They haven't started 'em yet. This Cromer seems to be more interested in buildin' a town before it's needed."

"I'm sure I don't understand it all, although I'm interested," Florence confessed. "But it will increase the value of our land."

"It won't do any such thing," Macy declared. "They couldn't get enough water out of the river to irrigate all this down here. An' when we're dried up, our land won't be worth a two cent stamp. I tell you that business up there is a bubble an' it's up to us stock raisers to puncture it."

"I don't just know what you mean by that," said Florence in a worried voice.

"We've got to get together an' fight for our rights," said Macy sternly. "An' if we can't get 'em any other way, we've got to take 'em."

"By that I expect you mean some kind of violence," said Florence. Well, there's one thing, Mister Macy . . . there'll be no violence on this ranch and no crossing of Marble range for any such purpose. I don't think the project is any bubble and I don't think they're going to cheat us out of any water. They may be taking considerable now, but it's a time when we don't really need it. Now I think we'd better get ready for dinner."

John Macy rose. "No, Miss Flo, I reckon we can't stay to dinner. We just wanted to find out if you intended to stick with the association. Sure enough, we've got our answer. We'll be going."

"I think you're making a lot out of nothing," said the girl with spirit. "You say I don't understand the situation, but it might be that the association doesn't understand it, either. Anyway, I've taken a step I can't take back, and don't forget the Half Diamond is running cattle, too."

"That's true," Macy drawled. "An' I'm not forgetting that the Half Diamond has the best grass on the north range an' will get first crack at what water's left over."

"That's unfair, John Macy, and you know it!" exclaimed Florence. "You're hinting that I'm going to get an advantage because I've invested up there. Well, I'm not."

"I'll take your word for it, Miss Flo," said Macy from the doorway.

Bannister slipped from the dining room. From the kitchen window he saw old Jeb bring the visitors' horses, saw them mount, and ride away. Then he went out into the courtyard as another horseman appeared in a cloud of dust. His eyes narrowed. It was Big Bill Hayes.

CHAPTER NINE

The big man brought his horse plunging into the courtyard, drew rein sharply, kicking up a cloud of dust that completely enveloped Bannister. He dismounted leisurely. "Take my horse," he commanded.

Bannister drew tobacco and papers from his shirt pocket. "I've got a horse," he drawled.

Big Bill Hayes stared in stupefaction. Then he scowled fiercely. "You're the new hand here, ain't you?" he demanded. "Well, I'm foreman of this ranch an' your first job is to put up my horse. Then take your roll an' beat it to the camp out at the Dome. I reckon you'll be able to find it."

"Yes, I know exactly where it is," said Bannister. "But Manley was going to send me up on the north range."

"Oh, he is, eh? Well, I need men an' I guess you'll work with me." Hayes started toward the house.

"Not so fast," Bannister said sharply, causing the burly foreman to whirl about in anger. "Manley isn't going to send me up on the north range. He isn't going to send me anywhere at all."

Hayes was puzzled. "Then you're not workin' here, after all," he decided. "I heard you was."

"Yes, I know. Link told you. Well, I am working here, but I guess Jeb here is able to take care of your horse."

"Now what's this?" It was Florence Marble who put the question. She had come out of the house, seeking Bannister after the conference.

Hayes scowled. He didn't brook interference by the mistress of the Half Diamond even though he was in her employ. "Is this fellow workin' here?" he asked.

"Yes, this is Bannister," she replied. "A new hand."

"I guess he is new," sneered Hayes. "He's sure got a lot to learn. I just ordered him to put up my horse an' beat it out to the Dome, where there's work to do. He stands an' gapes an' tries to sass me." He glared at Bannister, who smiled pleasantly at his fury.

"Bannister is taking orders from me only for the present," Florence explained severely.

Hayes drew back a step with a faint leer. Then he smiled broadly. "Oh, that's how it is," he said with a look at each of them.

"Hayes!" exclaimed Florence furiously. "If you ever look at me that way again, I'll get my quirt and cut you across the face!"

Red rage swam in Hayes's eyes, but he held his tongue.

"And now go about your business," Florence commanded.

Hayes strode toward the office in the front of the house, bent on a conference with Manley, but he gave Bannister a look that the latter returned with a tantalizing blank expression.

Having thus deliberately made a first-class enemy of a man he had disliked from their first meeting on the morning of the chase — a man he suspected, he did not know why, of something he was not sure of — Bannister turned to Florence Marble.

"I'm sorry this happened," she said, "but Hayes is a good deal of a bully. You heard what Macy had to say?" And when Bannister nodded: "Then you know what it is I want of you. I want you to keep an eye on things. I don't know exactly how to explain myself. But I suppose you would call yourself a sort of . . . detective? You see, I'm heavily interested in the project up there

99

and I have great faith in it. I believe the association is scaring itself ahead of time, and I have to protect my interests. I'll just give Manley a little hint that you are to be Howard's companion for a time."

Bannister laughed at this. "A chaperon, ma'am, but I'd like to suggest that as a first order you send me up to take a look at this project. Howard could go along if he wants."

"Excellent," said the girl. "But don't tell Cromer about this association business. It might be like pouring oil on the fire. I expect Howard will want to go."

She went into the house to send Howard out to eat with Bannister and old Jeb, the latter having been busy at his stove, as he announced proudly.

"Old Bull-Face will be out here to eat," he complained with a fierce scowl, "but he'll eat in the mess room an' we'll take ours in the kitchen. Tastes better out here, anyways."

But Jeb was mistaken. After a short time spent with Manley, Hayes came out after his horse. He rode away shortly afterward at a furious pace in the direction of the Dome.

"Reckon he don't like our company," was Jeb's comment. "Wal, he's sure welcome to his."

After they had eaten, Bannister and Howard started at once for the Marble Dome Land and Irrigation project in the north and the new-born town of Marble. Bannister pondered the coincidence that Cromer should use the name Marble so consistently. It stuck in his mind that the irrigation head must have some design in this. He might also find some of the things Macy hinted at to be correct. He thought of this probability, too, but his main thought was of the protection of Florence Marble's interests, and he conjectured the possibility that those interests might not entirely concern her investment and her property.

The plain flowed northward, as perfect a range as any experienced cattleman could dream of being made to order. Sleek herds grazed on the luscious grasses still green after the spring rains. The Half Diamond was indeed a paradise of a ranch, Bannister reflected. The man who would marry Florence Marble would indeed be lucky. He would secure, not only a beautiful and accomplished wife, but doubtless a lordship over this mighty kingdom. He remembered Cromer's irritation when he had seen him talking to Florence; he recalled vividly the half sneer on the man's lips; he could not forget the look in the eyes. Yes, it was possible the owner of the Half Diamond needed protection of a nature that didn't concern her riches. Howard noticed with surprise a new look come into Bannister's eyes, a new and rather fearful expression that flitted over his features.

"You still thinking about your run-in with Big Bill Hayes?" he chided. "You needn't worry. You stopped him."

"Maybe so . . . maybe not," said Bannister enigmatically.

Howard saw his companion did not wish to talk about it, so they rode on in silence. But Howard was thinking, also. He began to whistle and they quickened their pace.

The herds dwindled, and then the plain was free. They had passed the limit of the north range. The mountains appeared to march toward them. The river was off to the left, the small stream to the right. Their courses were marked by long, slender lines of timber. Between was a tableland, reaching straight and true, slightly rising, to the rolling foothills.

"We're on the project!" Howard called, pointing ahead.

But Bannister already was looking. In the middle distance were spots of gold — yellow roofs and sides of newly erected, unpainted shacks, struck by the bright sunlight. Beyond was the sheen of silver — the "soup dish", gleaming as a miniature lake. A gray ribbon threaded its way to it from the river — the main ditch.

Soon they were following lines of stakes that marked the courses of the contemplated laterals. Other stakes appeared, designating the corners of the projected farm plots. Bannister realized it was quite a business, after all, for a one-man job. And it was in this business that Florence Marble had invested a fortune. Every stake might be said to represent dollars of her money.

The town lay upon the open prairie. There were no trees. Its water came by pipeline from a mountain stream. As they neared it, Bannister saw rows of tents that were the abodes of the laborers, then shacks that housed foremen and engineers, then the town itself with its main street in the shaping. Small buildings were going up on either side of the street and many of them already were occupied. One he noticed in particular. It was larger, better constructed. He called Howard's attention to it.

"That's going to be the bank," said the boy. "Almost finished, too."

A bank already, thought Bannister. *Cromer is working fast.* They came into the street, passed a number of speedily constructed cafés, a small hotel, several resorts — always among the first in new towns or diggings — the bank building, the offices of the company, with gilt signs prominently displayed, and came at last to the huge tent that served as a livery. Scattered about were several large wagons used in the transportation of lumber and other materials, as well as supplies, from Prairie City, the nearest point of rail.

They put up their horses and repaired to one of the resorts to refresh themselves with mild drinks. It was called The Garden of Eden. Upon entering, Bannister received three distinct shocks. First, the place already was fully equipped with bar and gaming tables and devices, all with the proper fixtures; second, he saw Link at the lower end of the bar and he wasn't drinking, for even as Bannister looked, the evil-eyed dwarf (he might be called that as to stature) waved aside a bottle; third, a man said — "Hallo!" — and he turned to confront Sheriff Campbell.

"Well, if here isn't my old friend," said Bannister smoothly. "Are you trailing me or am I trailing you?"

"You seem to have a habit of turning up at the live spots," replied Campbell dryly.

"I always favored 'em," said Bannister pleasantly. "You see I own some stock in this project and I thought I'd look it over."

"Come far?" Campbell inquired.

"From the Half Diamond," was Bannister's reply. "Know the place?"

"Working there?" the sheriff asked, ignoring the sarcasm.

"Sure thing," was the ready reply. "Hooked up the night of the dance. Any objections?"

The sheriff had kept his eyes on him with that same glimmer of suspicion he had exhibited in Prairie City when he had hinted that Bannister might be the notorious bandit and gunfighter known simply as The Maverick.

"None a-tall," said Campbell cheerfully. "But I've got an idea in the back of my head that I'll have to trail you yet." He moved away without waiting for a reply.

"The biggest thing that man can do is wear a star," was Bannister's comment as he turned to Howard. "He's a confounded fool. Let's go somewhere else for a drink." He led Howard out, as he didn't want Link to see them.

When they had had their refreshment, Bannister suggested that they pay a visit to Cromer, and they headed for the office of the company.

"Out of town," was the information

vouchsafed by a suave clerk. "Back on the eight o'clock stage. Anything I can do?"

"Sure." Bannister nodded. "Keep your eye on the clock and quit on time."

They went into a café for supper. *So Cromer is out of town,* Bannister thought. *Prairie City, undoubtedly. Went down in the morning before Link could arrive, and now Link is waiting to see him. But Link came up from the Dome camp, not from the ranch house. Was he sent by Hayes? If so, just what connection could there be between Hayes and Cromer? Just a wild conjecture, of course but. . . .* At this point Bannister saw through the window that the hotel was directly across the street, affording a view of the company office.

"Reckon we'll hang around a while," he told Howard, "so we might as well slip across and get a room."

"It's a go with me," Howard agreed.

There were no front rooms, the hotel clerk told them. "Fair enough," said Bannister heartily, and reached out a hand. The clerk took it with a surprised smile. The smile faded as he felt a hard object in his palm. He stole a look, saw a glint of gold, and the smile faded.

"Maybe. . . ."

"I thought so," said Bannister cheerfully,

106

reaching for the register. Later, up in their room, Bannister confided the object of his visit to town, and swore Howard to secrecy. The boy was excited with the thrill of adventure as Bannister told him his plan.

Then they took up their vigil. The twilight had descended when the stage arrived. They saw Cromer hasten to his offices. One by one the lights went out across the street as the clerks left. Finally only a faint glow was in the window, coming from a door at the rear of the front room leading to a private office. They descended to the little lobby, where Bannister sat down at the front window. Howard walked out casually and directed his footsteps in the direction of the livery.

Minutes passed, but still the glow came from the office across the street. A diminutive figure slipped through the shadows and was outlined for a moment against the faint light. Bannister rose leisurely, but once outside the lobby he stole hurriedly across the street.

CHAPTER TEN

In the shadows at the corner of the building, Bannister reconnoitered. He looked hastily up and down the dim street but saw no one. He slipped around the building and saw an open window. Just as he reached it, he heard Link's voice: "I better close that window and pull the shade down."

Quick as light Bannister's gun was out. Standing to one side of the window, well out of sight, he slipped up his hand and thrust the muzzle of the gun across the sill at the extreme side. The window came down, but the muzzle of the gun prevented it from closing completely. Link, excited, noted nothing unusual. He pulled down the curtain and Bannister bent his ear to the crack.

"Well, he's down there," said Link in his thin voice. "Big Bill sent me to tell you."

"Who's down where?" Cromer demanded testily.

"That fellow Bannister," was the reply. "He's down at the ranch. Miss Marble's hired him."

"How'd Hayes know who he is?" asked Cromer curtly.

"I overheard him an' the girl talkin' last night," said Link impatiently. "An' two of the boys rode in from town with some more information. I guess you know the two."

"Never mind them," said Cromer sharply. It was plain he was no stranger to authority and was accustomed to be obeyed. "So Hayes sent you up to tell me that. Well, it's kind of him. I've only known it since night before last. But what's this about taking orders from Miss Marble only?"

" 'S fact," Link affirmed. " 'Fronted Bill this mornin' when Bill ordered him out on the range. Manley owned up to it. An' the lady boss horned into the play an' told Bill where to head in at."

There was a period of silence. "Well," said Cromer slowly in an ominous voice, "that's news. What's she set him to doing?"

"That's just it," Link answered eagerly. "I heard 'em talkin' last night an' she told him she didn't know what orders to give him. Said they'd been losin' cattle, though. An' then she told him he would make a good

109

companion for that young Howard brat. All rot."

"Can't tell," said Cromer dubiously. "She's a queer girl. And this Bannister did the kid a good turn by pulling him away from that killer, Le Beck."

"Now you're playin' blue checks!" Link exclaimed in triumph. "That Bannister drew on Le Beck. Do you think he'd have done that if he hadn't thought he could beat him to it? An' he did beat him to it. The boys say it was the fastest piece of gun work they'd ever seen."

"Oh, well, draws under such circumstances always look faster than they are," said Cromer with a yawn.

"Maybe you think so," said Link. Then, lowering his voice: "Do you know who the sheriff an' them thought this fellow was? Thought hard enough to follow him around?"

"Another secret, I suppose," said Cromer.

"It is, if he's the man," Link continued. "They think he's The Maverick."

"All crazy," was Cromer's derisive comment.

"He fits this Maverick's description tight as hide on a cow," Link asserted stoutly. "He's a mystery, too. Nobody knows where he comes from or anything about him. He's lightning with the cards, too, an' The Maverick's noted for that."

"You gazeboes down there have got the best imaginations I ever heard of," declared Cromer irritably. "Why don't some of you try him out and make sure. If the sheriff thinks this is The Maverick, why doesn't he arrest him? Answer that."

"The sheriff says he's been on so many false clues he isn't goin' to take any more chances," Link replied. "But he went to see him, the boys say, when this fellow refused to go to see him when he was sent for, an' he made the sheriff's idea as sound as butter in a hot sun. He's clever. You'll have cash in this bank, lots of it. He may be hanging around to get the lay for a job."

This caused Cromer to sit up sharply in his chair. It was the first suggestion during Link's discourse that caught his serious attention. "Link, you're a fool," he said. But his voice lacked conviction. "If this Bannister was that outlaw, he'd look like him. The Maverick's got a hard look, you can bet your stack on that. He's got a pair of eyes that go through you. But I want this fellow out of here, and I'm going to get him out. If you fellows help, it'll be salt in your tin. You've got him on the ranch where you want him. Frame him . . . anything except shooting him in the back. That'd look too bad for all of us. Now get out of here and go back and tell Hayes what I said."

"Sure," said Link in a purring voice. "But I thought I'd do just a little gambling tonight . . . if it's all right with you."

Cromer swore. "Here's a hundred," he snarled. "It's the limit. You fellows will break me with your loans, and the day you pay back, these mountains will move back a mile."

"That'll give you more land to plant suckers on." Link grinned, backing toward the door.

Outside the window Bannister straightened. As he did so that intangible sixth sense of the trail follower caused him to whirl about just as a body hurtled upon him. The impact drove him back against the side of the building and down on one knee. He grasped a leg and twisted it with all his strength. There was a grunt and his assailant was upon the ground. He flung himself upon the man who he couldn't see in the darkness. They rolled over and over in fierce, silent combat. Then another weight crashed down upon him and he was gripped from behind.

"Hold him!" a voice croaked.

But Bannister, with his great youthful

strength, braced himself on his knees and reared backward, wrenching his right arm free from the grip of the second attacker. There was a curse as they went over. He twisted and got a grip on a throat. The hold loosened, and he was out of it in a second, striking upward. He found a mark and drew a second curse. He ran blindly to the rear of the building. A horse snorted.

"Here," came Howard's voice.

Bannister saw the forms of the horses dimly, spoke to his mount, and was in the saddle in a twinkling.

Now angry tongues of red streaked the black velvet of the night. His hand whipped to his side, only to encounter an empty holster. They were out of the impenetrable shadow of the buildings now and Bannister called to Howard to wait. He had left his gun sticking in the window of Cromer's private office!

The firing had ceased, but excited exclamations came from the street and the front of the office building. Bannister slipped from the saddle and stole back to the shadow of the building, edging along the wall. The dim light from the shaded window guided him. He reached for the gun and jerked. But the gun sight caught inside the sash. He pressed his fingers into the small crack and pushed up the window to release the gun. It fell into his hand. In securing it his form had been outlined in the dim glow from within for a moment.

There was a yell from the street. A gun blazed as Bannister leaped aside, hot lead whistling past his ears. His right hand came up and streaked down across in front of him in a rain of fire. He ran back toward the horses, a shrill yell of pain cutting the night air. He recognized the high-pitched outcry as coming from Link. Then he was in the saddle and they were racing down behind the buildings. A tent loomed and they virtually went through it, the ropes giving way like threads under the flying hoofs of their horses. Beyond was the open ground. They gained it and struck southward at the fastest pace their mounts could command.

"What happened?" Howard shouted.

But Bannister didn't answer. He believed he had killed Link.

CHAPTER ELEVEN

When they reached the ranch and were looking after their horses, Bannister told Howard about the fight in the dark, and gave it as his opinion that two of Cromer's men had seen him peering in the office window and had attacked. They must have known who he was or they wouldn't have fired. Undoubtedly the irrigation head, eager to get him, had given orders to certain of his henchmen to do the job if they had the chance. The firing, of course, brought out Cromer and Link; the other two had shouted his name, or had seen him in the dim light from the window, and opened up.

"Anyway, I hit Link, for I recognized his shout, and now, I suppose, there'll be the devil to pay," he finished. "May gum up the works. More'n likely Campbell will be hot-footing it down here. Cromer'll want to know why I was looking in his window, and he'll know I heard what he said about getting me and who he thinks I am . . . dog-gone if I don't believe it's a mess."

"Why so?" Howard asked. "They was shooting at you first, and I don't believe Cromer'll want anything said about the window part of it, because you heard him tell Link to get you down here any way he could. How's Cromer going to explain why he wants you killed?"

"Well, there's something in that," Bannister conceded. "But on the other hand he can deny he ever said any such thing, an' how am I going to prove he did?"

"Didn't I see 'em blazing away at you?" Howard countered. "Still that doesn't prove anything, either. We'll have to wait an' see. Let's grab a wink. We'll sleep in the house so they can't surprise us in the bunkhouse if they come."

Bannister thought that a good idea and they stole into the big living room, where Howard dropped upon the sofa and Bannister took one of the huge easy chairs.

But no one came, and Florence found them there sound asleep, in the morning. The pair avoided mention of the shooting of Link and talked evasively of their visit to the irrigation town. No, they hadn't seen Cromer as he was in Prairie City. Yes, the bank building was coming along fine. Yes,

116

everything was going good. Something in the manner and tone of their casual replies aroused Florence Marble's curiosity and fed her suspicions.

"I know!" she exclaimed in triumph. "You two have been gambling! Did you lose much?"

"Not a thing," sang Bannister, with a sly wink at Howard.

After breakfast they went out to the bunkhouse.

"I don't understand," said Bannister. "You'd think Campbell would come down, wouldn't you? Or somebody? I never like it when it's quiet. I hate mystery. What would they do with Link if he isn't dead?"

"Isn't what?" This came from old Jeb White, who had suddenly appeared in the doorway.

"We heard Link was shot up in Marble last night," Bannister answered casually. "I was wondering what they'd do with him if he was just wounded."

"They'd take him to the company hospital," said Howard. "They've got a place where they take care of their men who are hurt."

"Wal, horns of Hades!" old Jeb cried. "If he's just hurt, my day's ruined, even if the sun's shining. That little black-faced double-

117

crosser ought to have been wearing more holes in his hide than a Swiss cheese long ago. How come?"

"No one's come down this morning with the details," Bannister replied, avoiding an explanation. "Maybe this is somebody now."

They hurried to the door in response to the thundering of hoofs and saw that somebody, indeed, had come. It was the foreman, Big Bill Hayes. He spotted Bannister at once, literally leaped from the saddle, flinging his reins for Jeb White to gather in, and confronted him just outside the bunkhouse door.

"So ye tried to knock him off, eh?" His eyes were bloodshot, thick lips drawn inward, rage in every inch of him.

"Off what?" Bannister drawled. "A fence?"

"You're sharp, you damned spy!" Hayes roared. "You shot Link up there last night."

"Did I kill him?" Bannister inquired.

This infuriated Hayes beyond any point of reason. He flung his huge bulk forward with extraordinary agility for so large a man. But Bannister's side-step was quick and sure as a cat can whirl. He went under Hayes's rush, met it with an uppercut to the jaw. This merely snapped his opponent's head back a bit. And, as Bannister went through, a huge arm caught him and hurled him

118

backward several feet.

Howard was jumping about excitedly and Jeb White was leaning with his hands on his knees, his eyes shining, his mouth wide open.

Hayes rushed again. This time Bannister did not try to hit him. He danced away. Hayes swung wide and so viciously that he threw himself off balance. It was Bannister's opportunity. He darted in like a flash. Hayes saw the blow coming — a tremendous straight right — but he was not set to avoid it. It landed flushly on his jaw and he swayed and stood as if looking vacantly at some distant object. Next he was in the dust, sitting there, with his hands on the ground behind him, a silly smile on his face, as if he had just at that moment thought it funny. But in another moment the smile was gone and the eyes were darting hate. He rose slowly, leaning to the left, and, as his right hand came up off the ground, Bannister's voice spoke sharply.

"Now, don't try that!"

Hayes glared as he saw that Bannister had drawn leisurely and was nodding his gun up and down.

"I'll get you for this," said Hayes, on his feet.

"Well, my friend," Bannister drawled,

"don't try too hard."

Hayes stalked angrily around to the porch, rapped loudly on the screen door. Florence Marble answered.

"Where's Manley?" he demanded gruffly. His jaw was swelling.

"I don't just know," Florence answered. "Your voice sounds kind of rough, Hayes, why don't you try cough drops?"

"I didn't come here for jokes, Miss Marble, but on mighty serious business. Since Manley ain't here, maybe you'll hear what I've got to say."

"I'm always ready to talk to my foreman, but I won't allow him to be the least disrespectful," she answered. "Come in."

His manner now underwent a change. He removed his hat and sat down. Then he spoke seriously.

"Miss Marble, Link was shot down up in Marble last night."

"Link . . . shot?" she asked in startled tones.

"Shot down in the dark." He nodded. "He's in the company's hospital up there. He may pull through."

"Who did it, Hayes?" she asked anxiously.

"That's it," he said somewhat eagerly. "We know, or they know up there, who did it. It was that new man, Bannister. He's had it in

120

for Link ever since he got here. But Cromer won't let us do anything about it because he thinks it might hurt your feelings or something."

"I don't believe it!" she exclaimed emphatically. "He was with Howard up there last night."

Hayes shrugged. "I suppose he was, but would that stop him being recognized. The men don't like it, Miss Marble, they think he's not on the square. If he was anything at all, why did he take this job . . . if you can call it a job . . . acting as young Howard's chaperon? That's no man's job."

"That's enough," said Florence sharply. "It's a man's job if he makes the kind of a man I want Howard to be. And you just remember that he might have taken the job because I asked him and. . . ." She paused, colored, and bit her lip. She couldn't tell anyone what Bannister's job was. "No, I didn't mean that," she continued. "Later on, he may do something else . . . but right now he's traveling with Howard."

"That may all be," said Hayes grimly, "but the men are complaining. They're threatening to quit an' go to work on the project if you don't ditch him."

"Then they can quit!" cried Florence. "Are they and you coming down here to

121

dictate to me how I'll run this ranch and who I'll employ?"

"I wouldn't say, ma'am," he said in a hard voice, rising and taking up his hat. "I was merely tryin' to tip you off."

"Then you can go back to your range," she said, pointing to the door.

He left without speaking.

Florence hurried furiously out the porch and called for Howard. When he came, she assailed him with rapid questions.

"Did you see Link up there last night?" she demanded.

"No, I didn't," he answered.

"Did Bannister see him?"

"I don't know if he did or not, for sure."

"Well, Hayes is trying to tell me that Bannister shot Link," she said sternly. "And in the dark, at that. Do you know if he did or not?"

"Can't say as I do," replied the boy, "but I know one thing. While I was getting the horses, there were a powerful lot of shots being fired at Bannister. And I know another thing. This outfit don't like him because they're afraid of him . . . every last one of 'em. He just licked the tar out of Hayes out in the yard because, when Hayes accused him of shooting Link, he started to kid him. Then Hayes made for him. He gave Hayes what he well an' good deserved and pointed the way to the house with his gun. Hayes went."

For a time Florence was silent. "Tell Bannister I want to see him . . . no, don't do that. Anyway, you can go now."

"Bannister's worth the whole crew of them," was Howard's parting shot.

Florence sat thinking. What kind of a man had she hired? He had the lure of an engaging personality. Next minute he was a raging, fighting demon. He had probably saved Howard's life against the gun terror, Le Beck. He had turned Howard away from the treacherous bars through sheer logic. He would do his job, she knew. And, deep in her heart, she believed he had shot Link. The thing that amazed her was the fact that she didn't seem to care.

CHAPTER TWELVE

Bannister and Howard left soon afterward for a tour of the badlands, that wilderness of twisted ridges, ragged gulches, soap holes with their treacherous sands, and timber patches that reached for miles below the ranch along Indian River. Howard led the way, explaining the various trails so that Bannister could become acquainted to some extent with the district. All Bannister knew of it was the Marble Dome trail leading to the widest and best ford in the badlands, but Howard showed him many other fords and cross trails and one trail in particular that led along the river under a hanging bank. They didn't follow this trail as it was time to eat, the sun having crossed the zenith.

"We'll go to Old Luke's cabin," Howard announced. "There's few of 'em that know where it is."

So they went back half a mile on the

Marble Dome trail to where a huge cotton-wood tree leaned out over the plain. Howard led the way in behind this tree and through a screen of bushes. Here they came upon a dim trail that was well concealed. They followed it about a mile and suddenly burst upon a small meadow, at the farther end of which was a cold spring, by which stood a small cabin, a corral, and a three-sided horse shelter.

"Old Luke once lived here alone," Howard explained, "and everybody thought that he rustled cattle."

They ate their lunch and followed a trail across the river to the south side. Here they proceeded northward until they reached the big Marble Dome ford, where they crossed again. Then they headed for the ranch. They had hardly arrived there when Manley came galloping in from the Dome range. Florence came out on the porch, astonished, because Manley very seldom rode so furiously. He brought his horse to a rearing stop below the steps. Bannister and Howard came running.

"The men!" exclaimed Manley. "Every man of them has gone. North, I suppose, perhaps because they can get better wages up there."

"Hayes threatened that they might do that

this morning," Florence explained, her face paling.

"Well, he's gone with the rest of them," said Manley bitterly. "There's something behind this besides more money for the men."

"I reckon I'm the cause of it," said Bannister. "He doesn't want me here. He's made that clear. And we had some trouble this morning . . . a fight in the yard . . . and I licked him."

"Maybe," said Manley, "but I can't help believing there's more to it than your being here. Anyway, we'll have to look after the stock till we can pick up a new crew."

"There's three of us to see they don't stray too far," said Bannister, "and old Jeb can come along and cook."

"Yeh, an' I sure kin do more'n thet," said Jeb, who had come up to find out what it was all about. "I'm still able to sit a hoss an' I'm still able to ride one. So's there bein' only four of us, I kin help out on the range 'tween times."

"And meanwhile," said Florence in a determined voice, "I'll ride to Prairie City and pick up what men I can. I'm sure of getting a few, anyway, even if I have to ask them to come for a short time till we can fill out an outfit as a favor to me."

"Just the thing!" Manley exclaimed enthusiastically. "You can go up in the morning. Sure you can pick up some men. You can do it better than I could. You ought to be able to get a dozen. If it wasn't for this irrigation business . . . us being for it and him being against it . . . we could borrow some hands from John Macy."

Florence shook her head. "We can't do that," she said.

"You know, I'm wondering," drawled Bannister, "if there might not be someone who prevailed upon Hayes to entice the crew away."

"What do you mean?" asked Florence with a puzzled look.

"I say I'm just wondering," Bannister replied. "Maybe, later on, we'll find out something."

"Oh, you and your mysteries!" Florence exclaimed, stamping her foot. "I like men who come right out in the open with what they think."

"That's all right, too," said Bannister, lifting his brows, "but I'm not going to make any accusations I can't back up. I just put that in because later you will recall the remark."

"Well, we've had enough parley," said Manley impatiently. "Now let's get back to

127

the cattle."

"After this, Bannister," said Florence in a tone of annoyance, "if you can't tell me what you're thinking about, don't try to confuse me with veiled hints and mysteries."

Bannister bowed as she flounced into the house.

"Would you mind my asking what you were driving at?" asked Manley later, when they were saddling in the barn.

"Not a bit of it," Bannister replied, drawing him aside, "as long as it doesn't go any further. I think Cromer had a hand in it. I think he wants to bring pressure to bear on the Half Diamond for personal reasons of his own. That's all I'll say."

He turned on his heel, leaving Manley with a thoughtful look on his face, and went for his horse.

In a few minutes the quartet was on its way to Dome range, where they arrived at dusk. Joe found the cook wagon in good order, with no supplies or utensils missing, and went to work at once preparing supper. Manley arranged the night-watch shifts and, despite the situation, they were cheerful at supper.

"I'm going to bring down a couple of men from the north range tomorrow," Manley announced, "and a couple from the lower herd. So we won't be so awful bad off, after all. Miss Flo is sure to bring back a few from Prairie City, and then I. . . ." He stopped short and looked keenly at Bannister. "Could you take charge of the outfit for a few days? I mean, do you feel capable?"

"I reckon so," Bannister drawled in reply.

"Then you can take hold for a few days and I'll go cut and rustle men and a foreman," said Manley. "Oh, we'll come out all right. It isn't so hard to pick up a crew for such a ranch as the Half Diamond. We've got too good a reputation."

"I reckon so," Bannister said again.

Next morning Florence Marble was off for Prairie City with the first faint light of dawn. Before noon she had gathered nine experienced hands — all that were available in town. She stood their dinner at the hotel and started back with them right after the meal. Several of them had no mounts, but she borrowed horses, as she could easily do, and they would get their remudas at the ranch.

They passed above the ranch house and headed straight for the Dome. There she turned them over to Manley, told him to look after the borrowed horses and see they were returned, and then rode back to the house, well pleased with her day's work.

"Hayes tried to cripple me," she explained to Martha, her housekeeper. "Why, I should have gotten rid of him long ago."

Manley was in rare good humor that day. They now had a good emergency working force for the Dome range and he sent the men he had borrowed back to their stations in the north and south. He planned to take a trip in a day or two to pick up more men, leaving Bannister temporarily in charge. The latter already had successfully demonstrated that he was a cowman from the high heels of his boots to the crown of his Stetson, and he was more than ever a god in the eyes of Howard Marble.

This was the situation on the morning of the second day when he stared in surprise at a whirling cloud of dust in the north.

"What the . . . ?"

"Those are your men coming back," Bannister told him mildly. "Remember I mentioned there might be somebody besides Hayes mixed up in this?"

"The devil!" Manley exclaimed. "Well, Hayes will never work on this ranch again."

"Don't worry," said Bannister with a cryptic smile. "He won't be with the bunch. Anyway, Manley, it's just as well they don't see me. I'll streak for the ranch and tell Miss Marble. I've a reason in going back, too. Sure it's your crowd?"

"Sure as shootin'," Manley responded. "I could tell that mob of Indians just by their dust. All right, go ahead. And tell Miss Flo that, if Hayes is with them, I'm going to fire him and to pay him off. I reckon she won't have any objections."

Bannister was off like a streak. It was all as clear to him as day. Cromer, working hand in glove with Hayes, had told him to take the men away. Now the men were coming back. Cromer would ride down to the Half Diamond ranch house and tell Florence that he had refused to hire the men, knowing that she needed them, and had compelled them to return. Her foreman had been furious and had refused to return. He was sorry. It was a well-laid scheme to further his interests in her favor. Bannister laughed outright and loped, whistling, into the yard.

" 'Morning, ma'am," he said with a great sweep of his hat, as she came out on the porch wearing a wondering look.

"Well, did you come on business or just to pay a call?" she said. She couldn't forget his innuendo the last time she had seen him.

"Business," he sang cheerfully, dismount-

131

ing. "And I am the bearer of good tidings. I bring a message of great good cheer, and later I shall make a prediction . . . a prediction, Miss Florence, that I would bet my horse, gun, and money belt will come true."

"Stop that nonsense," she said with a pretty frown. "I know what your tidings are. The men are returning to the Dome."

He arched his brows in mock surprise. "A mind-reader as well as a rancheress," he said. "Yes, they have returned, pack and parcel."

"I'll not take Hayes back," she said in a determined voice.

"Hayes won't be with them," he declared.

"How do you know?" she asked. "Oh, I might have known. You've seen them, of course."

"No, I haven't seen them, except coming in like a fury on their sturdy and, I suspect, Half Diamond beasts," he said. "But I don't think he'll be with them, because . . . well, because I don't think he'll be along."

"Another mystery," she said disdainfully. "I'll soon know without your help."

"Are you interested in my prediction?" he asked in a plaintive voice.

"If it has to do with my business," she returned.

"Very well," he said complacently. "You

will receive a visit, probably this very morning, from Mister Cromer, who will explain that he refused to engage your men and sent them back because he knew you needed them. He will say your foreman was angry and quit, and he will express his sorrow because of the fact."

Her face had flushed and then gathered in stern lines. "Just what do you mean by that, Bannister? You mustn't forget there are lines beyond which hands on this ranch cannot pass."

"Exactly, Miss Florence," he said with a bow, "and that's why I'm going to stop at this one. There! You see? Dust on the north trail. I've got to look after my horse."

He left her staring northward where a golden streamer proclaimed the approach of a rider.

CHAPTER THIRTEEN

The dust spiral lost its golden luster as horse and rider reached the top of the bench and dropped down the winding road to the ranch house. They disappeared a few moments around a bend, came into sight again trotting through the windbreak, and next drew up in the yard near the porch.

Cromer dipped his hat with a smile to Florence, slid out of the saddle, and called to Bannister.

"Take my horse," he commanded abruptly.

"I have a horse," Bannister returned innocently.

Cromer halted on his way to the porch. "I say, aren't you working here . . . or do I have to put my horse up myself?"

"Oh, oh," drawled Bannister. "*Put* him up. That's different. I thought you were trying to give him to me. Sure, I'll put him up, Mister Cromer. Glad to do it. Take good care of him, too. See, he's been ridden powerful hard. He'll need a blanket and a rub down . . . and he'll get it. Don't worry, go right in."

Cromer bit his lip under his thick mustache and glared. He was being made a fool of and insulted in the bargain, but there was no come-back because of the way in which Bannister had put it. He whirled on his heel and went up the porch, a smile of genuine pleasure routing the scowl.

"Florence, you look prettier than any flower in your yard," he said, taking her hand.

"As a brazen flatterer, you are even more able than an engineer," she returned, although anyone could have seen that she was pleased. "Come in, Mister Cromer." It was noticeable that while at all times she addressed him by his last name, he invariably addressed her by her first.

He tossed his hat on the table and dropped into an easy chair. "Well, you may think it is flattery, but it isn't," he protested. "You are beautiful and someday I'm going to tell you just how beautiful you are, and how dear you are to me. But not today, Miss Spitfire, for I see it is not the time, and . . . we are both so busy." He laughed, and to his unmitigated satisfaction she laughed with him.

"I didn't think you came down here to tell me things like that," she observed.

"I could, though," he asserted. "I could tell 'em all day. What do you think I came down for?"

Florence remembered Bannister's prediction of this visit and his forecast as to its nature. Well, it was merely a guess on his part and she couldn't by any means be sure.

"I haven't the slightest idea," she told him.

"I come with glad tidings . . . if you haven't heard," he said with a smile. Florence started, for Bannister also had stressed glad tidings at the start. "Your men are returning to work," he said impressively.

"Yes, I heard they were seen coming back," she said.

He seemed a bit set back at this, for it sort of robbed his announcement of its drama. "They came up on the project and asked me for work, and, while I surely need men, I turned them down flat."

Florence nodded and waited expectantly.

"I could have used them," he went on, "but I realized that you needed them more than I did. So I shooed 'em home where they belonged."

"That was very kind of you, Mister

136

Cromer," said the girl soberly.

He glowed with satisfaction. "Oh, nothing," he protested with a dramatic wave of his hand. "Florence, I'd do anything for you." He paused for just the proper interval. "But I'm afraid I am also the bearer of bad news as well as good." His brow wrinkled with concern.

She remembered again what Bannister had predicted. Why, the interview was progressing just as he said it would. She could think of nothing to say to this at the moment, so remained passive, merely lifting her brows a trifle.

"You see," said Cromer, clearing his throat, "that foreman of yours, Bill Hayes, is accustomed to having his own way, you know?" She nodded. "Well," he went on wryly, "he became very angry when I refused them work. Said they could make more money up there . . . which they could . . . and that I needed men, and why should I discriminate?"

"He was always bull-headed," Florence observed.

"I started to tell him that his place was here on the ranch and that, in any event, he and the others of the outfit should not quit, if they had to quit, until after the beef shipment. That's as far as I got. I never received

137

such a cursing . . . well, I haven't received any cursing to my face . . . in my life. He called me everything he could think of. I took it all calmly and told him he was taking advantage of me because I couldn't, in my position, afford to get into a brawl with him." He paused at this point.

"And I see where you're right, Mister Cromer," she said with spirit. "I suppose he quit the outfit. Well, I would not have taken him back under any circumstances."

He stared at her a moment, and then sighed with relief. He even wiped a few imaginary drops of perspiration from his brow. "You don't know what a relief that is to me," he said. "I was afraid you might think I was in some way responsible for his quitting, that I kept him and sent the others back, or something of the sort. And I'll try my best to help you get a man to take his place."

"No," said the girl, "you've enough to do. Manley will look after that. Don't you bother. Of course you'll stay to dinner." She went to the dining room door. "Martha. Martha! Oh, there you are. Mister Cromer will be with us for dinner."

She came back, to find him sitting with a gloomy look on his face. "You look like the start of a rainstorm," she observed. "What's the matter? Don't worry about Hayes. Or maybe it's something about your work?"

"No, it's neither," he returned, "although, goodness knows, I have enough responsibility on that job up there. No, it's something else, Florence, but the trouble is, if I tell you, I know you'll think I'm trying to edge in on your affairs."

"Not at all, Mister Cromer," Florence declared, intrigued by his hesitant manner.

"I'm not so sure," he said dubiously. "No, I don't believe I better speak of the matter in my mind." He looked at her as if he had suddenly become imbued with a fresh idea. "Why, certainly I'll tell you," he said loudly. "It's my duty to warn you. I hadn't thought of that angle of the case before."

"Do tell me," she said, very much interested.

"Well, Florence, did you ever hear of an outlaw called The Maverick?"

"I . . . think so," she answered. "I don't pay much attention to such things."

"Well, all I need to say is that he's a bad man. Bandit, gunfighter, and a killer. A deceiving cuss in the bargain, as you'd never know what his . . . *er* calling was to look at him. He's notorious and dangerous."

He paused just long enough to permit his words to make their impression upon her.

When he saw by the look in her eyes that his end had been accomplished, he resumed: "A short time ago a young man . . . this gunman is young . . . arrived in Prairie City. Deputy Van Note spotted him first and saw that his description tallied perfectly with that of the outlaw. He told Sheriff Campbell, and the sheriff scoffed at him because Van Note had sent him on so many false clues. But then something happened that caused the sheriff to sit up and take notice. He sent for him to interview him and the fellow . . . with just such sheer audacity as The Maverick would have . . . sent back word that, if the sheriff wanted to see him, he was at the hotel." Cromer paused again as if he were getting his narrative all straight in his brain. Then he continued: "This fellow baffled the sheriff, evaded his questions in a clever manner, and finally told him in a menacing way that, if he thought he was this Maverick, before he did anything, he'd better be sure first . . . or words to that effect. He was bold, insolent, and exceedingly clever. As the sheriff didn't want to put the wrong man in jail, having been fooled before, and perhaps get himself in a mess of some kind, he let him go. The fellow then proceeded to gamble and he made the most accomplished professionals in Prairie City . . . and there are some good ones there . . . look like abject beginners. That was another point. The Maverick is a notorious gambler."

Again Cromer hesitated. He wanted the gambling point to sink deep.

"His next step was to drift out into the country, and after a bit he showed up in Marble. Sheriff Campbell was up there and looked him over again. Now he is almost sure he is the man known as The Maverick . . . a ruthless killer with a price on his head."

He stopped, nodding his head.

"But what has all this got to do with me or the Half Diamond?" asked the interested but perplexed girl.

"Now we come to the point," said Cromer earnestly, leaning forward in his chair. "This is what I must tell you. He is the man who drew on Le Beck that night when Howard got into the mix-up. His very lightning draw showed him up, and he didn't draw so much on Howard's account as to get Le Beck into a gun play, for gun play is his very heart's blood. You know what he has done since, and you can bet he has had an object in every act he has done. That man is the man right here on your ranch who calls himself Bannister."

Florence held her breath. Horror, perplexity, fear were all commingled in the look in her eyes.

"You . . . you think . . . ?"

"We all have reason to believe that Bannister is none other than this Maverick," said Cromer soberly. "Now, why would he take this job here when he can make so much at the green tables? Undoubtedly he has a money belt containing thousands. I'll tell you, Florence, why I think he's here. He's masquerading as an honest person, but he's just hanging around until we open that bank up there, and you know we are going to carry an enormous amount of cash. Do you see?"

"Why . . . doesn't . . . the sheriff take him then?" she asked.

"He's not an easy man to take, and he has to be taken through a ruse," was Cromer's reply. "I got most of this from the sheriff last night. He has a plan, and we're keeping him on ice so to speak. Oh, he won't touch any of us till he sees he can make a big haul. But there's no question but that he shot Link. He didn't like him. It was just luck . . . dim light . . . that he didn't get him."

"This is awful," said Florence. "What should I do? Here he's going around with Howard and. . . ."

"Fire him," said Cromer sternly. "Give

142

him no reason, or think up a reason, anything . . . but let him go. He'll probably head straight for Marble, and there's where we're going to get him."

"He doesn't look like such a man as you describe," said Florence, the first flicker of doubt showing in her eyes.

Cromer shrugged and stood up. "As you wish, Florence. I've only told you because, as I said, I considered it my duty."

"But, Mister Cromer, he has a good pair of eyes, and he stopped Howard from drinking, and Howard worships him. Wouldn't he show his true self in some way to Howard?"

"Perhaps he has and Howard hasn't noticed it," replied Cromer. "Anyway, think it over, Florence. Great guns, girl, you don't think I'd lie to you, do you? And I'm all-fired hungry."

"No, I don't think you'd lie to me," said the girl. "And I'll see if dinner is ready. I believe it is."

When they came into the yard after dinner, Bannister, who had eaten in the kitchen and listened to every word Cromer had spoken, had the latter's horse ready.

"Pretty work," said Bannister as Cromer mounted.

"What's that?" snapped Cromer.

143

"I say, pretty work," Bannister repeated.

"Meaning just how much?" demanded Cromer with a scowl.

"I mean pretty work up on your irrigation project," said Bannister. "I've a notion to buy some more stock." With that he walked toward the bunkhouse.

Cromer nodded to Florence, gave her his hand and a significant look, and rode away. Florence hadn't looked at Cromer in farewell, but had stared, awed, fascinated, and fearful at the broad shoulders of the retreating Bannister.

CHAPTER FOURTEEN

For some length of time Florence remained standing in the yard after Bannister had entered the bunkhouse. She was stunned, bewildered, half afraid. In her present state of mind she would never have talked to Bannister. Indeed, if he had come out at that moment, she would have fled precipitately into the house. And now she did start for the house, but as she neared the porch, Howard came thundering in from the east.

He brought up near her. "Where's Bannister?" he asked eagerly.

"He's in the bunkhouse," she replied.

"Good!" cried the boy. "I was afraid he might have run off somewhere without me. The bunch is back on the Dome range. I guess he told you that. Hayes isn't with 'em. They didn't need me an' I came back. I'm coming in to get something to eat soon's I can put up my horse. Old Jeb's following, but he don't ride very fast."

145

He rode on to the barn and Florence went into the house. She'd clear up one or two items, anyhow. Howard must be some kind of a judge of character. She decided to question him. But when he sat down at the table, she found it hard to start. She asked him some questions about the conditions over at the Dome. Howard then said that Bannister had called him a reckless rider.

"Why, he's one himself, isn't he?" Florence queried.

"He's everything," said Howard enthusiastically.

This gave Florence the opportunity she desired. "Everything!" she said incredulously. "I suppose he's an outlaw, too."

"Nope. He isn't that. But I'll tell you what, Florence, if he ever started out to be one, he'd be a terror."

"Listen, Howard," said the girl in an earnest voice, "we don't know much about Bannister. In fact, we don't know anything about him. And he's a stranger who is being talked about. I've heard hints . . . I won't tell you where or from whom . . . that he is an outlaw and came up here to get away . . . things were getting too hot for him and. . . ."

Howard had put down his knife and fork. "That's enough," he insisted. "Tell me who's been saying these things, an' I'll put a slug of hot lead into him. It's a danged lie. Don't you think I'd know if there was anything wrong, me being with him so much? I know a little about men if I am under-age. He's clean as a whistle. He's faster than a bat out of the hot place with his gun, but that doesn't make him an outlaw. Just you tell whoever made these statements to ask Bannister if they're true. Ever think of that? Sneaking around behind a woman. An' you listening. They're afraid of Bannister, an', what's more, the big thing, they're jealous of him. Now please don't talk any more such nonsense to me. You'll spoil my digestion."

Florence left him at the table and went into the living room. She felt a little thrill as she realized that she believed every word Howard had said.

Came a clatter of hoofs — many hoofs — a shout or two. Florence hurried out on the porch to see six men — stockmen they were, for she knew every one of them. They were led by John Macy, who was dismounting.

"Howdy, Miss Half Diamond," he boomed facetiously. "An' how's the world treatin' you?"

"Can't complain," she answered, smiling and taking his hand as he came up on the porch. She had always liked John Macy better than any rancher in the Marble River district. "Won't you come in?"

"Wal, we haven't much time, Miss Flo. I reckon this will do. We're a committee from the Cattlemen's Association on our way to Marble to interview the great high-lord of this here irrigation project, Mister Sydney Cromer. We want to find out how we're going to be used on this water question this summer. You were named as a member of the committee with full power to talk, vote, take drinks, and sech. Will you go along?"

"John Macy, I can't," she said earnestly. "And I wouldn't be any good anyway."

"All right," boomed Macy, "that's just what I expected you to say. We had you pegged right an' we provided for it. This being a committee, an' not an association meeting, we decided you could send a proxy. Now who do you want to send?"

Florence's heart leaped. In the space of seconds she made up her mind. "I'll send Bannister," she said. And then to Howard, who had heard them and was at her back: "Go tell Bannister to get his horse and ride up here."

Macy and Florence chatted a few minutes until Bannister appeared on his mount. John Macy stared at him intently and slapped his knee.

"Why, I know you," he roared. "You stopped at my place on your way up here an' wouldn't take a job from me on a bet. Then you come on up here an' Miss Flo here hooks you. Wal, I can't say I blame you, young feller."

"Bannister," said Florence, her face flaming, "these men represent a committee from the Cattlemen's Association to confer with Mister Cromer as to the water rights in the south. I was named as a member but do not wish to go. You are to go as my proxy, do you understand?"

"I reckon so," Bannister drawled.

"Then let's go," John Macy thundered, clambering into his saddle.

They rode northward at a fast pace, Macy riding with Bannister, kidding the life out of him, and Bannister shooting it back at him. "But I'll bet you'd make a danged good man to run thet ranch," was Macy's parting shot as they trotted into town.

They put up their horses and sought Cromer's office in the little building of the Marble Dome Land and Irrigation Company. As they approached it, Bannister, who was well to the right of the others, saw a figure behind the office. He was so startled on the instant that he stopped. Then he hurried on with the rest, his lips pressed firmly

149

together, a cold, hard look in his eyes — a complete change of countenance that vanquished the cheerful, youthful lines and the clear, frank eyes. He was glad he had been accorded the opportunity to attend this meeting.

They entered the front office and the clerk there called Cromer, who came out with a cold smile on his face.

John Macy explained who they were, what they represented, and why they had come.

Cromer actually bowed. "I'd been expecting you gentlemen," he said courteously, although there was a certain hard reserve about his manner. "Let's go into my office, where there is more room."

They passed into the rear office and Bannister saw at once that Cromer had anticipated their visit. He had moved his desk to the rear, near the rear door. There was a screen about the wash basin on one side of him and a coat rack on the other. In front there were several chairs.

Cromer went around behind his desk. "Sit down, gentlemen. I guess there are enough chairs."

They all seated themselves, Bannister keeping near Macy, as seemed natural since he was the only one present he knew to any extent. And now Macy rose and addressed

Cromer.

"As you know, we represent the Cattle-men's Association, and you represent the Marble Dome Land and Irrigation Company. This meeting needn't be long. All we want to know, Mister Cromer, is what protection us ranchers south and southeast along the Indian River are to have for water this summer."

"That will depend," Cromer answered vaguely.

"Depend on what?" asked John Macy, while the others stirred in their chairs.

"It will depend on the season," said Cromer. "We shall take our stipulated allowance under our acquired water rights in any event for our project. If it's a wet season, you people will get more. If it's a dry season, you'll get less. So you see it really isn't in our hands. It depends on the weather, and we cannot control the weather."

There was more stirring in chairs and faint mutterings at this, and John Macy turned a warning eye on the other members of the committee.

"You mean there is no provision for a certain amount of water to come down Indian River to us?" he asked.

"None whatever," replied Cromer coldly.

A committeeman rose at this, but Macy waved him down.

"Thet's one thing the Cattlemen's Association wanted to find out," he said. "Now, according to that, there could be such a thing as Indian River going dry?"

"That's highly improbable and you know it." Cromer scowled. "Now, listen here, we know you people are sore. We know also that you are hostile to our enterprise. We know other things. You don't like the idea of farms in here and you won't recognize the fact that this project will increase the value of your land. . . ."

"It can't increase the value of our land when there isn't enough water to go 'round, can it?" Macy broke in.

"Of course it can," Cromer declared angrily. "On natural principles it will to begin with, or, at least, within a year. But the water supply can be increased. We haven't tapped all the streams in the hills and. . . ."

"You talk like a fool," Macy scoffed. "How much water could you get out of those little streams? Middle of August, when we need it most, you couldn't get a hatful. You don't talk like a practical irrigation engineer an' you're not one. Just the same we want to know *one* thing. Are you going to protect

152

water for us?" Macy, using his very best English, striving to keep himself in control, looked Cromer straight in the eye. The others leaned forward in their chairs. Bannister himself was tense.

"To a certain extent," said Cromer sharply, "but we're going to protect ourselves first, you can lay to that. However," he added in softer tones, "if things get too bad we . . . I'm not saying we would, understand, for we pay good for our water . . . but we might sell you some."

Every member of the committee was on his feet in a second.

"Sell us some!" shouted Macy, pounding a fist on Cromer's desk. "You'd take our water . . . the water we've always had . . . and sell it to us, eh? Or let our cattle starve? You're a dirty, rotten skunk an' I believe your damned company is a fake!"

"Don't say any more," said Cromer loudly, his face white.

But Macy's anger had gotten beyond his control. "You'll give us our share, you sneaking scoundrel, or we'll take it!" he shouted.

"You threaten violence, do you?" said Cromer with an evil look. "There's a law in this country . . . don't forget that."

"Law, hell!" cried Macy. "The only law

153

you know about is the two hundred rifles you've got stored up here."

"You're a liar!" shouted Cromer.

Bannister leaped to Macy's side and struck his hand from his weapon, and it was into the bore of Bannister's gun that Cromer looked.

"Drop it!" Bannister commanded sharply.

Cromer's gun clattered on the floor and Bannister made a flying leap for the curtain about the washstand. He ducked low just as a shot rang out, jerked the curtain down from below, and had the right hand of a small, dark-faced man in his grip in an instant. Another gun clattered on the floor. He thrust his own in its holster. Macy was covering Cromer.

"You see this man?" cried Bannister. "Why was he there? Why did he fire at me? Because he's Cromer's gunman, just imported." He shook the smaller man, whose eyes were darting pinpoints of light. "This, gentlemen, is the notorious Le Beck."

Cromer was shaking like a leaf with rage and chagrin.

Then Bannister deliberately caught up Le Beck, rushed him across the room, and sent him hurtling through the window as though he were a sack of wheat.

"Out!" cried John Macy, pointing with his

gun toward the front office and the door to the street. "Out! The meeting is over!"

CHAPTER FIFTEEN

In the street the members of the committee hurried toward the hotel in a bewildered, flustered state of mind, able to comprehend only two things: Cromer didn't intend to protect them for water when they needed it, and Bannister had disclosed the fact that Cromer had hired an infamous gunfighter — and had routed that gun artist in a way, which, if it got about, would make him the laughing-stock of Marble range.

"Boy," said John Macy, "you sure made him look like something a coyote had left on the prairie. I'm right proud to shake your hand."

"You do not quite understand what I did," said Bannister slowly. "Of course this won't happen for a time . . . but it will come. I made it absolutely impossible for Le Beck not to meet me in a gun play. He has to do it to redeem himself, don't you see? And don't you ever get it into your heads that he's not fast. He's one of the fastest gun-fighters north of the Missouri River, and I don't care how far north you go. But I wanted to establish, before reliable witnesses, the fact that Cromer had hired a gunman."

"Well, son," said one of the others, "if anybody was to ask me, I'd say you sure enough did it."

They laughed at this — all save Bannister. He did not laugh. In his case, it wasn't so much Le Beck as it was the look on the faces of the cattlemen when Cromer had announced he would sell water to them. He knew that look and he knew full well its portent. It was the last appeal they would make to Cromer. They meant to fight. A water war would certainly involve the Half Diamond. That meant it would involve Florence Marble. He didn't like that idea. He knew — and it worried him not a little — that Florence was heavily involved in Marble Dome Land and Irrigation Company stock. She stood to lose unless. . . . His lips closed in a fine, white line. He might be able to carry out what he had in mind and he might not. But he'd try. Bannister told himself that he would do anything for Florence. And before he would see Florence marry Cromer, he would kill him.

"What do you think of it all?" asked John Macy as they entered the hotel dining room for supper before their return.

"I think he's a crook," said Bannister abruptly.

"An' that's the end of it," Macy agreed. "What do you intend to tell Miss Marble?"

"I'll tell her what happened and what the conference amounted to and that's all . . . which will be enough, I reckon," replied Bannister with a grim smile.

"Are you going to make any suggestions?" asked Macy, curious.

"Yes," replied Bannister. "I'm going to suggest that she keep out of it as far as possible. And in making the suggestion, I know danged well she can't keep out of it. But I want you to remember, Macy, that I like you and all that, but I'm following Miss Marble's orders. So don't count me in on any of your schemes unless you have her sanction."

"Schemes?" said Macy. "We have no schemes."

"But you will have them," said Bannister with sinister conviction. "I know your breed like a book. You mean to fight. And, while I won't come right out with it and embarrass us both, I'll say that I know your first move. I'd bet my life on it."

158

They were silent after this.

Soon after the meal the stockmen made their preparations to return. But Bannister lingered. He wanted to encounter Le Beck to ascertain if Cromer had given Le Beck orders to get him. In such an event Le Beck would draw on sight. Bannister, while he had the advantage of the little gunman in weight and muscle, realized that he had a worthy opponent in that same small man when it came to the expert use of shooting irons. Le Beck was as dangerous as dynamite. He had notches on his gun from butt to front sight and was not averse to filing in a few more.

So Bannister wandered in and out of the resorts of the town until finally, in a large tent, he saw his man. He passed close to him, stood and drank near him, gave him every opportunity to promote hostilities. But Le Beck did not notice him. This showed, in Bannister's mind, that Cromer was not ready to start things, that he had another card up his sleeve. But if Cromer was not prepared to start anything at that time, Sheriff Gus Campbell was.

When Bannister returned to the hotel, he found Sheriff Campbell and Deputy Van Note awaiting him. Campbell greeted him civilly and invited him into the little parlor

159

of the small, new structure.

"Bannister," he said briefly, "I'm being criticized."

"No doubt." Bannister scowled. "All men in public office are criticized."

"But I'm being criticized on your account," Campbell said.

"Yes?" drawled Bannister. "Through the good offices of our friend Cromer, I suppose. And you have to listen to Cromer because he doubtless commands a lot of votes. Is that it?"

The sheriff flushed. "No, that's not it," he declared. "And I'm not up here catering to votes. In fact, none of these men working here, except a very few, vote. The criticism started in Prairie City. There are a lot of people there who insist that you're this Maverick and a dangerous person to have around."

"So that's it again," said Bannister, with a smile that was very much like a sneer. "I suppose when the people around here get a thing in their heads, it can't be pried out with a crowbar."

"It isn't a question of what the people think," said the sheriff with a show of irritation, "it's a question of what I think, and I've come to think pretty strongly that you're The Maverick."

"There's two or three things I want to ask you, Sheriff," said Bannister with a cold gleam in his eyes. "First of all, it looks pretty much to me as if Cromer was urging you on my trail and dictating to you in general. Is that so?"

"Absolutely not," insisted Campbell in indignation, while Van Note also murmured a denial.

"Then why is it," Bannister demanded, "that you pick on me and let this Le Beck, who is Cromer's hired gunman . . . and you know it . . . run loose?"

"The minute I get anything on him he'll be roped in," the sheriff asserted.

"Have you got anything on me?" asked Bannister mildly.

"If you're the man I think you are, there are people who've got plenty on you," the sheriff replied grimly. "That's the difference."

"Another thing," said Bannister, leaning forward in his chair. "Do you like Florence Marble, owner of the Half Diamond?"

"I think the world of her," Campbell declared. "Her father was one of the best friends I ever had."

"Then I suppose you'd be willing to help her in an emergency," said Bannister. "Well, let's see . . . no, I've no more questions."

161

"Well, I don't know what you were getting at," growled the sheriff, "but I know one thing. You look enough like this Maverick, and you've shown enough of his characteristics to warrant being arrested on suspicion. Bannister, I've got to take you in."

"No, Sheriff," said Bannister, smiling and shaking his head. "You can't do that."

"And why not?" Campbell snapped out angrily, while Van Note moved in his chair.

Bannister was on his feet like lightning. His right hand flickered and held his gun. His face was a different face, cold and stern; the eyes were narrowed, shot with a steel-blue light. "Because," he said in a voice of ice, "I am The Maverick."

Campbell and Van Note sat motionlessly, staring at him. It was as if an altogether different person had suddenly been put into the place of Bannister. Here was a man who fairly radiated menace. The sheriff, who had encountered many bad men, almost shivered as he looked into the eyes of The Maverick — reputed to be the worst of them all.

"Now, Sheriff" — The Maverick's words fairly crackled in the little room — "you and I are going to make a deal. Are you willing to talk it over?"

Sheriff Campbell considered. "Yes," he

said finally, seeing there was no way out of it.

The gun went back into its holster and the face changed like magic. Again the man Bannister sat down before them.

"First of all, Sheriff," came the old, smooth voice, "my real identity must be kept a secret among us three, and I'll continue to be known as Bannister . . . which, by the way, is my real name. Now, Sheriff, you can't take me. There isn't a chance in the world for you to take me unless I'm willing. Maybe you don't know it, or believe it, but I'm as safe right here with you as if I was fifty miles out on the prairie. I just won't be taken, and there's plenty that know that." He paused and looked steadily at the sheriff, who grunted. "But there is a way you can take me," Bannister went on. "Now Miss Marble is going to have trouble. There's no doubt of it. The irrigation forces and the stockmen's forces are going to clash. I went to the conference between the two here today as her representative, and I know it. Also she has Hayes against her. And while she may not realize it, she has Cromer against her. And the Half Diamond is directly between the two factions. Do you see what I am getting at?"

The sheriff nodded thoughtfully.

163

"Now Miss Marble has hired me, not so much a companion to Howard, as most people think," Bannister continued, "but to keep an eye out and protect her in this dangerous situation. That is what I want to do, Sheriff. It's the first big thing in my life, this helping Florence Marble, and I'll be absolutely loyal. Look into my eyes, Sheriff, and tell me if you believe me."

Sheriff Gus Campbell knew men. "I believe you," he replied readily.

"Good," said Bannister in a satisfied tone. "Now here is my proposition, Sheriff, made in all sincerity. I want to be of what assistance I can to Florence Marble during this trouble. I'll serve her faithfully and will indulge in no activities of any kind or description outside of those required in her interests. I'm not The Maverick, understand, but Bannister of the Half Diamond. Lay off of me and permit me to do this and I give my word and promise that, when the trouble is over, I'll come in and lay my gun on your desk."

Sheriff Campbell sat silently for a space of fully two minutes. Not once did he take his eyes from Bannister's. Finally he looked away, out the window into the fading light. He turned quickly. "It's a deal!" he said, holding out his hand.

CHAPTER SIXTEEN

On the ride back to the Half Diamond, Bannister had much to occupy his thoughts. He did not start until the purple twilight was flooding the land and the first brave stars were swinging in the darkening sky. It was cool, with a sweet-scented breeze blowing gently. Everything about him — the shadowy land, the great arch of the sky — signified freedom. And Bannister was going to give up his freedom, which was his very heart's blood, for Florence Marble. But he was resolved that she should not learn his true identity. Sometime she would know, of course, and that would be soon enough.

Bannister loved to ride at night, with the sweet wind in his face, and a canopy of stars overhead. He was something of a dreamer, but this night there were no dreams. Outside of his service to Florence Marble his world was empty. He was stirred by resentment as he thought of the many acts that had been laid at his door though he had been blameless. Every misdeed in the southern country during the past two years had been attributed to him until his manufactured reputation was a thing to conjure with. All through one mistake, he thought bitterly. And then he exulted. He was doing a genuine service in a good cause. It is easy to dampen the spirit of youth, but it recovers rapidly. He hummed snatches of range songs as he rode at a leisurely pace across the dim stretches of the plain. He took his time. Consequently it was past midnight when he arrived at the Half Diamond, put up his horse, and started for the bunkhouse. He was surprised to see a light in the windows. When he entered, he received another surprise. Old Jeb White rose from a bunk.

"I figured you'd be gettin' home late," said the old man in his cracked voice, "so I waited up. Now don't be ornery, fer I'm boss tonight. I know you young buckaroos, an' don't fergit it. You've had a long ride from town an' you're hungry. I've got something ready an' you're goin' to eat it if I have to cram it down your throat with a stove poker. Take off your coat an' hat an' gun an' mosey along into the kitchen."

Bannister laughed in delight as the old

fellow passed through the door into the kitchen. He was hungry, and above all things he craved companionship this night.

When he entered the kitchen, he saw that Jeb had prepared a most palatable lunch. Cold chicken and salad, which undoubtedly had come from the house, jelly and cold biscuits, pickles, and on the stove the coffee pot was emitting a savory odor. He fell to eagerly enough.

"What went on up in Marble?" Jeb asked in what he meant to be a casual tone.

Bannister told him most of it, between mouthfuls. But he made no mention of Le Beck; why, he didn't know. Somehow he felt that it would be just as well if Le Beck's part in the affair did not get around the ranch and thus into Florence Marble's ears if it could be helped. She would probably hear of it, but not from him.

"Just what I thought," was Jeb's comment. "That feller Cromer just ain't on the square. He put up that job of the men leaving an' I'll bet anything he's kept big Hayes away for some evil purpose of his own . . . or else Hayes has got something up his sleeve on his own hook."

"Have you got any idea what it might be?" Bannister asked curiously.

"Wal, yes . . . in a way," said Jeb, peering

167

at Bannister out of his watery blue eyes. "But it might sound silly, and it's a serious charge, one I wouldn't want it to get around that I even hinted of."

"You can depend on me, Jeb," said Bannister. "A clam is noisy when it comes to me telling secrets."

"Wal . . . wal . . . ," old Jeb considered, "I'll tell you, Bannister, because . . . wal, you see, I kinder like you, an' I more'n like Miss Flo, an' I reckon by the way you've acted that you're a loyal cuss. Now, I'll say one thing, an' I'll say no more. I won't tell you why I think what I do or anything else. There's no use asking me any questions, none a-tall. I don't know where this hunch came from, but I've got a powerful lot of faith in hunches. You know, I believe this Hayes has designs on Half Diamond cattle. That's all. No more. Don't ask any questions."

Bannister started, and stared at the old man for some time. The nature of Jeb's hunch was positively astounding. It left him stunned. He said to himself: *Could there be a conspiracy to steal Florence Marble's stock as well as get her money into Marble Dome Land and Irrigation Company stock?* "All right, Jeb," he said, when he finally found his voice. "I won't ask any questions about

168

your hunch. But I'll ask one question that has nothing to do with it. Something about past doings. I understand some stock has been reported stolen. Do you think Hayes had anything to do with that?"

"I don't know a god-damn thing about it," Jeb replied. "Now have another cup of coffee an' then go to bed. Miss Flo will be wantin' details in the morning."

Bannister found it hard to sleep with old Jeb's intimation on his mind. He thought and thought and at last decided it was nothing more than a vague conjecture on Jeb's part, the wandering of a senile mind. Men of age lean toward the dramatic. At last he fell asleep. He woke with Jeb shaking him and saying he had hot cakes for breakfast and not to bother going to the house. So Bannister obliged him.

Howard was over soon after to make sure Bannister had returned all right, and later the two of them went to the ranch house and entered the living room, where Florence Marble was waiting.

"How does it look, Bannister?" she asked, coming to the point at once.

"None too good," he confessed. "I reckon there's going to be some trouble."

"I expected it," she said with a troubled look in her eyes. "Well, tell me about the meeting."

Bannister recited in detail what had happened, being interrupted at times by ejaculations from Florence. He avoided reference to the appearance of Le Beck on the scene. When he had finished, Florence spoke indignantly.

"I think John Macy and the others lose their heads too easily," was her comment. "Calling the project a fake. Why, the idea. They'll get water. Why, I'm a stockholder up there and I need water down here as well as they do."

"But you have a creek flowing past the Dome," Bannister pointed out.

"What of it?" Florence flashed. "I can use water in the river, too. They'll get their water, of course. Why, Sydney Cromer told me so himself."

"Don't you think perhaps there might be a reason for him telling you that?" Bannister suggested mildly.

This question only served to annoy Florence the more. "I don't like these veiled hints directed at Mister Cromer," she said with a toss of her head.

"An' I wouldn't trust Cromer any farther than I could throw a bull by the tail!" Howard blurted.

Florence turned on him in surprise. "Why,

170

what's the matter with you, Howard? You've never said anything against him before. Why are you against him all of a sudden?"

"Because Bannister don't take to him much, for one thing. I'll back Bannister's judgment any day. And I'll tell you something else that I didn't intend to tell you and that's this. When I was gambling my head off, Cromer was always glad to lend me money and take my I.O.U. and egg me on to get more. What was his idea in doing that?"

"Howard," said the girl sternly, "I'm ashamed of you. He loaned you that money because of me, probably." She flushed slightly. "Anyway, he thought he was doing the Half Diamond a favor. Don't you ever borrow another cent from him and we'll pay this money back at once."

"No chance of my ever borrowing any more from him," growled the boy. "And he's been paid back."

"Paid back? Where'd you get the money to pay him back . . . gambling?"

"From Bannister," said Howard almost in triumph, despite Bannister's signal to him to keep still. Florence looked at Bannister queerly. "Why did you do it?" she asked quietly.

"Because it didn't look exactly right to

me for Howard to be owing Cromer money," Bannister answered. "I hadn't the slightest idea in the world that you'd ever hear of it."

"I'll pay it at once," she said briskly.

Bannister shook his head. "I wouldn't take it from you. Howard can pay it back easy enough when he sells his cattle in the fall."

"That's right, Florence," said Howard. "I'll tend to it."

Florence was thoughtful for a spell. Did Bannister have an ulterior motive in aiding Howard? Or had he done this to irritate Cromer? And how did he come to have so much money? Again Cromer's hints were uppermost in her mind; again she felt a surge of doubt. Why should she be beset by doubts when they could be routed by a frank talk with this man before her.

"Howard, please go out a few minutes. I want to talk with Bannister."

Somehow Bannister had a premonition of what was coming. He could tell by her nervous manner and by the look in her eyes. Someone had been talking — Cromer, probably. He decided to evade the issue, whatever it was, without directly lying to her.

"Bannister," she said, when Howard had gone, "the range country is a great place for talk." It was a lame start and she realized it with his answer.

"So I've heard," he said.

"You know I engaged you without knowing anything at all about you except that you had befriended Howard," she said with increasing spirit.

"That's true," he agreed.

"And I've heard rumors that you might not be just as you've represented yourself," she said slowly.

"Who's been doing this talking?" he asked so sharply that her eyes widened.

"There isn't any need to go into that," she answered tartly. "This concerns no one except you and I. I'll come to the point. I don't know where you come from or anything about your past. But you were suspected in Prairie City of being . . . well, of being a well-known character."

"I was, while I was there," he said lightly. "I showed the professionals several thousand dollars' worth of fine points at stud poker, and that little incident where Howard was involved didn't put me in the background none."

"I don't mean that," said Florence, showing a trace of annoyance. "I mean elsewhere. It was said you bore a remarkable resemblance to an . . . an outlaw known as The

173

Maverick." She looked at him keenly.

"So?" he drawled. "Well, I suppose almost every man has a double. Do you think I'm this Maverick person?"

"I'm not saying any such thing," she returned, "but you can see my situation. Do you blame me for being curious?"

"Not at all," he replied heartily. "But, Miss Marble, if they thought I was this outlaw you mention, how does it come that the sheriff didn't grab me?"

She frowned at this and tried to remember what Cromer had said on that point. "Well, I don't know," she confessed. "The whole matter is more or less of a mystery to me, just as you are. But because of these rumors and the fact that you're employed here, I feel that I'm privileged to ask you a direct question. Bannister, are you The Maverick?"

He had decided upon his play before she put the question. His face froze. "I thought you could tell a man by his actions and by his eyes," he said sternly, rising and taking up his hat. "I won't answer such a question, because I thought you put more trust in me. Since you think, or maybe have some kind of an idea that I'm an outlaw . . . that I'm The Maverick . . . I'd best be leaving the ranch."

He turned and walked out the door. He

crossed the porch, but before he reached the top of the steps she came running after him.

"Bannister!" she cried. "I don't think any such thing, and never did!" She grasped his arm with both hands. "Bannister," she pleaded, "please don't go."

CHAPTER SEVENTEEN

After the cattlemen had left his office, Cromer stood for some minutes at his desk, white-faced, white-lipped, his hands clenched. Then he took to pacing the room.

"I was a fool," he muttered over and over. "Let my anger get away with me. Why didn't I stall 'em off? Fool . . . fool!"

He closed the door into the outer office and continued his pacing. He knew his reply to the association committee's questions meant trouble. He believed he was prepared to meet it. But he realized that had he used more tact in the delicate situation this trouble could have been avoided. He had thought it best to deal with the southern stockmen with an iron hand. Even now — he felt a thrill of hope at the thought — what could they do? He kept repeating the question: what could they do? His inability to answer this to his satisfaction made him uneasy. He was politically secure, since he had paid enough for that security. His was a small project, the first on the north range. The enterprise was a private one, as the great government projects were yet to come. It might be looked upon in the light of being an experiment. He had started it on a shoe string and was running it on a shoe string. Coming out from Chicago with the scheme in mind, he had invested such money as he had in securing the water rights and the land on time payments. There was a provision that one-third of the acreage was to be put under irrigation each year for three years. This he hoped to do. But he was selling the whole acreage on time payments at the start.

He had interested small town bankers and big stockmen to the east and west, and had sold a huge block of stock to Florence Marble, but he had not been able to interest the stockmen south of Indian River, who failed to see how the project would in any way benefit them and who regarded his flattering promises of big stock dividends with stoic reserve. So far his expenditure had not been so great. One great ditch from the river and the building of the dam. He had expert salesmen out selling stock as far south as the Montana-Wyoming line, other salesmen in Minneapolis and St. Paul and Chicago, and they were making good. Every mail brought a sheaf of checks, to be deposited in Prairie City and Big Falls until such time as he would open his own bank. He controlled the bank as he did the irrigation enterprise. Sydney Cromer was president and general manager of the Marble Dome Land and Irrigation Company for one reason — to get the money.

But when he met Florence Marble he realized there was something he wanted besides money. He realized, too, the vast acres and fat herds of stock that would go with the prize. Cromer could not be said to be altogether scrupulous in his dealings and schemes, yet things were going nicely until the advent of Bannister and his employment by Florence. Cromer could recognize ability and cleverness on sight, and he saw at once that Bannister possessed both. Therefore, Bannister was dangerous and a man to be gotten rid of as soon as possible. But how? In his position Cromer had to be careful. There could be no boomerang to fasten the blame on him for anything that might happen. Even after his warning to Florence about the man, she had sent him with the association committee as her representative!

It was this more than anything else that caused Cromer to walk the floor of his private office, numbing his brain in a futile effort to seek a loophole through the net that Bannister apparently was weaving. He wondered what Bannister would tell Florence and what affect his report would have upon the girl. This uncertainty increased his uneasiness. He would have to go down to the Half Diamond and find out. But what excuse could he make for the trip?

On his desk was a pad of gaudy stock certificates for the Marble State Bank. His eye brightened. Of course! He was offering a limited amount of stock in the bank. An excellent excuse. He might see Bannister, but. . . . Cromer stopped dead in his tracks with a startled look on his face. There was one thing he hadn't tried on Bannister. Money. And now Cromer imagined that he had discovered the cause of all his trouble. Bannister was carrying out a clever scheme to compel him to buy him off. Cromer resumed his pacing at a much faster gait in his excitement. He reasoned that it was as plain as day. Bannister was a gambler, a rover — he might be The Maverick. In the latter case Cromer knew he would be right beyond the peradventure of a doubt. Bannister had gotten into Florence Marble's good graces through Howard. It had been clever work. It was ridiculous that a man such as he would be working in any capacity on a ranch at a nominal wage. Cromer was certain he had struck it. Bannister was blackmailing him, but doing it in a way that was well within the law. He was covered at every angle in such manner that Cromer himself would have to make the overtures.

"Well, he can have it!" Cromer exclaimed aloud. The only question would be as to the amount. At this juncture there came three light raps on the rear door. Cromer started and his eyes fairly glistened. "Come in," he invited amiably.

The door opened and Le Beck slipped into the office, carefully closing the door after him. Two fingers of his left hand were bandaged. There were numerous patches of court plaster on his face where he had been cut by the glass when he went through the window. His eyes gleamed fiercely.

"Decorated up for some kind of a carnival?" asked Cromer sweetly.

"Bah!" Le Beck spat the word out with venom.

"Looks as if you'd had some kind of an accident," Cromer ventured pleasantly.

Le Beck came around the desk like a cat. "Don't you fool with me," he whistled through his teeth. "No like."

"Well, somebody's been fooling with you

and I've an idea who it was," observed Cromer, evidently unafraid. "Why did you fire that shot? Did you think you could scare him?"

The half-breed — for such he was, as everybody knew — snarled like a wild animal. "I theenk to stop heem . . . make heem shoot."

"That would have been fine business," sneered Cromer. "I told you to keep your gun in the leather unless they started to shoot first. In that case . . . well, I'm entitled to a bodyguard and it would be all right." He scowled heavily.

"How he know I'm there?" Le Beck pointed to the washstand and the fallen curtain.

"Probably saw your feet under the curtain," Cromer replied.

"Leeson," said Le Beck, with an evil glare in his eyes, "I no fight with the hands. An' he ees too beeg. I fight with the gun." He tapped the butt of his weapon with long, slender fingers. "Now I keel heem. You savvy?" The light in his eyes changed to one of savage anticipation.

"You'll do no such thing," said Cromer, sternly showing he was startled.

"Ah, you will see." Le Beck nodded his head energetically.

"Get that out of your fool head!" Cromer thundered. "Don't you know that cattle bunch saw you here, saw Bannister throw you through the window after you fired a shot at him?"

"But that is eet," Le Beck interrupted, holding up a finger. "That give me the right, you see?"

"No, I don't see," said Cromer angrily. "It would come right back on me. You lay off him till . . . till the time comes. Are you going to take my orders?"

"Oh," lisped Le Beck, "I take thees orders, but I no like the insult."

"Well, you've got to stand for it at the present," growled Cromer, looking at his henchman speculatively. "He did that more on my account than on yours. He wanted to show off in front of me, understand?"

"Mebbe so, but he show off with me," hissed Le Beck. "I no like." He shook his head ominously.

Cromer wasn't sure of Le Beck. He might obey orders and he might not. If he went gunning straightaway for Bannister, it would be well nigh fatal. He reached into a pocket and brought out some gold pieces.

"Here, take these," he said, "and go gamble and forget it. Forget it, understand, until you get orders from me."

Le Beck's eyes glistened as he caught the yellow gleam of the gold in Cromer's palm. He hesitated. Then, without a word, he took the money and went out the rear door, leaving Cromer to sigh with relief and wonder if he hadn't engaged a spirit too wild to control.

He sat down at his desk and fingered the bank stock certificates. It was time he began offering the stock. The bank building would soon be completed and ready for business. The vault was already at the railhead, and would soon be transported to Marble. Cromer's eyes gained luster as he thought of the large sum of cash that would be carried. Most of the farm tracts already had been contracted for and a down payment made. In another month a big drawing would be held and the tracts allotted according to the numbers drawn by the purchasers. Thus everyone had an equal chance for choice locations. It was a gamble that appealed to purchasers, most of whom were from the Middle West. At the drawing another payment was due. Cash. Cromer's eyes glistened, but his face clouded again as he remembered the threatened trouble with the Indian River cattlemen. Above all things this trouble must be averted until after the drawing at least. If it were to come before the drawing, it might scare off the prospective purchasers. He had a sudden inspiration. He would ride down and see John Macy, chairman of the Cattlemen's Association committee, tell him they had misunderstood him in some ways and that he had reconsidered and would guarantee to protect them for such water as they needed.

He thumped his desk in exultation. An excellent way out of the mess he was in, and he could shoot the water down there so far as that was concerned. In fact, he could live up to the bargain without endangering his supply of water for the project — until the main ditches and laterals were in. And on the way down to see Macy, he could stop and see Florence Marble, explain the purpose of his errand — which was sure to please her — and indirectly ascertain what effect Bannister's attendance at the conference had had at the Half Diamond. Then, if conditions appeared favorable, he could approach Bannister. His plans fully laid, he decided to start early next morning.

CHAPTER EIGHTEEN

It was hardly 9:00 next morning when Florence, who was tending the flowers in the yard, looked up quickly as a horseman came riding in through the cottonwoods and saw that it was Cromer. Surprised at the early visit, she was surprised also that she should be assailed by a vague feeling of annoyance.

" 'Morning!" called Cromer with a wave of the hand. Then after he had dismounted: "I know I'm early, Florence, but I'm on my way down to the Macy Ranch to see John Macy, and I thought I'd stop in and say hello."

Again she was conscious of the feeling of annoyance, this time because of the use of her first name, although she hadn't particularly resented it before. "You're welcome any time, Mister Cromer," she said, trying to shake off her irritation, "but I don't understand your going to the Macy Ranch. I understand he was chairman of that committee yesterday and that they came away from your office pretty mad."

"Well, they misunderstood some things," he answered with a depreciatory gesture, "and I got mad myself when I thought they were going a little strong, and . . . well, there was a general misunderstanding. We didn't get at the thing right on either side."

"But Bannister tells me you refused them water and offered to sell it to them," Florence contended.

"I meant I would sell them what they wanted in excess of the amount left after we had exercised our water rights," he explained.

For the first time a doubt as to Cromer's intentions and his principles surged through Florence's mind. "But you said nothing about selling water to the stockmen when you explained this irrigation proposition to me," she accused.

"Nor do I intend to sell them any," he said uncomfortably. "I've changed my mind about that since cooling off after yesterday's conference. I'll protect them for what they need and I'm going to tell them that. That's why I'm going down this morning to see Macy."

"Well, you won't have to go down," she said, "for here he comes."

John Macy rode in through the cotton-woods and waved a cheery good morning to Florence, but, when he recognized Cromer, his smile froze and he frowned heavily. Bannister sauntered from the bunk-house.

"You're on the job already, I see," said Macy angrily, eyeing Cromer with a malevolent stare. "Putting more trash into Miss Flo's head, I suppose. Telling her how you're goin' to make suckers outta the cattlemen an' tryin' to get her to buy more stock, an'. . . ."

"I was on my way to your place," said Cromer.

"My place," Macy returned. "If I ever catch you on my range, I'll give you a treatment with a sawed-off shotgun."

"I was going to tell you that a mistake had been made yesterday," Cromer explained with a great show of dignity.

"There sure was," Macy agreed, nodding his head. "You're right there. An you're the one that made the mistake. Telling us you'd sell us water, sticking a hired gunman behind a curtain where he could shoot us up if need be. Good thing Bannister was along, at that, I reckon. That's one thing I came up to tell Miss Flo about."

Florence saw Cromer's face go white. She

looked from him to Bannister and caught Bannister in the act of signaling to Macy to keep still. "What is this, Bannister?" she demanded. "You didn't tell me anything about a gunman behind a curtain."

"I was entitled to a bodyguard after all the threats that have been made by that bunch down here," Cromer declared in a loud, blustering tone. "How did I know what might happen, with every one of the committee armed and boiling over about nothing."

"I suppose it would be a small item if our cattle were to die of thirst or something like that?" sneered Macy.

"But they're not going to die of thirst," insisted Cromer desperately. "That's why I was on my way to see you this morning. But you won't give a man a chance to talk."

"You had plenty of chance to talk yesterday," Macy pointed out. "But you didn't talk in the right direction."

"We were all excited," said Cromer in a modulated voice. He was striving to save his face before Florence Marble and to avert the dreaded prospect of trouble with the cattlemen before the big drawing. "I cooled down, thought it over, and looked for you after the conference, but you had already gone. So I decided to see you this morning.

There's no use having trouble over this, for there will be enough water for all of us."

"That's more'n you could say yesterday," growled Macy, staring at Cromer doubtfully.

Bannister also was looking at Cromer with interest, a smile suggesting derision showing faintly on his lips.

"I told you we were all excited yesterday," said Cromer impatiently. "There never was any intention on the part of the Marble Dome Land and Irrigation Company to keep water from the Indian River stockmen. Our contract calls for so many inches from the river. We are entitled to that flow. If it doesn't leave sufficient water for you folks down here, we could ask pay for water if we wanted to, I suppose. But I'm down here this morning to tell you that we have no such intention."

Macy considered this, while Bannister and Florence looked on as interested spectators. "Funny you changed your mind so quick," Macy observed suspiciously.

"Not funny at all," Cromer protested. "And I didn't change my mind because of your threat to take the water if we didn't give it to you. In fact, I didn't change my mind at all, for we had no intention of working a hardship on you people. Do you think

189

it would pay us . . . in a business way, I mean . . . to do that? Of course not. It wouldn't pay us to antagonize anybody." He saw with great inward satisfaction that his bluff was going over.

"You would tell the other members of the association committee that?" Macy inquired.

"I would," Cromer answered readily.

"You'd make an agreement as to that?" Macy asked.

"At the next meeting of the board of directors on July Tenth," said Cromer. He had decided while they were talking to hold the drawing on the Fourth of July and make a gala event of it.

"Well, it sounds all right," said Macy, "an', anyway, I've two witnesses."

"You won't need them," Cromer snapped out with a show of indignation. "My word is good."

"Then we'll take it," John Macy decided, with his first smile of the morning. "Miss Flo" — turning to Florence — "my visit up here this morning turned out better than I expected. Now I'll be ridin' over to headquarters to spill the news."

Cromer watched him go, satisfied that he had convinced him, and knowing very well that he was playing a dangerous game.

"I told Bannister that you would not keep the water from the southern stockmen," said Florence in a tone of relief. She still was thinking of Macy's statement about the gunman, and Cromer's contention that he was entitled to a bodyguard, but she did not intend to refer to it again. It did not, however, set Cromer forth in a very good light; she realized that.

"Never had any intention of doing anything of the kind," declared Cromer. He was conscious of an intangible barrier forming between them. "They came at me the wrong way, that was all. I guess I was rather tired, for I'd had a hard morning with the engineers." Then, turning to Bannister: "I wonder if I could have a little talk with you about a . . . a problem I have up there."

"Sure thing," said Bannister. "Come right along."

A commonplace or two with Florence, and Cromer followed him to the bunkhouse. Inside, Cromer sat on one of the chairs by the table, took off his hat, and wiped his forehead with his handkerchief, then eyed Bannister curiously as the latter took his place across from him. He was about to play a trump card.

"Bannister," he said slowly, "I'm not going to exact a promise, but I'll leave it to your sense of fairness not to mention anything about what I am going to say to Miss Marble, if you are not interested. If you are interested, use your best judgment as to explanations."

"Sounds important," was Bannister's comment.

"Now, that incident of yesterday," Cromer began uneasily, "I had Le Beck around in case of . . . well, I don't know these fighting Westerners any too well, and I'm not a gunman, and I thought it would be as well to have him handy to stop any trouble. I discharged him for firing that shot."

"Le Beck was lucky I didn't fire back," said Bannister quietly.

"I expect so." Cromer nodded. "Well, now, I don't want to appear as butting in or anything like that . . . but there's no question but that you're worth far more money than you're receiving here, and that you could really be of more service to Miss Marble elsewhere." He was watching Bannister closely and was gratified to see his eyes light up with interest.

"In just what way?" Bannister asked coolly.

"Miss Marble is heavily interested in the Marble Dome Land and Irrigation Company," Cromer pointed out. "She has considerable at stake, just as I have . . . just as all of us have. The success of the project means much to her, as it means much to all of us. Now, the company needs men, not merely laborers, but men of unique ability able to assume unusual duties and difficult tasks. You are such a man, Bannister." He ended in a subtle note of flattery.

"You think so?" said Bannister pleasantly.

"I know so," Cromer declared, feeling that he was making headway. "I could use you, Bannister, if Miss Marble could spare you, and I could use you at a very good salary . . . at a very large salary, in fact."

"You offering me a job?" Bannister inquired mildly.

"I am that," replied Cromer, "and, as I say, at a big salary."

"I'd rather have a lump sum," said Bannister coldly.

Cromer's eyes shone. It was just as he had expected. He patted himself on the back mentally. Bannister had been playing a game, just as he had reasoned. Now Bannister was willing to be bought off. "How . . . how much would you expect?" he asked, smiling and lifting his brows significantly.

"One hundred thousand dollars," Bannister answered nonchalantly.

"A hundred thousand . . . but that's

preposterous!" Cromer gasped.

Bannister leaned his elbows on the table and looked Cromer straight in the eye. "You don't want me to work up there and you know it," he said evenly. "You want me to slope out of here. All right, I'm willing to slope . . . for a hundred thousand. And I'll see that you get a hundred thousand dollars' worth of Marble Dome Land and Irrigation Company stock in exchange."

Cromer's eyes were bulging. "Where would you get that much stock?" he demanded derisively.

"Florence Marble has about that, hasn't she?"

"What's that got to do with it?"

"Just this," said Bannister, tapping his forefinger on the table top. "You turn over the hundred thousand, Miss Marble will turn over the stock . . . and I go."

"Miss Marble never said anything to me about wanting to turn over any stock," said Cromer warmly. "I don't get you at all."

"Of course not. So far as I know at the present moment she doesn't want to turn over any stock. But I believe I could induce her to do so. Don't you think that's quite a chunk of money for that girl to have invested in your . . . enterprise?"

"I fail to see where it's any of your business," Cromer retorted hotly.

Bannister shrugged. "I am in Miss Marble's employ," he said mildly, "and naturally I have her interests at heart. You paid me a compliment about having certain ability a while back. Let's grant, then, that I can see this girl is in pretty strong. If anything was to slip, say, if those stockmen down there were to go on the rampage or something, if your bookkeeping staff was to get tangled up . . . sit down!" Cromer, red-faced, his eyes glaring, sank back into his chair at the command. "As I say," Bannister continued, "if anything was to go wrong, she'd stand to lose more'n she could afford, maybe. And her house is papered so she'd have no use for those stock certificates. I've never mentioned these things to her, but I think she's beginning to wonder whether she was hypnotized or not. You came down here to buy me off. I've shown you how you can do it. Do you agree to the terms?"

"No!" shouted Cromer, slamming the table with his fist. "It's the most impertinent proposition I ever listened to."

"So I guess we can't make a deal," said Bannister, rising. Then, as Cromer, white with fury, plunged toward the door, he called to him: "Cromer!"

The other swung about, his fists clenched.

"Be careful," Bannister warned. "Watch your knitting up there, or I'll take that irrigation project away from you."

CHAPTER NINETEEN

Cromer's rage was at such white heat that he did not dare risk further conversation with Florence Marble that morning. As she had gone into the house, he did not even take the trouble to tell her he was going, but dashed madly through the cottonwoods and spurred his horse up the road to the bench land at a cruel pace. Then he straightened out for Marble, pushing his horse to the utmost to keep pace with his racing thoughts. He actually had a feeling that Bannister had betrayed him. He had been sure that Bannister would take his price and quit the country. His manner as Cromer had talked indicated such action. And then Bannister had sprung his bombshell. What rankled as much, and more, was the fact that something had come between himself and Florence Marble. He felt, somehow, the overwhelming conviction that so far as ever obtaining Florence for a wife, he might as well give up. He did not blame this on his own actions, but on Bannister. It was all plain now. Bannister was after the girl. He was using Howard as a tool. He would doubtless use the proposition Cromer had made this morning as another wedge to gain further favor. He would play up the story of Le Beck being in the office during the conference with the committee. He would discount Cromer's promise to Macy.

Cromer ground his teeth in bitter and futile anger as he sped northward. Take his irrigation project away from him! How far did the fool think he could go? There was only one solution to the whole problem, and that was to get rid of Bannister in any way that offered. This Cromer decided to do if it was the last thing he did on earth. With this determination deeply rooted in his mind, the man cooled down considerably, and, when he rode into town in record time, he was comparatively calm.

Florence Marble had been standing just within the front doorway when he left at such a furious pace. She went out on the porch as Bannister came from the bunk-house.

"Whatever has got into Mister Cromer?" she asked wonderingly.

"Reckon he's in a hurry," was the cryptic reply.

"He didn't even pause to wave good bye," said the puzzled girl, eyeing Bannister keenly. "Bannister, what did he want with you?"

"Oh, just explaining how that gunman happened to be in the office yesterday sort of by accident," Bannister answered casually. "Wanted to know where he could pick up some good men, and one thing and another."

"Bannister, you're concealing something," she accused severely. "But we'll let that go. Who was the gunman in the office up there? I've a right to know, remember, because you were there as my proxy."

"Well . . . ," Bannister hesitated. But she had put it up to him so he could hardly get out of it. "It was Le Beck," he finished.

"Le Beck!" she exclaimed. "So he's hired that killer as a . . . what did he call it? Bodyguard?"

"That's what he called him," Bannister replied dryly.

"And you didn't say a word about it. You were protecting him. Why, the man's a coward. And him coming down here trying to tell me you were The Maverick. I don't care if you do know now, after what's happened."

"I had a hunch it was him," said Bannister.

She was looking at him queerly. "You're not much for talking about people behind their backs, are you, Bannister?" she asked in a lower voice.

"Not so you could notice it," he conceded. "But there are emergencies when I reckon it has to be done. I haven't met up with any of 'em yet, but there's no telling."

She walked over to him and held out her hand. As he took it, a series of thrills vibrated through his whole being.

"Bannister, I took you for what you are from the start," she said simply. "You're just naturally all man."

Something tugged at his throat. All man. The Maverick? The horrible futility of his situation kept back the words that were on his tongue. Finally: "Where'd Howard go?" he asked lamely.

"I sent him to town for a sprayer," she told him. "Oh, here's Manley in from the Dome."

Bannister turned and saw the manager, who had taken charge of the big herd of beef cattle at the Dome, jogging out of the trees. He was mighty glad of the interruption.

"I'll take your horse," he said to Manley as the latter dismounted. But he didn't have a chance to do so for old Jeb came at a swift hobble and took charge of the animal.

"How's everything at the Dome, Manley?" asked Florence by way of greeting.

"Not so good," said the manager, wiping sweat and dust from his face and forehead. "I took count out there an' we're some hundred an' sixteen steers short." He paused as if lost in thought. "I can't understand it," he resumed. "That many couldn't stray without our knowing it. An' if they're being stolen, they're being taken a few at a time. The hell of it is, I haven't a chance of taking a look around right now."

"Well, I have," Bannister put in, "and, if it's all right with you, I'll do a little snooping around below the Dome and see what I can see."

"It's sure all right with me," said Manley. "If you could strike a trail that's being used, or see some sign, we might get a line on this business."

"You really think we're up against rustlers again?" Florence asked in a worried voice.

"I can't see any other reason for a hundred an' sixteen head being missing at a crack so soon after the roundup," Manley replied. "An' we've been watching 'em close, too, damn it."

"They'd take 'em through the river breaks," said Bannister with conviction. "And that's where I'm going to look."

"Might be," Manley agreed. "Pretty likely, in fact. Suppose you do take a look around down there. I've got to make out the time of a couple of hands I'm letting go, or . . . but there's nothing more to tell you. You know the Half Diamond brand . . . it's a big Half Diamond over a small M. But you've seen it, of course, so what am I talking about? Well, I'm going into the office. If you find out anything, let me know. The whole outfit's ready to take the trail if we have something to go on."

"I'll have Martha get a lunch ready while you're getting your horse," Florence told Bannister as she started for the house.

Bannister rode eastward just outside the timber fringe along the river. This was a new angle to Florence Marble's troubles. Although she might not realize it, she really was menaced by Cromer on the north, by the stockmen on the south, and now rustlers were operating in the east. He remembered old Jeb's hint that Hayes might have designs on Half Diamond cattle. He hadn't seen

Hayes anywhere in town. Link was still in the hospital. He recalled, too, how incensed Hayes had been because of Bannister's presence on the ranch and his inadvertently calling him a spy. Why spy? Had it been a slip? And Hayes had been exceedingly interested that first day when Bannister had come on the ranch from the south. But this, of course, was all wild conjecture. Still, as a skilled trailer, Bannister was ready to grasp at any clue or sign.

He rode slowly eastward, and, whenever he came to a trail, however dim, leading into the wilderness of the badlands, he paused and looked for signs to ascertain whether it had recently been used. He saw no such sign, and eventually reached the main road or trail from the Dome which led to the wide ford of the river. Here there were tracks, comparatively fresh tracks, but they had been made by horses. As this was the main trail north and south, Bannister decided that the Cattlemen's Association committee members had crossed the river here on their way to and from the town of Marble. He rode on.

He came finally to the trail by which he and Howard had entered the badlands the day they were exploring the district. Cattle had been on this trail, but not recently. He followed it in and soon was involved in a labyrinth of trails and cross trails, running in every direction, with tracks everywhere. He checked his horse with an exclamation of disgust. A few head of stock could make all those old tracks, and there were strays in the breaks. He was getting nowhere. Next he decided to ride down to the trail that ran east and west above the banks of the river.

It was well past noon by this time, with the sun past the zenith and poised for its drop toward the western mountains. He came to a little meadow with good grass and a spring and dismounted. After refreshing himself at the spring, he watered his horse, loosened the saddle cinch, and turned the animal out to graze. Then he had recourse to the fat lunch Martha had put up for him. After he had eaten, he lay back on the soft grass in the shade at the edge of the meadow and smoked.

As a matter of fact, Bannister was not so much concerned with the rustling operations — though they were important — as he was with the activities of Cromer. The Marble Dome Land and Irrigation Company project didn't look good to him, as it was being managed. He could not get the impression out of his mind that there was more interest on the part of Cromer in selling stock and plots than in the work of the project itself. He smoked and dozed until midafternoon before he resumed the saddle. When he reached the river trail, he stopped dead at first sight. He had found his sign! Plain and fresh were the tracks left by two horses that had gone east. Bannister decided they had been made early that morning. That being the case, there was an excellent possibility that the horsemen might be expected to return at nightfall. He considered his next move carefully. If he followed those tracks, he would leave a fresh track of his own. This would be bound to excite suspicion when it was seen by the men who had ridden down this way. Even if he was to follow the tracks and discover a rendezvous, it might avail him nothing because of the sign he would leave himself. If the tracks led to where stolen cattle were cached, he would have to investigate, ascertain how the stock was being driven in, and how the rustlers were to be taken. And the chief of the band must be taken above all things.

Bannister knew of no other trail by which he could parallel the river trail. Then he came to a decision. He would not risk going on the river trail, but he would take up his station on a low ridge above it and wait for night — wait all night, if necessary. If the riders returned on their way out, he would then ride down the trail, assuming they would be gone some time. If they didn't return, he would take the down trail in the morning.

He turned off the trail he was on and rode over a ridge into a wide ravine. Here he turned his horse loose to graze and spent the time until sundown. Then he returned to his station, tied his horse among the trees, inspected the river trail to make sure no one had passed since he had been there last, and took up his vigil on the ridge, which was more or less open, with scanty tree growth. The twilight played with all colors of the rainbow on the weird, tumbled land about him, then was swallowed by the black velvet cloak of night. The stars broke forth in clusters and a new moon slipped up out of the east, a gleaming, celestial bangle. The night wind whispered inquiringly among the leaves.

Bannister waited for what seemed hours and hours, and finally his sixth sense — the intuition of the man of the open — was aroused to a premonition of impending danger. He looked about at the dim reaches of the breaks, down at the trail, lighted somewhat by the sheen of the moonlight on the river. An owl hooted and his hand darted to his gun. He swore softly under his breath. What was it? He was not a nervous man. Yet there was the feeling — that feeling of a presence near. He couldn't shake it off. It was there. The feeling. . . .

He saw its shadow before he could dodge. The rope dropped over his shoulders, tightened in the instant he pulled his gun. He was jerked backward, dragged. But as the rope became taut, he fired in the direction it led. Three times his gun blazed, for his right forearm was free. The rope suddenly loosened and he leaped to his feet, shaking it free. Red flame streaked across the shadows under the trees to his left. Bannister now was under a stunted pine. He fired three more shots in the direction from whence the flashes had come and dropped to the ground to reload his gun.

Silence.

Bannister wriggled away from his position. He could hear nothing. How they had discovered he was on the ridge, he did not know, but he surmised that there had been a look-out somewhere in the vicinity or that he had been seen by accident, perhaps from across the river. He lay still for some time. Then he rose slowly to one knee, gun in hand. The wind whispered; the owl voiced its complaint. Bannister rose to his feet.

There was a burst of fire and the heavens crashed upon him. He stumbled forward into black oblivion.

CHAPTER TWENTY

In his delirious sleep, Bannister was riding like mad — riding like mad from white specters that pursued him on great blue horses. The smell of smoke was in the air; there was fire somewhere. He could not seem to make his feet move to spur his mount to greater exertion. He looked behind and his pursuers had changed to little brown men with peaked caps like those of a chimney sweep. Funny, he thought. Then his horse stumbled and he went whirling through the air. They were upon him in a minute — scores of them. The white heat of a branding iron dazzled his eyes. It came down upon his head and he shrieked with pain. It came down again . . . again. He came out of it with a jerk — conscious.

His first sensation was that of a burning pain on the left side of the head. It was as if a red-hot poker was being drawn backward and forward, relentlessly, just above his left ear. He squirmed with the torture of it. He started to put his hand to his head but couldn't move it. Vaguely he realized that he was bound hand and foot. Then the events preceding that burst of flame and his loss of consciousness came back to him. He opened his eyes.

At first he could see nothing. Then, twisting his aching head a bit, he saw a patch of light — a square patch, such as would be made by a window. He was lying on something soft — a bunk. He realized he was in a cabin. He cried aloud several times but received no answer. He groaned with the excruciating pain. His mouth and tongue and lips were dry; his whole being cried for water. He shouted and twisted and turned in the bunk until a sharp pain, like the stab of a knife, stopped him with a moan. Then he was off again. Riding — riding — riding. Florence Marble was with him. She disappeared and Howard Marble was with him. Green and yellow lights broke forth in wreathed clusters and in the center were the leering faces of Cromer and Le Beck. A great, black cloud came down and he plowed into it, choking . . . choking.

When he again opened his eyes, it was daylight. He stared up at the rafters. Then he twisted his head again, wincing with the fire above his left ear. Yes, he was in a cabin. There was a table under one of the windows, a few empty shelves, an old, rusty stove, a bench. It somehow had a familiar look. He racked his aching brain, and then he had it. He was in the cabin behind the leaning cottonwood, the cabin Howard had shown him the day they had gone into the badlands together. In the old rustler's cabin, wounded, bound hand and foot — a prisoner.

He clenched his teeth against the agonizing pain in his head, twisted and squirmed and strained at his bonds with every iota of his strength, but it was no use. Whoever had bound him had been no amateur. The job had been well done. He desisted in his efforts, and tried to wet his lips with a dry tongue.

"Water," he croaked, looking at the closed door. Could any one be out there? "Water! Water!" It was a torment to breathe.

Once more he drifted off into delirium, and this time he was back in another country where there were pepper trees and mesquite and dust — always dust. He was riding again, shooting over his shoulder, racing for the hills that stood out in jagged purple outlines like the pieces of a purple puzzle. A buzzard soared overhead. He yelled to it and it swooped down, its great beak plunging into his head.

He awoke again with the pain. It was a steady, deep, aching pain now. He knew its portent. That horrible burst of flame on the ridge had sent a bullet into his head. They had seen him and stolen upon him from behind. There must have been more than one of them. He had been a fool to get up from the ground. His work for nothing. They had him now — the rustlers, of course.

The ripple of water came to his ears, and suddenly he was beside a running stream. He lay down upon his stomach and buried his face in its cool depths. But he couldn't swallow. There it was, the water, but he couldn't drink it. He crawled into it and splashed about. But he couldn't swallow. . . .

The sunlight was streaming into the cabin and his eyes were wide open. How long would they leave him here? Perhaps they didn't intend to come back. He wouldn't mind dying if he could only quench his thirst. He strained futilely at his bonds with diminishing strength.

"Water!" he shrieked in a cracked voice. "Water!" He felt a madness creeping over him.

And then, against the fulgent rays of the

sun in a window, he saw a shadow — a head and shoulders. He cried out inarticulately. There came a crash at the window and the sash flew inward as glass splintered and rained on the table. The head and shoulders came through with a strong body after them.

"Howard!" croaked the man on thc bunk.

In a jiffy Howard Marble had out his knife and was cutting the ropes that bound Bannister.

"Lucky I came this way," he was saying. "Florence told me you'd gone to the badlands, and, when you didn't come home last night, I came to look for you. I cut through here, saw the door padlocked, and stopped because I thought it was strange. Then I heard you cry out. Now . . . sit up, Bannister."

He helped Bannister, who was steadily growing weaker, to sit up on the edge of the bunk.

"Water," Bannister mumbled.

"Right away," said Howard. He hurried to the spring, where there was a drinking can, filled it with the cold water, and brought it back.

"Not too much at a time," he warned. "Suffering Jupiter, man, you're hit."

He didn't wait for further words. Tearing the blue bandanna from about his neck, he ran to the spring and soaked it, together with his pocket handkerchief. Then he bathed the ugly wound on Bannister's head, placed the dripping white handkerchief over it and bound it in place with the bandanna.

"Come on," he said, "we're getting home quick as we can."

Bannister's horse, gun, and hat were missing. Howard didn't ask for explanations. He surmised what had happened, for he knew the nature of the mission upon which Bannister had been bent. He helped him into the saddle on his own horse and climbed up behind him. They proceeded along the trail and out upon the plain from behind the leaning cottonwood. Then they turned west toward the ranch.

Bannister was beginning to sway and mutter incoherently. Howard's strength was easily equal to the demand made upon it. He held Bannister securely in the saddle and spurred his horse into a gentle lope. But he soon checked the animal to a fast walk as Bannister began to rave in the throes of delirium. It took strength to hold him then.

They came finally to the pastures and fields, then the windbreak of cottonwoods and the road to the yard. Florence was at her flower beds and saw them as soon as they broke through the trees. With a little cry she came running as Howard drew up at the porch.

"Bannister's hit," said Howard crisply. "Call Jeb. We must get him upstairs to bed."

Florence's face had gone white. For the space of a few moments she faltered. Then she was suddenly calm and, running toward the bunkhouse, called Jeb. He came quickly and they got Bannister out of the saddle and up the stairs to a front room. Howard undressed him and got him into bed.

Then Florence and Martha began to work over him, cleansing the wound and bandaging it with clean, cool strips. He moaned and muttered in his delirium as he burned with fever.

"I'm going for the company doctor," Howard announced, "an' I'm going like all hell!"

In a few minutes he was flying northward on a fresh mount, one of the fastest horses on the ranch. He passed the north range herd, crossed the line, and dashed between the little white stakes on the project. In record time he reached the tents and then the dusty street. He pulled up where some men were standing.

"Where's the doctor?" he called.

"Over there in the hospital tent," said one

215

of the men, pointing to a tent of brown canvas.

Howard was there in a twinkling. Inside there was no doubt as to who was the doctor. Howard approached the man in the white coat with the Vandyke beard.

"Doctor," he said breathlessly, "there's a man badly hurt down at the Half Diamond. Can you come down right away?"

"Well, very soon," was the answer, "but I have to have an order from Mister Cromer in the meantime."

"I'll get it," snapped Howard, and he was out of the tent.

He found Cromer in his office. "There's a man badly hurt down at the ranch," he told the irrigation manager, "an' we'd like to have your doctor come an' look after him."

"Who's hurt?" Cromer asked calmly.

"Bannister," Howard replied. "Shot in the head, I guess."

"Well," said Cromer, "according to our insurance arrangement, our doctor isn't supposed to leave the project."

"What!" cried Howard. "With a man maybe dying within reach?"

"He isn't here now, anyway," said Cromer with a wry smile.

"He's in the hospital tent," Howard flashed, "I just saw him. He said he could come soon, but he had to have an order from you to go."

Cromer's face darkened. "Oh, he said that, did he? So he's down in the hospital tent. Well, I'll go down and see him shortly and see what we can do. It's against regulations. . . ."

"You're a white-livered rat if one ever lived!" shouted Howard, and he called Cromer a name that caused the man's teeth to clamp shut.

Fire was raging in Howard's eyes. He started for the door. Then he whirled. "You don't intend to send him," he said through his teeth. He leaped for the desk, pulling his gun, and struck Cromer squarely between the eyes with the heavy barrel. Then he was out of the office, on his horse, and streaking past tents and piles of supplies for the road to Prairie City.

No horse could have caught him on that ride. He reached Prairie City shortly after noon and turned the animal over to the liveryman.

"Save him if you can," were his instructions, and he ran for the doctor's office.

Dr. Holmes had attended the Marbles ever since he had come to Prairie City. He had been a friend of Florence Marble's father. He was putting on his hat and getting his medicine bag and instruments before Howard finished explaining the purpose of his errand.

Howard left his exhausted mount and rode back to the ranch with Dr. Holmes in the latter's buckboard behind a pair of fast-stepping grays. On the way he told the doctor about his experience with Cromer.

"They offered me that place up there," said the doctor dryly, "at good money. So much a head per month for the workers and a bonus. But I couldn't see how I could leave my regular practice."

It was the doctor's way of expressing his loyalty to his old patients.

Old Jeb took the team when they arrived at the ranch and Dr. Holmes and Howard hurried into the house. Florence Marble's eyes lighted with pleasure when she saw the elderly physician.

"But I thought you were going for the company doctor," she said to Howard as they followed Dr. Holmes up the stairs.

"Yeah? Well, so I did, and that rat of a Cromer wouldn't let him come," said Howard scornfully.

"He . . . what?" Florence stopped and stared at Howard, her face gone white.

"Just what I said," Howard told her grimly. "An' that settles his hash with me for all time an' then some."

Florence pressed her lips into a fine white line as she went on up the stairs.

Dr. Holmes removed his coat and got busy at once. Bannister was raving in acute delirium. He had a raging fever. The doctor examined the wound on Bannister's head and proceeded to dress it property.

"I tell you I am The Maverick!" Bannister cried shrilly. "Tell 'em all. What the hell do I care. Take your hand away from that bridle or I'll fill your heart with lead!" He lapsed into coma.

Florence Marble stood, white-faced, her hands crossed on her breast.

Dr. Holmes stepped back from the bed. "That bullet made a pretty deep groove in a bad place," he said soberly. "When he comes out of this, he'll have a mind, or . . . he won't." Florence gave a queer little cry, and he looked at her quickly. "Come, I must give you something," he said gruffly, "you look as if you'd faint any minute."

He administered a strong sleeping potion and had Martha lead her away to lie down. He ordered Howard out. Then he turned to his medicine vials and began the long, wearisome fight for Bannister's life — and reason.

CHAPTER TWENTY-ONE

Dusk had fallen with the blue velvet skirts of the night flung over the land, when a rider dashed out of the whispering cottonwoods and into the yard by the porch. He dismounted hurriedly, disengaged the handle of a black case from his saddle horn, and walked briskly up the steps. Howard and Florence came out of the dining room to the front door.

"I'm Doctor Reynolds from Marble," said the visitor, as Howard recognized him. "Mister Cromer sent me down. I couldn't come sooner, as I had a minor operation up there that proved troublesome."

"That's a first-class lie," said Howard. "You go back and tell Cromer to go to blazes. He can't save his face this late."

"Howard." It was Florence who spoke. She went out on the porch. "We don't need you now," she said. "We have our regular doctor from Prairie City. You can tell Mister

Cromer I'm sorry to have bothered him."

The doctor bowed. "I hope you understand my position, ma'am," he said courteously. "I am held strictly to orders according to my contract. Mister Cromer . . . ah . . . seemed very much put out."

"I should think he would be," Howard stormed. "Tell him he's worn out his welcome on this ranch."

Again Florence admonished the youth. Then to the doctor: "I understand your position. The only reason Howard had in going up there was that he thought he could perhaps save some time. Mister Bannister is in a critical condition."

"Well, since I can't be of service," said the doctor, "I'll be going back." He lifted his hat and went down the steps.

Later that night Cromer listened to his report in silence, merely nodding his head and waving him away when he had finished. Alone, Cromer swore roundly. He had missed a chance that morning to redeem himself, and his hatred of Bannister had caused him to throw it away. Now all was lost so far as the Half Diamond and its fair owner was concerned. There was but one thought that brought any consolation. Bannister's condition was critical, Florence Marble had said. He might die, then.

221

Cromer wished with all his heart and soul that he would.

Meanwhile the nerve tension of those at the Marble ranch house was almost at the breaking point. Dr. Holmes was maintaining a constant vigil at the bedside. Martha was officiating as nurse. Florence and Howard were in the living room. Strong as had been the potion the doctor had given her, it would not put the girl to sleep. He dared not give her more.

"But who did it?" she kept asking Howard.

"For the last time, Flo," said the boy impatiently, "I don't know. He had no chance to tell me how, where, or when it happened. He went down there looking for trace of the rustlers. Evidently he met up with some of them and the shooting started. They knocked him down with a bullet, tied him up, and put him in that cabin. Now you know as much as I do."

"Howard, go send Jeb to the Dome for Manley," she ordered. "I'd send you, but I want you here."

The boy went out, and Florence followed him, to walk on the grass in the lower yard. It was such a night as only mid-June can bring to the semi-altitudes. The air was soft and sweet, gently stirring. Myriads of stars hung low in the great arch of the sky and the new moon tipped saucily in the east.

Florence could not get out of her head the last words she had heard Bannister cry in his delirium: *I tell you I am The Maverick!* Over and over the words repeated themselves. But he had as much as told her he wasn't the outlaw he was suspected of being. But, if he wasn't, why should he make that declaration in his delirium? Truth will more often come out than not under such circumstances, as she well knew. She bit her lip and forced back the tears. He had been injured in her service and might lose his life or his reason. She would never forget that. And she would never tell him what he had said if he recovered.

Manley came with the first glimmer of dawn to find everyone in the house still up. He listened keenly as Howard told what had happened.

"I'll take a dozen men an' go in there," he said grimly. "We may be able to track back from the cabin. Howard, get me a fresh horse an' a fast one while I'm taking on some breakfast."

Howard wanted to go with Manley when he departed, but Florence wouldn't permit it.

Bannister's condition remained the same all that day. He was delirious by spells, but his talk was all inarticulate and broken. Florence and Martha both got a little rest. Dr. Holmes never closed his eyes. He drank huge cups of strong, black coffee and remained at his post. Late in the afternoon he discovered he was out of a certain strong sedative that he needed. He wrote a prescription and Howard was sent to Prairie City to have it filled.

When he rode into town on his lathered horse almost the first person he saw on the street was the former Half Diamond foreman, Big Bill Hayes. He passed him without a second glance.

Leaving the prescription at the drugstore, he rode on to the livery, where he found that the horse he had ridden so hard the day before was all right. He changed mounts and thus had a fresh horse for the ride back to the ranch. When he returned to the drugstore, the medicine was ready. He stuffed the package into a coat pocket and started back.

The night was an hour advanced when he reached the river crossing west of the ranch. He thought he saw a shadow sweep across the road where it entered the trees. His heart leaped and he drew his gun. Then he drove in his spurs and dashed ahead. Leaning forward in the saddle, his eyes straining into the darkness, it was as if he deliberately rode into a noose. He was jerked from the saddle and landed in the road, stunned.

Vaguely, as though through a mist, he was conscious of hands fumbling at his pockets. Then the sky seemed to clear overhead and he saw the stars. He sat up. All was still. He could see the darker shadow of his horse standing to one side of the road. He put out a hand to rise and it touched the cold metal of his gun. In a flash he remembered. He felt in his pocket and cried out. The needed medicine was gone. Howard wasted no time in conjectures. It was plainly another move against Bannister by Cromer or the rustlers. Someone knew he had gone for that medicine, and. . . .

As he caught his horse and mounted, he trembled with outraged excitement. Hayes had seen him go into town and into the drugstore. Could he have had his horse handy and gotten the start on him while he was at the livery? Hayes hated Bannister. He had quit the Half Diamond, and must now hate the Marbles, too. Howard turned back in another dash for Prairie City.

This time, when he reached town, he ordered the prescription refilled, and then made a hurried circuit of the various resorts where Hayes would be liable to hang out.

He did not see him, nor had any of those he asked seen him that evening. He went to the livery and engaged a fresh horse, after which he hurried to the sheriff's office. Sheriff Campbell listened attentively, scowling the while in thought.

"I'll send Van Note back with you," he said when the youth had finished. "And I'll have the town searched for Hayes. As for sending a posse into the river breaks, as I first contemplated, I think it would be useless. Your men know more about the badlands than I do. We'll have to wait until Bannister can tell what took place and where. Get your horse and medicine and I'll send for Van Note."

In a few minutes Howard and the deputy were on their way. When they reached the trees at the river, they drew their guns and each kept a keen watch on either side of the road. But this time there was no attack. They rode on into the ranch and Howard hurried into the house with the parcel for the doctor, while Van Note tarried in the kitchen for a cup of coffee. It was well past midnight and the deputy decided to get some sleep in the bunkhouse before going back to town in the morning.

Florence was asleep at breakfast time, and, as she hadn't seen Van Note, Howard decided he would tell her nothing of what had happened the night before. It would only add to her worries. The deputy started back shortly after breakfast. Next came a messenger from Manley with the information that they had made no progress in the search of the day before, but were going out again.

Dr. Holmes took an occasional brief nap on the couch that had been placed in the sick room and at such times Martha or Florence kept watch at the bedside. These were trying periods for Florence, beset by doubts as to Bannister's identity, anxious for his recovery, conscious of the impression his personality had made upon her. She realized now that it was this extraordinary personality that had caused her to give way to the impulse to engage him. Yet she did not look upon him as any ordinary employee of the Half Diamond. In fact, to her surprise, as she looked upon the tanned features and the tousled hair above the bandage on the pillow, she realized that she hardly looked upon him as an employee at all. It was almost as though he were a member of the family.

When Dr. Holmes learned of the visit of the company physician, he was disappointed because he had not seen him. Regardless of the feeling between the Marbles and Cromer, he would have liked to have had the other doctor in consultation.

Another day and night wore through with Bannister tossing and turning and muttering, and the doctor fighting the fever. The others tiptoed about the house and looked at each other fearfully. For sickness is an unnatural thing on a ranch, rendered the more so because of the isolation.

On the third day, Dr. Holmes announced the crisis. Florence went out into the yard. There were her flowers, bright splashes of color against the green of sward and shrubbery. The tall, graceful cottonwoods nodded and whispered in a scented breeze, over all the glorious, golden sunshine of a perfect June. But the girl saw none of this. She walked aimlessly here and there, unseeing, her mind in a turmoil of hope, doubt, perplexity. Old Jeb came to her for news.

"He'll make it," said the old man when he had heard. "He's too well made to go off with a scratch of the head. Damn! Miss Flo, Big Bill Hayes had something to do with this. I'd bet my last chaw of terbaccer on it. But he'll make it . . . you see."

Florence was startled. "What makes you think Hayes had anything to do with it?" she asked quickly.

Jeb taped his head mysteriously. "A hunch," he answered shortly. "I've had hundreds of 'em an' they always come up to scratch. Hayes don't like Bannister, an' he don't like us, an' he ain't the kind that'll light out without tryin' to get even. That's all I got to say, an' I won't say no more."

Florence looked after him thoughtfully. The doctor came out on the porch. His eyes were sunken, his face drawn with weariness as he ran his fingers through his shock of gray hair. Florence hurried to him.

"He's sleeping at last," said the doctor in a tired voice. "The fever has gone down. When he wakes, we shall know. His mind will be in darkness or in the light."

All afternoon Bannister slept and far into the night. At midnight Martha called Florence and Howard, who were in the living room. They went upstairs. Two lamps were burning in the sick room. Dr. Holmes was bending over the bed, his arm under Bannister's head, giving him a drink of water.

Florence's heart seemed to come into her throat. Bannister's eyes were open. They were clear. He finished the water and murmured his thanks to the doctor, from whose face all trace of weariness had fled before the victory. Then he saw her and smiled faintly.

Dr. Holmes pushed them firmly out of the room. "He'll be back to sleep in a minute, and now you folks go to bed," he commanded sternly. "I'm going to catch a few winks myself. Do as I say. I'm boss here. Now hurry along."

In her room Florence knelt by her bed, her arms crossed on the counterpane. The moonlight streamed through the window upon her head. The wind played an anthem in the waving branches of the trees. A great peace came over her.

CHAPTER TWENTY-TWO

Dr. Holmes stayed another day, making sure that Bannister was out of danger, and then, after giving strict and implicit directions as to the care of the injured man, he left for town, promising to come out to the ranch regularly to change the dressings on the wound.

And then Bannister's magnificent physique and splendid constitution began to assert themselves. He mended rapidly. He was not permitted to talk for two days to any extent, and, when the doctor lifted the ban, Florence sent for Manley so he could be present when Bannister told in detail what had happened. Quite unexpectedly, Sheriff Campbell came out from Prairie City the same morning. But Bannister could tell them very little. He explained how he had seen the fresh tracks on the river trail, told them as nearly as possible the location of the ridge upon which he had taken up his vigil, and of the rope, the firing, and the burst of flame in his face when he had been shot. That was all he knew until he regained consciousness in the cabin.

It wasn't much to go on, but Sheriff Campbell left at once with Manley to get a number of Half Diamond men and explore the eastern terminus of the river trail. Bannister didn't expect them to find anything, and he proved to be right. He was much put out by the accident, complaining that it was his own fault, and that as a consequence the rustlers had been scared out and might not operate again all summer, thus lessening the possibility of their capture. He said nothing about his vague suspicions of Hayes, nor did Florence tell him what old Jeb had said about his hunch.

Both of them would have been interested in Howard's experience the night he went for the medicine, but Howard decided to keep the details to himself until sometime in the future. The sheriff had told him that Hayes was not in town that night and Howard was convinced Hayes had ridden out ahead of him, roped him, and stolen the medicine, thinking it would retard Bannister's recovery. The sheriff was noncommittal in the matter, but he had done considerable thinking.

Meanwhile Cromer had postponed the grand drawing of plots in the project until July 10, and had put off the meeting of the company's board of directors until July 15. Howard Marble was responsible for this, as the blow that Cromer had received across the bridge of his nose from the gun barrel had caused both his eyes to turn black. Looking as he did, it was impossible for him to go to the city in the south and other places as would be necessary to complete his arrangements. He did not once think of reporting the matter to the constable stationed in Marble, as he would have to tell the whole story, and it would put him in a bad light or make him appear ridiculous. Therefore Howard heard nothing more from that quarter.

But Cromer still had a card up his sleeve that promised ill for Bannister. When he heard that Bannister was recovering rapidly, he thought more and more of this next move. It would be taking a chance, but Cromer was used to taking chances. Wasn't he taking the biggest chance of his life with the irrigation project? But this new move had to be put off until after the drawing and the directors' meeting, because it meant a long ride for Cromer far to southward. But the idea was ever in his mind and he nursed it until it grew to such proportions that the plan seemed incapable of failure. During these days Cromer became more cheerful than in months. His vindictive nature also whispered to him of the water in the river. If he were to open his intake full. . . . It was another weapon, but one that would have to be used with studied care. And what effect would it have on the Half Diamond? He would have to figure that out. He could make it count, and count big in some way. Florence Marble should be made to see that Bannister constituted a menace to her investments, her property, and her peace of mind. With these thoughts, and the prospects of big cash payments at the time of the drawing, Cromer became more cheerful than ever.

Summer came in a day, riding in on a hot wind with the sun a burning ball of fire in a sky of slate. The beef herd at the Dome was slowly moved northward along the creek on the east side. The herd on the north range moved over nearer the creek and grazed both north and south. All the cattle now were on summer range.

Bannister was soon sitting up, and it wasn't long before he could be taken out on the shaded porch. He chafed at the inactivity, but then there really wasn't much to do.

But he did not for a minute assume that the trouble was over. The very quietness of things was to him alarming — the lull before the storm.

Then one afternoon, when the heat waves were shimmering on the prairie, and Marble Dome was buried in a blue haze under a broiling sun, Howard told him about the night he had gone for the medicine, about Hayes's sudden disappearance from town, and what he suspected.

Bannister was silent for some time, his eyes gleaming from between narrowed lids. "You mustn't say anything of this to Miss Florence," he said finally. "You mustn't say anything about Hayes to anyone. I think I have his number. Somehow I can't shake off the feeling that everything is going to break at once. But we've got to keep what we know to ourselves."

Howard pondered this remark, for he did not altogether understand it. But he went on to tell Bannister about Cromer's refusal to send the company doctor down the day Bannister was brought back to the house, and how he had had to ride on to Prairie City.

Bannister merely smiled and reached over to lay a hand on his arm. "I reckon you saved my life twice that day," was his only comment.

Bannister spent most of his time on the porch now, although he could walk around the yard. He stood by and watched as Florence worked with her flowers. Her chief pride was a long, wide bed of pansies. She would work among them for hours and Bannister would sit on the grass and watch. They didn't talk much. Since his illness a peculiar situation had arisen between these two. They seemed to understand one another better, to have something in common, although Bannister never could determine what it was. Florence felt that she had needed more companionship on the ranch, and had found it in Bannister. She liked to have him around. She liked to look up from her work and see him sitting there, looking off into the distance dreamily, liked to have him smile at her and say something — anything. And Bannister liked to see her look up, her face flushed, the hand trowel tilted awkwardly, her eyes sparkling.

They would sit on the porch of an evening and at times their conversation would take on an intimacy by subtle instinct that left her breathless and wondering and a bit afraid. She never told him what he had said in his delirium. It gradually grew dim in her mind as she made the astounding discovery that she didn't care.

Then there came a night. Howard had been with them all evening, sitting on a lower step while they had sat on the upper. Howard had been telling of a girl he knew in Prairie City who had gone away to school and come back so high-toned there was no living with her. They had laughed, and, when he left, Florence confessed that she had gone away to school herself.

"But it hasn't spoiled you," said Bannister quickly.

"It did the first year." She laughed. "But Dad soon took it all out of me by saying that I had changed so he believed he'd sell the ranch and go East where I liked it better."

"I reckon you didn't take to that," said Bannister.

"Take to it? Well, I should say not. I was born here. I'm just as much of the West as those cottonwoods. Dad had to argue some powerful to get me to go back that fall."

Bannister laughed softly. "Florence, you're a right good sort," he said, using her first name as if he had never called her anything else.

"That's rather a dry compliment," she observed, looking at the moon that was edging up above the cottonwoods with its following of stars.

"Oh, I didn't mean it that way," he said in a low voice, putting an arm about her shoulders. "You see, Florence, after this sickness and your . . . your kindness, and yourself, I'm traveling a dangerous trail."

She didn't understand him, but she thrilled at the contact with his strong, young body, at the manly, vibrant notes of his voice. It was as if she had suddenly found protection from something. From what? Loneliness? Danger? Then in a flash she remembered what he had said when the fever was afire in his brain.

"Why is it a dangerous trail, Bannister?" she asked breathlessly.

"Because it has no end," he answered slowly, with a hint of despair. "It can take me nowhere."

Instinctively she leaned toward him. He drew her head to his shoulder and patted her hair.

"What is this trail?" she asked softly, her eyes on the drifting slice of silver moon. "Tell me about it."

"I reckon it's the trail to heaven," he said in that same slow, hopeless voice. "It's you, Florence. You're sweet and dear . . . pure gold. You're the only girl I ever wanted, and I want you with my heart and soul and all that is me. I can have you maybe for a minute, but that is all."

She looked up at him out of eyes that were swimming wells of light. His arms were about her. He kissed her — and once again.

She drew away and rested a hand on the floor of the porch. Now she knew. She knew why she liked to look up and find him sitting there by the flower bed with that far-away look. She knew why she liked to see him come down in the morning with his hair ruffled up and a sleepy frown on his face as he went to the wash bench just off the kitchen. She knew why his flashing smile thrilled her. She knew why she wanted to call him by his first name.

"A minute, Bob, isn't a very long time," she said almost in a whisper.

"In my case it is an eternity," he said, looking straight ahead. Should he tell her? Should he tell her all — all? And have her draw away from him as if he were some odious thing? There are limits to a brave man's courage. And would it be altogether fair to her after . . . ?

"Bob," she said, putting a hand on his knee, "do you want me to . . . to tell you something?"

It was as if he could read her mind and fathom what she intended to say. "No," he answered. "It would only make it the harder for me, Florence. The end of the trail just isn't in the picture."

"But why?" she persisted petulantly. "Why, Bob?"

He looked at her out of eyes brimming with pain. Wild oats come home in shock. He couldn't trust his voice to answer, even if he had known what to say.

She saw his look and her arms went about his neck. "Another minute, Bob," she whispered. "And there is no trail that has no end." She kissed him and ruffled his hair while he held her as if he would never let her go.

Then she broke away, rose quickly, and went into the house.

He sat there, stunned, gripping his hands until the nails bit into his palms. Then he rose and went down on the grass.

From her window, Florence watched him pacing the yard in the moonlight. In her eyes the white bandage that he still wore formed a halo about his head. She waited until she heard his step upon the stairs. Then she flung herself upon the bed and gave way to the tears.

CHAPTER TWENTY-THREE

"Well, folks," said Howard at breakfast the next morning, "I suppose you know what's going on day after tomorrow."

Bannister and Florence looked at him blankly.

"Haven't any idea as to the date, I suppose," he went on in a superior tone.

Florence glanced at the calendar on the wall near the window. "Why, it'll be the Fourth of July," she said. "I had lost all track of the date."

"You're right," said Howard. "Day after tomorrow will be the Fourth of July, and they're figuring on doing things up brown in Prairie City. Big celebration, rodeo, dance, and all the trimmings."

"You going in?" Bannister asked.

"That depends," said the boy. "I was wondering why you two couldn't drive in the buckboard with me for an escort."

Florence shook her head. "I wouldn't go,"

241

she said, "and I don't think Bannister should be taking in any celebrations just yet."

Howard looked at Bannister with widening eyes. "Why, he's all right," he declared. "He don't have to ride any broncos, and I guess we could prop him up at a poker table in a pinch."

This brought a laugh from Bannister, while Florence eyed her cousin in evident disapproval. "Howard, you have a queer sense of humor," she said severely.

"How so?" demanded the youth. "I suppose you knew that Bannister plays stud like he made up the game in the first place."

"Howard." It was plain that Florence was annoyed.

"Oh, well, if that's the way it is, I won't go in, either," said the boy in resignation.

"Go in and have your fun," said Bannister sternly. "I'm not hankering to go in or I'd probably go. Go on in and see if that dame of yours hasn't got over some of her uppishness."

"That's what I intended to do in the first place." Howard grinned. "I was just entertaining with conversation, seeing as how you two seem to have forgotten how to talk."

Bannister looked at Florence, but the girl didn't raise her eyes from her plate.

Martha appeared in the kitchen doorway. "Little evil-eye is out here," she announced. "Wanted to see Manley, and I told him he was over north of the Dome. Then he said he wanted to see you, Miss Flo."

"It's Link," Florence concluded. "Wants what pay is coming to him, I suppose. Well, he can have it, and the sooner he gets off the ranch the better."

"Must have just got out of the hospital," Bannister commented. "Maybe he wants his job back. If he does, give it to him, Miss Florence. I've got an idea or two about that fellow. Just between we three, I wouldn't be surprised if he knew something about this rustling business. No . . . don't ask me any questions. It's just a hunch. But he'll hang himself with his own rope with the outfit quicker than anywhere else."

Florence looked at him intently. Here it was again. Hunches. Old Jeb had a hunch about Hayes. Now Bannister had a hunch about Link. And the pair had always run together. She thought she began to see the portent of these hunches. Hayes and Link were suspected of being implicated in the cattle thefts.

"Tell him to go around front," she said to Martha, finishing her coffee. "I'll see him."

Bannister and Howard dallied over their

breakfast while she was gone. Bannister was not inclined to talk and Howard didn't press him. When Florence returned, they both looked at her questioningly.

"That was it," she said, nodding to Bannister. "Wanted his job back. I gave him a note to Manley with instructions to take him on and send him out to the camp."

Bannister was silent, thinking rapidly. Link wouldn't come back to an outfit he knew was hostile to him. He must have friends among the men. Perhaps there were several of them working with Hayes. Bannister had surmised from the first that the cattle had been spirited away with the aid of some of the outfit. He was well satisfied to have Link back on the job and he intended to acquaint Manley with his suspicions at the first opportunity.

When they went out, Bannister told Jeb to saddle him a horse. Then he pulled himself into the leather for the first time since he was shot. He and Howard rode for an hour, and, when they returned, Bannister dismounted on the run with his old snap and vigor.

That night the bandage came off his head for good.

Howard went in to Prairie City early on the morning of the Fourth. He was commissioned to bring back a gun belt for Bannister, who luckily had an extra gun and holster in his pack.

"Keep your eyes open," Bannister told him, "and don't forget your promise. I've an idea we're going to have work to do before the moon gets dark."

Howard kept his word and came back to the ranch early on the morning of the Fifth. He found Bannister, just returned from a ride, standing by Florence, who was working among her flowers. He appeared greatly excited.

"Now what do you think is up?" he asked, signaling to old Jeb to take his horse.

"I suppose you and that girl over at Prairie City are going to get married," Bannister drawled.

Howard looked at him scornfully. "She isn't in my class," he declared — which told them much. "No, it's another celebration, the biggest celebration the Marble range country ever had." He displayed a lurid handbill printed in red and blue with wide, white borders. "Cromer's staging it up at Marble on the Tenth. They're going to hold a big drawing of farm plots, and the folks who've bought plots will get 'em according to the numbers they draw. That's supposed to be so everybody will have an equal chance to get a good location. But that isn't half of it." He paused, noting with satisfaction that his two listeners were showing considerable interest. "He's going to stage a Fourth of July and rodeo celebration combined," he went on enthusiastically. "He's offering prizes for bucking contests, roping, bull-dogging, wild horse races, shooting, and everything else that make the prizes at Prairie City look like glasses of soda water. Why, Buck Adams and twenty other riders are coming down from Canada. He's got scouts out rounding up the worst bunch of end-swappers that ever was collected for a bucking chute. He's paying expenses for a flock of Indians to give the thing color. They're going to run special trains from south and east, and every wagon on the project and in Prairie City and all the stages are going to be used to get the people up there." He paused again, breathless, his eyes shining.

"Go on, let's hear all of it," Bannister prompted. "You haven't got a part of it off your chest yet."

"You bet I haven't," sang Howard. "They're going to use all the loose lumber on the project for a big dance floor with a canvas top, and the stand for the drawing and such, and he's bringing a ten-piece orchestra and a band from Big Falls. There's going to be a big display of fireworks. And people are coming from as far as Saint Paul and even Chicago, I heard, to say nothing of Canada. He's ordered about a million tents and cots to put the people up, and the celebration's going to run over to the Eleventh and maybe the Twelfth. All the men working up there are going to get a time off, and the new bank's going to open and the first fifty depositors get a share of the company stock free. I can't remember all of it, but that ought to be enough."

"That's plenty," Bannister agreed. "Where'd you get all this information?"

"From men that were in Prairie City from the project and . . . well, everybody was talking about it, and Cromer was in town spreading the news personally, although I didn't talk with him. Why, don't you believe it?"

"Of course I believe it," said Bannister. "It's his big grandstand play. He'll get healthy deposits from all those who've bought plots and he'll sell what plots haven't already been taken. He'll sell a lot of stock, too. He'll rent gambling concessions and booths and all that sort of thing and take a rake-off. He won't lose anything. And he'll draw the biggest crowd, and the toughest

247

crowd, that northern Montana ever saw."

"There's another thing," said Howard. "Sheriff Campbell is appointing special deputies right and left to preserve order, and Cromer is buying the badges for 'em."

Bannister laughed. "I wonder if he'll pin one on Le Beck. I know just about how much good a special deputy is in a pinch when the guns get hot. Did you bring my belt?"

"I brought three of 'em," was the reply. "They're on my saddle. You can take your pick and send the other two back."

"Fair enough," said Bannister, pleased. "I sure aim to take in this celebration."

Florence had been listening and reading the handbill at the same time. Now she looked at the two of them, her eyes wide. "Sounds like they figure on shaving the prairie," she commented, using a favorite expression of her father's.

Bannister and Howard both laughed.

"Well, Miss Florence, I reckon you'll have to go along with us," said Bannister. "You're a big stockholder up there and you've got to keep your eyes on the proceedings. And I aim to deposit a dollar and get another share of stock whether they like it or not."

This brought another laugh, and excitement ruled the day on the Half Diamond.

Nor was it confined to the ranch house. Manley came riding in that afternoon with a heavy frown on his face.

"I don't know what the idea was in taking Link back on, but I took him as you said," he told Florence. "Now he's handed out a piece of news that's got the men milling like a bunch of steers before a storm."

"I suppose he's told them about the celebration they're going to have up at Marble," Florence conjectured.

"You've heard about it, then," said Manley in a cross voice. "Yes, that's what he's done. Spread the news all around about what a big time it's going to be, an' the big prizes offered, an' everybody going that can ride or walk, an' such, until the men are all worked up. They all want to go an' let the cattle take care of themselves, the way it looks."

Florence puckered her brows over this new problem.

"What's more," he went on, "we've got some men that can ride. Your dad and Hayes and I all saw to that in picking men for the outfit, an' all those fellows say that they want a crack at the bronco-busting prizes or they'll quit flat. What am I to do?"

"You'll have to let them go," Florence decided. "I understand this affair is going to last two days at least, so, to keep peace in the camp, let half of them go the first day and the other half go the second day."

"I suppose that's the only way out of it," Manley grumbled. And it was so agreed.

The morning of the Tenth dawned hot and clear. Bannister and Howard were stirring before dawn. Bannister had been riding more every day and so far as he could tell had regained all his former strength. They brought three splendid mounts from the pasture, Florence having signified her intention of riding up rather than using the buckboard.

Old Jeb was going to trail along, too, and had laid out all his finery. He was as excited as a schoolboy on the day before vacation. Martha refused to go, saying that celebrations tired her too much.

They started shortly after 9:00 in order to reach the new town before noon. They were a gay party, prepared and resolved to amuse themselves. But they still did not realize the stupendous nature of the entertainment enterprise upon which Cromer had embarked. Given *carte blanche* by his board of directors, he had gone the uttermost limit. In the last few weeks the great drawing and celebration had become an obsession with him. All other business had been swept

250

aside. Almost the entire working force on the project had been recruited to make the preparations. And his agents had seen to it that the advertising angle was not neglected.

This morning of the first day, as Florence, Bannister, and Howard reached the crest of a knoll south of the town, they checked their horses as of one accord and stared in amazement at the panorama spread out before them.

CHAPTER TWENTY-FOUR

The newly born town of Marble was plumed in color like some gigantic flower that had suddenly come into bloom on the sweeping prairie. The white tents glistened like silver in the sunlight; the unpainted board buildings were splashes of gold; flags and buntings waved and fluttered, flaunting the colors of red and blue, and even at that distance the holiday attire of the women and the gay shirts and scarves of the men who crowded the town added their flaring, flaming hues to complete the marvelous picture. Off to the left a long line of wagons, buckboards, stages, and horsemen streamed into town from the west. Great corrals at the outer edge of the ring of tents were filled with horses. Conveyances of every description formed long lines still farther out. A great, golden cup on the east proved to be the stadium where the contests would be held. A miracle had been accomplished there in a vast setting of golden brown plain with the silver-crowned peaks trailing their robes of royal purple far beyond.

The three of them caught their breath at this imposing sight. None of them ever had seen anything like it before. And, curiously enough, the same thought was in the mind of each of them — the matter of expense. Bannister was first to speak and he gave voice to what they were all thinking about.

"Well, Cromer's doing it up brown and then some," he said. "Still, flags and bunting don't cost such a lot, and they had all that lumber and can take down those things and use it again. And by the way that street has lengthened out I'd say he's renting about a hundred concessions, which is more than enough to pay for everything and leave a snug profit. This jamboree is going to be a money-maker, if I ever saw one."

The others nodded. It could hardly be anything else with all those people coming into the town with money to spend. Cromer was no fool. They all agreed to that. But the magnitude of the undertaking impressed them nonetheless.

They were suddenly aware of the pounding of hoofs behind them and turned quickly. It proved to be John Macy, riding up the gentle slope. With him was a girl of sixteen or thereabout, fair to look at, with her eyes lighted with excitement and wisps of golden hair flying from under her hat.

Florence greeted them and Howard waved his hand.

John Macy and the girl reined in as they gained the crest and both stared, wide-eyed, at what they saw.

"Well, I'll be." But the stockman could not find the words with which to express himself further. He stared in stupefaction, bewildered to the point where he could hardly believe his eyes. Then he looked at the others and caught Bannister's eye.

"Looks like he means business, eh?" he said with a wink.

"Looks so," drawled Bannister. "I reckon business is the word."

Florence and the girl were talking, and now Florence turned to Bannister. "This is June Macy," she said by way of introduction.

"I knew that the minute I saw her," said Bannister. "You've got your dad's eyes, June."

The girl laughed, and then Howard edged his horse in beside her.

"C'mon, June, let's lead 'em down there," he challenged.

In a moment the two young people were

off, flying down the slope, with the others following. Long before they reached the outskirts of the town, the din from Marble's swollen street came to their ears. When they reached the south end of the street, they saw at once that it would be impossible to ride in. The street was jammed; the dust from hundreds of feet soared in clouds; some of the great strips of bunting that had been stretched across the street had come down and were being dragged along on the heads and shoulders of the throng; vendors in the gaily decorated booths were screaming their wares despite the fact that they couldn't work fast enough to supply the demands of customers.

A man wearing a star and mounted on a big, gray horse rode in front of them.

"You'll have to go around!" he shouted, waving a hand toward the left. "The corrals are around there."

They rode around as directed and came to the corrals. There was a man with a ribbon badge stationed at the entrance to each.

"Right here!" called a man at the first corral, where there were but few horses tied to the rails. "Check your horses in. We feed an' water 'em."

They stopped, and the man hurriedly adjusted tickets to their saddle horns, giving them checks with corresponding numbers before they could dismount. "Two dollars apiece, an' leave 'em as long as you want," said the man.

"This is a new one on me," said John Macy, "but I'm thinking it's a good scheme. Guess we better leave 'em. See that the cinches are loosened or take off the saddles," he finished, addressing the man.

"We'll take 'em off," said the corral tender. "Hang 'em on the rail. Ready when you come for 'em an' we'll put 'em back on."

They dismounted and left their horses. Then they walked up the line of corrals some distance and turned in between the tents to an opening that led to the street. There they were caught in the tide of surging celebrants. There were men in business suits and women in smart frocks from the East; farmers who were unmistakably from the Middle West; stockmen in soft shirts without neckties, huge watch chains across their middles, trousers tucked into riding boots, great, gray hats; ranchers' wives and daughters in white with colored sashes and ribbons in their hair; cowpunchers and rodeo contestants in green, pink, purple, and yellow shirts and flaming scarves, topped by wide-brimmed, high-crowned hats of gray and brown and black; girls with rouged cheeks and lips, eyes unnaturally bright, accompanied by pale-faced men, whose glances roved furtively about the crowds; teamsters and laborers in mud-stained overalls; engineers in smart khaki uniforms; youths in mail-order, blue serge suits — their Sunday best.

All were talking, shouting, laughing, calling out to one another, crowding against the booths where lemonade and soft drinks were being served; struggling for an opportunity to play the wheels of chance in the hope of winning one of the gaudy, worthless prizes; screaming for hot dogs or sandwiches; bombarding the ice cream stands; buying souvenirs — making carnival to the point of pandemonium. And over all, the dust — and the hot, glaring sun.

The two girls, in their neat riding habits, attracted attention. Friendly salutations were flung at them. Their men crowded in about them to keep the party from becoming separated.

"Where will we go?" said Florence in bewilderment.

As she put this question, they were passing the office of the Marble Dome Land and Irrigation Company. It was answered immediately. Cromer saw them from his station at the front window, where he was surveying the long line of people filing through the office, registering their numbers of plot purchase contracts with clerks, so the company would know who was present and could later check up on those who had not attended the drawing and made their second payment. He pushed his way through the line and caught up with them.

"Hello, Macy!" he called, grasping the rancher's arm. "And Miss Marble! This is good. I thought maybe you folks would be up from the south and I've got three front rooms in the hotel saved for you and any other of the stockmen and their families who come up. Good place to rest and see what's going on in the street before the big show." His face was beaming with excitement and satisfaction. He looked like a different Cromer this day. But he took no notice whatsoever of Bannister or Howard. The pair winked at each other.

"Well, that sounds good," said Macy. "I reckon we'll take you up on it . . . if we can get to the hotel."

"It's right across the street," said Cromer. "Come, we'll make a wedge and push through."

With Macy and Cromer in front, Bannister and Howard behind, and the two girls in between, they fought their way through

258

the crowd to the hotel and edged through the mob in the little lobby. Upstairs they found the rooms cool and quiet; the green window shades, drawn halfway, shut out the glare of the sun, and the screens kept out most of the dust that swirled above the perspiring throngs below.

"I'll send a waitress up," said Cromer genially. "She'll bring you cold drinks and anything you want to eat. It's all arranged." He was looking at Florence, who regarded him coolly. So far none had spoken to him save Macy. And Macy it was who spoke now.

"Tell her to fetch along a barrel of lemonade or something," he said, taking off his hat to wipe his forehead. "It's hotter than Billy-be-damned."

"Right," said Cromer, smiling at the girls. He had not altogether given up hope that Florence would relent. Perhaps this show would have a favorable effect on her. For the first time he looked straight at Bannister. "I'm glad you've recovered," he boomed heartily.

"Funny, but I was just now expecting to hear you say that," drawled Bannister.

Cromer's eyes clouded as he left the room. Bannister's veiled insolence and challenge caused him to remember. Never in his life had he hated a man so fiercely as he hated

Bannister at that moment. His lips pressed into a white line and his eyes shone with sinister resolve as he went down the stairs to give his orders.

"Well, I don't hanker for any lemonade, exactly, but I'd like to take a look around, so I guess I'll go down for a while," said Bannister.

"Me, too," said Howard. "I'll go along, if it's all right with you, Bannister."

"I'll wait for the drinks an' then mosey down into the lobby," John Macy decided. "There's some others coming up from Indian River today, an' I suppose they'll hit for the hotel. I'll steer the womenfolks up here."

In the street, Bannister's interest was quite apart from that of John Macy or the girls. He had no time for the colorful crowd, but led Howard through the dense mobs until they came to the entrance of a huge brown tent over which was a cloth sign reading: *DOME PALACE.*

They went in to find that a board floor had been laid, a long bar built of rough boards ranged the entire length of the tent on each side, and the center was strewn with gaming tables, while in the rear were the roulette wheels, crap games, faro layouts, and blackjack tables. It was thronged with a milling crowd of men who were drinking and gambling. Big Stetson hats reigned supreme here. There were scores of cowpunchers and riders in colorful garb. There were rough-looking characters, too, and plenty of them. Here was a place for trouble to start.

"Made to order," Bannister muttered, thinking of that very thing.

"What did you say?" Howard asked.

"Nothing," said Bannister. Then he started. Cromer was making his way out of the place on the opposite side. Cromer didn't drink or gamble, so why should he come in here? To keep a check on his rake-off, probably. Bannister's lips curled scornfully.

They circled the place, and, when they were midway to the bar on the side across from the side by which they had entered, Bannister's face froze into an expressionless mask. Le Beck was standing close against the bar. With him were two men who Bannister took to be Canadians. And at the second Canadian's left stood Big Bill Hayes.

If Howard saw them also, he made no mention of it. The boy was excited, and Bannister suddenly felt a desire to be rid of him. They went out of the place into the heat and dust. As they moved with the throng up the street between rows of tents and booths, they passed a dozen other tent resorts, but none as large as Dome Palace.

"Suppose we go over to the riders' camp," Howard suggested. "Some of our men figure on riding this afternoon."

"You go over and see 'em," said Bannister in a tone that virtually left Howard no alternative. "I'll meet you later at the hotel."

So Howard left him and Bannister turned back. Alone, Bannister's mood changed. He temporarily forgot Howard and Florence and the Half Diamond. His eyes gleamed and he thrilled with the rush of blood in his veins. Here was an element at his elbow that he knew well. Tough characters, wily gamblers, gunmen — lots of them. Stacks of gold and silver on the gaming tables. An avowed enemy at the head of it all. His eyes narrowed, his step quickened. Two fingers slipped into his holster against the cool cylinder of his gun. A man jostled against him and he gave him a belligerent look. Then his shoulders seemed to straighten more than ever. He plowed through the crowd and hurried through the entrance of Dome Palace.

CHAPTER TWENTY-FIVE

They saw no more of Bannister at the hotel before the time came to go to the rodeo contests. Florence inquired of Howard as to his whereabouts, but Howard suspected, and rightly, that Bannister wished to be left to his own devices. He suspected also that Bannister had gone back to Dome Palace, but he said nothing about this. He pleaded ignorance as to where Bannister might be, pretending that he had lost him in the crowd.

Although Florence said nothing more, she felt worried. She thought she knew something of Bannister's wild spirit. It was a trait that had first roused her interest in him, but it could be called interest no longer. It was more than that. She was really concerned. Had the others not been there she would have gone searching for him. It would be so easy for him to yield to his passion for gambling and get into trouble.

She accompanied John Macy, Howard, and June and some others they knew to the stadium to see the contests, hoping that she might catch a glimpse of him there. But while she saw men she recognized as members of the Half Diamond outfit, she saw nothing of Bannister. Nor were they to see him for some time after the contests and the big drawing itself was over.

As for Bannister, he had practically forgotten them. The moment he entered Dome Palace the gaming lust was upon him, gripping him with a hold he could not loosen. He yielded readily, but before slipping into a place at a stud poker table, he walked to the bar and wedged in almost at Le Beck's elbow. He meant to give Le Beck every opportunity to start things this day or night. For he hadn't believed Cromer when the latter had said he had discharged Le Beck. And he believed Le Beck had his orders. Bannister was in no mood to attempt to prevent him from carrying those orders out — if he were capable of doing so. He caught Le Beck's glittering, snaky eyes regarding him surreptitiously, and his lips curled. Le Beck wet his lips and his gaze was shot with fire. For Bannister's look was like a slap in the face. He turned back to his drink and said something to the two Canadians, who forthwith stole a look at Bannister. Hayes kept his eyes straight ahead, although he must have known. Something seemed to whisper in Bannister's ears that the pair with Le Beck would be in on whatever play came up. He smiled grimly, though his voice had never sounded more cheerful than when he ordered beer.

He drank the stuff slowly, seeking every opportunity to catch Le Beck's eye. The gunman began to appear ill at ease and finally stopped stealing glances at Bannister as he talked to his companions in low tones. They were drinking steadily, and Bannister knew no good would come of that. Nor did he care what happened. The old reckless spirit was alive and throbbing within him. He was just beginning to become thoroughly angry over his wound and the theft of his horse and gun. If he had thought it would do any good, he would have called the turn on Hayes then and there — even to the point of compelling both him and Le Beck to draw. Florence Marble didn't know this Bannister who stood at the bar, sipping his beer, his eyes cold and hard, a storm gathering in his mind.

When his glass was empty, Bannister turned abruptly from the bar. He knew the eyes of the four followed him and he found a place at a table where he could see in their direction. Then he forgot them and everything else as the dealer shoved yellow and blue and red stacks across to him in exchange for the yellow roll of bills he had tossed on the table.

He had chosen a table where the play was high. He watched the deal closely, and, when he caught the eye of the man who had dealt, he raised his brows slightly.

"Pass," he said, without looking at his hole card. The man frowned slightly. Others looked up. And at once it was understood that a man had entered the game who was well acquainted with all the tricks of the tinhorn and the professional houseman. The play changed somewhat.

Bannister watched every dealer in succession like a hawk. He discomfited them, took the cleverness out of their flying fingers; by sheer hypnotism, it seemed, he made the game a straight one. They caught him between the pinchers and he bet them to a standstill and raked in a hatful of checks. All that afternoon he played. The housemen changed off with men from other tables until the best professionals who had come for the clean-up were pitted against him. And still he won. It was uncanny, his opponents thought. He destroyed their poise.

They became rattled and forgot themselves, showing their hands at times in their faces. Spectators crowded about the table three deep.

He looked up from a winning hand, stacking his checks. He had a bulwark of yellows and blues before him. He glanced casually about him and his gaze froze on a face — a lean face, tanned to the color of leather; blue eyes, blond brows, a good mouth and a firm chin under a great black beaver hat. His head inclined ever so slightly in a move imperceptible to the others.

"Deal me out," he said crisply to the man who was shuffling the cards.

There was a stir at this but Bannister paid no heed. He quickly counted a stack to be sure it contained twenty chips, sized the others up to it, and began pushing the stacks across to the man in the slot.

"Three thousand, nine hundred and twenty," he said, "and an extra red." He tossed over the lone check with a short laugh, stuffed the roll of bills the dealer passed him into a hip pocket, and left the table.

Instead of going out the front entrance, he strolled back to the big rear entrance and walked out on the grass behind the tents. The short, blue-eyed, youthful-looking man who had caught his eye at the table strolled casually after him. Bannister was waiting.

"Tommy Gale," he said as the other came up with a glad grin on his face. "Tommy, how'd you get up here?"

"I've still got a hoss," drawled Tommy.

"Tell me, Tommy," said Bannister seriously, "are there any others up from below?"

"None as I knows of," was the reply. "I come by accident, you might say. Heard about these doings down in Billings, an', as I didn't have anything else to do for the time being, I came along."

"Seen anybody here you know?" asked Bannister.

"Seen you, that's all," Tommy answered. "Say, Bob, ain't you sort of takin' a chance?"

"Yes, I'm taking a chance," Bannister agreed. "But I'm all right if none of those danged star flashers down there don't get wise to where I am. They'll see me soon enough."

"Eh? You goin' back?" Tommy appeared very much surprised.

"In time . . . when my work here is finished," Bannister said slowly. "Yes, sooner or later I'm going back. Did I get blamed for that Sheridan racket, Tommy?"

"You sure enough did," said Tommy with a scowl. "You get the blame for everything.

I suppose you know that."

"Yes, I know it," said Bannister grimly. "They'll try to hang it on me right when they get me and I suppose they can do it."

"I dunno." Tommy appeared doubtful. "They're electing a new sheriff down there this fall. The present incumbent, old John Wills, isn't as popular as he was. He'll go out of office sure as shootin' this next election. The handwritin' is all over the prairies down there."

"Then maybe there'll be a chance for a square deal, or something near it," said Bannister. "Tommy, I'm sure mighty glad to see you. If you're not doing anything, as you said, maybe you'll stick around for a while. I can use you, Tommy, and you're the only man from down below that I'd trust. Oh, don't squint. This is all on the level, all clean as a blue bird's wing. C'mon. We've got to have a talk somewhere."

The two of them walked behind the tents until they came to an opening where they could gain the street. As the drawing now was in progress, the street was practically deserted. They walked up between the rows of booths and resorts and finally dropped into a drinking place near the end of the street. There were a few games in progress and at the rear of the tent there were some tables and a small lunch counter. They sat down at one of the tables and ordered sandwiches and beer. Then Bannister began talking in a low voice intended for Tommy Gale's ears alone.

He told his friend from the south everything that had taken place from the time of his arrival at the Half Diamond and in Prairie City to the present moment; explained how he had met Howard Marble and had the run-in with Le Beck; how he had met Florence and then Cromer; how he had come to go to the ranch; his visits to Marble; the irrigation situation; the rustling and his encounter with unknown persons he believed to be rustlers with the resulting loss of his horse and gun, and finished with the presence of Le Beck and Hayes in town this day, conniving, as he believed, in a plot against him.

Tommy took a bite of his sandwich, a swallow of beer, and looked at Bannister respectfully. "You sure can do it," he said, more or less in admiration. "You get more action for your time an' money than any man on earth. The only way I can have an adventure is to get drunk an' get in a fight. An' then I'm liable to get licked. I got licked once."

Bannister chuckled. "Well, it looks as

though you could have an adventure up here, Tommy, if you want to trail along with me a while." He hadn't seen fit to tell Tommy about the deal he had made with Sheriff Campbell, but now he decided to do so and accordingly did.

Tommy stared, wide-eyed, this time. "Everybody's got their soft spots, I reckon," he observed. "Do you think that much of her, Bob?"

Bannister frowned. "Well, if you want to put it that way," he said slowly, "I do."

Tommy whistled softly. "All right, I'll trail along," he said finally. "What do you want me to do first?"

"First and last I don't want anybody to see us hobnobbing together if we can help it," said Bannister. "Now it's getting along toward six o'clock and I'll have to show up at the hotel. Suppose you wait around up here till I get back. And say, Tommy, don't go for the hard stuff. We may have work ahead of us tonight. Somehow I've got a hunch that the pot's going to boil over."

"I hope so," said Tommy cheerfully. "Go ahead. I'll sit in a game till you get back."

When Bannister reached the hotel, he ran into Sheriff Campbell. He addressed the sheriff at once, appearing pleased that they had met.

"Campbell, I suppose you know Le Beck is in town," he said in a tone of interrogation.

"I'm watching him . . . and you, too, for that matter," said the official.

"I'll stand watching, putting the meaning both ways," said Bannister with a frown. "I suppose you know he's in Cromer's pay? Well, whether you know it or not, I know it. He's been traveling with Hayes and two mean-looking Canadians all day, and I think they're hatching up something. Now I'm playing square as a die with you, Sheriff" — Bannister's tone was firm and convincing and he looked Campbell straight in the eyes — "and I'll keep my word. I've found out a few things, and every move I make is in the interests of Florence Marble. I want you to know this and remember it. If that outfit of cut-throats starts anything with me, I'm going to get 'em all."

With that he strode away, leaving the sheriff to stare after him.

He found his company in one of the rooms upstairs. To their questions as to where he had been he made evasive replies. But he knew by Florence Marble's look that she suspected what he had been doing. Her eyes were troubled. It thrilled him through and through to think that this girl thought

272

enough of him to worry about him.

"Are you going back with us after the fireworks, Bob?" she asked, when they were together for a few moments near the door.

"No, Florence, I can't go back tonight," he answered. "Don't look that way, please. I'm investigating some things besides aces and kings. I've got to stay. But be sure you take Howard with you."

"Oh, I guess he'll want to ride back with June Macy well enough," she said. Then impulsively: "Bob Bannister, I don't want you to get into any trouble on my account. I . . . I can't stand the thought of it."

He laid a hand on her arm. "Don't worry about me," he said in a low voice. "That . . . that other down there was a blind accident. But I'm working for you, just the same . . . every minute. And it's the one real joy of my life." He moved away and spoke to John Macy. "I'm going down to see that the horses are being taken care of," he said, and went out the door.

It was already growing dusk as he walked through the crowd again thronging the street and made his way to the rear of the tents. He passed the long line of wagons and buckboards and corrals and finally came to where they had left their horses. The corral tender told him the horses had

273

been watered at the ditch behind the corrals and he could see the hay on the ground himself. They were still eating. He lingered, talking aimlessly with the man, who was one of Cromer's teamsters. Something might slip out that would be of interest. But nothing did, and he started back along the corrals in a twilight that was just on the verge of melting with the night.

Two men approached him. He paid no attention to them until one of them bumped into him with a force that nearly threw him off his feet. He whirled as the man spoke.

"What's the matter? You blind? Or maybe you've got all this space rented for a sidewalk."

Bannister recognized the two Canadians who had been with Le Beck and Hayes. They had seen him and had followed him. It all came to him in a flash. These two could pick a fight with him and get away with it, even if they killed him. They were strangers. Cromer could disclaim any knowledge of them. Le Beck and Hayes would keep silent. It was as raw as it was vicious.

Bannister didn't answer and he didn't hesitate to act. His right came up with the power of a sledge-hammer against the man's jaw, knocking him flat on the grass. Before the other could move, Bannister brought his left crashing against his ear. He went down like a log. But he was out of it in a twinkling and getting up.

Bannister's eyes were flaming with the lust for combat. He met the man as he got to his feet with a straight right that he brought clear from the next county. The man stayed down this time. But Bannister caught a glint of metal just in time to leap aside as a gun roared. His own weapon was in his hand like a flash of light. Two thin tongues of flame licked at the deepening dusk and the other man grasped his right arm with a cry and dropped his gun. There were two bullets in that arm.

"When your friend comes around," Bannister drawled, breaking his gun to extract the empty shells and reload the two chambers, "you better hot-foot it for headquarters and tell 'em you're leaving."

That's all he said aloud. *Round one,* he mused to himself as he walked on along the corrals. *I wouldn't wonder if this would prove to be an evening.*

Suddenly he stopped dead in his tracks. A horse in the corral he was passing nickered. Somehow the nicker seemed familiar. He looked and stepped close to the rails. The nicker came again from right ahead of him.

He looked sharply and came near crying out. There, tied to a rail within three feet of him, was his own horse that had been stolen the night he had been shot.

CHAPTER TWENTY-SIX

The corral tender sauntered toward Bannister. "Got a hoss in here?" he asked casually, more because he wanted to talk to someone than anything else.

"Yes, but I don't want him now," Bannister replied. "Quite a scheme, this checking business." He was wondering if it would do any good to ask the man who it was that had brought in his horse, but decided it wouldn't, as the corral tenders had doubtless changed shifts.

"Big boss thought up the scheme," said the corral tender. "Said it would stop hosses bein' stole an' keep things orderly. Anyway, there wasn't any place to tie 'em an' you can see how many there are here."

"Plenty," said Bannister, noting that this was the fourth corral from the upper end, and all were filled. "And at two dollars a head it means a sweet bit of change."

"You said it." He chuckled as Bannister

moved off.

Then Bannister bethought himself of something. He stopped, and, when the tender strolled up to him, he asked: "I'm curious if this is a concession or if the company is running it . . . which is it?"

"Company scheme, company profits," replied the tender.

"Well, Cromer isn't overlooking anything," Bannister observed. "If this celebration isn't a money-maker, then I'm a sheepherder."

"Yep," said the man cheerfully. "Well, they've got a brand new bank vault to put it in."

"That's right," said Bannister, remembering. "The bank opened today, didn't it?"

"Sure did," was the answer. "Nine this mornin' to ten tonight is opening hours. Then the fireworks."

"Well, so long," said Bannister, starting off. Somehow the man's last words — *Then the fireworks.* — struck him queerly. There was a lot of cash in the Marble State Bank this night. The payments made by purchasers on their plot contracts must have amounted to thousands and thousands. The resorts and concession holders would bank big sums. And all this was cash — gold, silver, and bills. A perfect lure for cracksmen or even hold-ups.

Bannister hurried up the street through the milling crowd. He found Tommy Gale in a place across the street from where he had been when Bannister left him. He was playing poker.

Bannister went to the bar without appearing to notice him, and, after taking a glass of beer, he left. In a short time Tommy followed him out. Bannister led the way around the upper end of the street and behind the tents. He told Tommy quickly what had happened at the corrals. Then: "Where's your horse?"

"Around back of the stands," Tommy replied, waving a hand toward the east side of town where the temporary stadium was located.

"Listen, Tommy," said Bannister in guarded tones, "now you know my horse, don't you?"

"Pretty near as well as I do my own," Tommy replied.

"All right," said Bannister with satisfaction. "Now you go and get your horse. Ride around to the corrals and up to the fourth from the upper end. My horse is tied just above the gate. You can spot him in no time. Put your horse up there. Act like you'd had a little bit too much. Get to talking with the corral tender. He wants to talk, for he's lonesome out there away from the crowd. You better pack a bottle along and give him a drink. Give him all he'll take. Sit down and lean against a post, or go over in the shadow of a tent and pretend to go to sleep . . . anything so long as you keep an eye on my horse. We want to see who comes for him and we don't want whoever does come for him to get out of town. That is, unless I follow him. They probably thought I was too much under the weather to get to the celebration. But by now they must know different. They'll be planning to whisk that horse away now that night has come. Do you gather my drift?"

"Sure do," said Tommy. "I gathered it before you said it."

"All right," said Bannister, "go to it. Now I'm going to try and see who those Canadians report to. They'll beat it to the doctor's place to get that arm fixed up. Then they'll edge around to headquarters, whoever or wherever that is. I aim to find out. But don't you let anyone get out of town with my horse, if you have to shoot him out of the saddle. Whoever comes for him is mixed up in the rustling, I'll bet on that. When I'm through with my sleuthing, I'll beat it over there where you are. Got it all straight?"

"Straight as a string," said Tommy softly.

"An' I'll sure keep the saddle on my hoss. I'll mosey over an' get that cayuse, but first I'll get a bottle like you said. I can fake my part of the drinking."

He went back into the resort where he had been playing cards and Bannister proceeded down the street. He continued on until he reached the hospital tent at the lower end of the street. There he stealthily peered within. He saw immediately that his surmise had been correct. The Canadians were there and the man he had shot in the arm was being treated.

He stepped into the shadow between the tents on the upper side and waited for the pair to come out. They didn't come out for some time, and, when they did, one of them had his right arm in a sling.

They turned up the street and Bannister did not have much trouble following them, despite the crowd. Indeed, the crowd acted as a cover for his movements. They crossed the street and continued up the other side. This also was as Bannister had expected, for it was on this side of the street that the Dome Palace was located. They were making for that place, he felt sure.

But when they reached the big resort they did not go in the entrance but picked their way through ropes and stays between the tents on the lower side to the rear. Bannister was suspicious of this move. He made his way to the rear of the big tent on the upper side and, peering around the corner of the canvas, could plainly see the two men in the shadow. There was no light behind the tents, although the street was lighted by gasoline torches.

One of the pair went into the tent by the rear entrance and Bannister could see the white bandages about the forearm of the other. He waited quietly. In a few moments two men came out. One of them was short and slight, with a great hat that seemed to overbalance his diminutive figure. Bannister recognized him as Le Beck. The four slipped from behind the tents and walked rapidly among the parked vehicles to the temporary bowl that had been erected for the rodeo sports. They disappeared underneath the largest stand. Bannister followed as closely as he could without being seen. But when he reached the rear of the stand, he could see nothing but inky blackness underneath.

He moved in under the tiers of seats cautiously. But for all his caution he bumped against posts and stumbled over pieces of wood and uneven ground. All was still. The only sounds were those Bannister made himself. He halted, listened intently, and endeavored to accustom his eyes to the intense darkness. Then he saw a faint glimmer of light some distance off to his left. He moved carefully in that direction, holding out his hands in front of him, taking one slow, careful step at a time.

The needle of light shone brighter, and, as he progressed, he saw the pale starlight beyond it and realized that this light came from the extreme northern end of the stand. There, though he did not know it at the time, quarters had been boarded in for some of the more prominent riders and officials of the rodeo. Thus, when he finally could make out the source of the light, he saw it came from a crack between the boards of a room. There were other glimmers of light, too, from other cracks. The sound of voices came to him as he approached stealthily. Then he heard a louder voice that he did not recognize.

"Remember," this voice said sharply, "when the first rockets go up."

Then came silence. The light suddenly went out. A door opened and closed somewhere. Murmurs of voices came to his ears, but he could make out nothing of what was being said. They died away. Then the silence again.

Bannister crept toward the opening

around the rooms. When he stole out from under the stand, he could see no one. The men had disappeared. From the inside of the bowl, however, came the pounding of hammers, and Bannister knew they were completing the frames for the setting off of the fireworks.

When the first rockets go up, he recalled. *Now what?*

Something was afoot. This doubtless explained the attack the two Canadians had made upon him when he had taken the initiative after they had accosted him. They planned to beat him up or shoot him — get him out of the way somehow. But what did they intend to do when the fireworks began?

Bannister picked his way through wagons and buckboards to the rear of the Dome Palace, his alert gaze roving everywhere. He saw no one and entered the tent at the rear. Although he circled about the inside, looking at those who stood before the bars and the players at the tables, he saw neither Le Beck nor Hayes or either of the Canadians. This led him to believe they had been under the grandstand and consequently were involved in any scheme that was being cooked up.

He went into the street, which was rapidly becoming deserted as the throngs made

their way to the stadium to view the fireworks. Men were filing out of the canvas-
covered resorts to see the show in the skies.
Bannister instinctively looked up and instantly became aware of two things — two
changes in the elements of air and sky —
that he had not noticed as he concentrated
on his trailing of the men. The sky eastward
and southward was alive with stars. But
directly overhead it seemed as if a line had
been drawn, cutting the zenith. To the north
and west of it, the sky was dark. Clouds
were scuttling, rolling the line of stars before
it. The wind had freshened, but it was a hot
wind, hotter even than the breeze that had
dallied during the day as if being blown
gently from the jaws of a furnace. Then suddenly all motion of air ceased.

Bannister knew the signs. One of those
sudden, terrific electric storms that are a
terror of the northern semi-altitudes was
sweeping down from the northwest. It
would come with the speed of an express
train, wreak its havoc, and rush on. Even as
he stood looking upward, a flash of dazzling
white fire crinkled in the north, as if leaping
the peaks in a celestial ecstasy over the
advent of the storm. The air was perfectly
still, with the heat weighing down, until the
earth seemed a cauldron fed by unseen fires.

Bannister was standing still in the center of the deserted street, torn in this moment of emergency by indecision. He had started for the corrals to see if Tommy Gale was still there. But how about the safety of Florence Marble, who most certainly had gone to see the fireworks? And the unknown move on the part of the men he had followed that was set for . . . ?

There was a rush of flame to the east as a dozen rockets soared into the sky, leaving a trail of fiery sparks to rain down almost to the earth. Blue, red, and yellow balls blossomed in the high heavens and were flung headlong by the racing wind, which now dipped and plunged and burst with a wild, deafening roar. The storm came in with all the ferocity the elements could muster.

Bannister braced himself against the terrific blast of wind and saw a horseman galloping up the street. The form in the saddle appeared familiar. He recognized Tommy.

"Behind the bank!" Tommy shouted. "Run like . . . !" His words were taken out of his mouth by the blast and hurled away.

Bannister was on the run down the street in a moment, the wind hurling him on. Tommy galloped ahead of him. He could see the light streaming from the front windows of the bank. *Behind the bank!*

Tommy had shouted. The warning had come on the heels of the signal of the bursting rockets. So that was it — the bank. The lure of gold and silver — of cash — had done its work. Blue flame from the gasoline torches streaked out, giving practically no light. Some were blown out. The street darkened. The shrieking wind brought other hideous sounds — shouts and cries and screams. The world seemed to be spinning.

Bannister dodged into a space between the bank and the next building. He brought up at the rear of the new building as red arrows of fire stabbed the blackness to the sharp barking of guns. His weapon was in his hand. Then of an instant all was brighter than day in a blinding sheet of lightning. In that long instant Bannister saw a man running out the rear door of the bank. A horseman beyond the door was Tommy. To the left were horses. Bannister and Tommy both fired as the blackness shut in, and the heavens exploded in a deafening crash of thunder that seemed to rock the very earth.

A yellow beam of light shone from the open door. Bannister ran for it as a shadow flashed through it. He fired. There were red streaks in front of him in answer. Another lightning bolt shot across the sky and a ball of blue-white fire burst to eastward. The crash of thunder that followed almost threw him to the ground. "It struck!" he shouted, and came into the beam of lamplight.

He saw a man dashing for the door through a short, narrow corridor, a gun in his hand. He leaped upon the one step as the man reached the door. It was Cromer, his face bloodless — a ghastly white. He fired pointblank at Bannister and Bannister's hat was knocked from his head by the impact of a bullet. Then the door banged shut and shots rang out behind.

The rushing black terror above winked three times with its blue-white lightning. The thunderbolts and the thunderclaps came instantaneously. A riderless horse passed by Bannister and he leaped for the dragging reins, grasped them, and brought the animal up. He swung into the saddle and the feel of it told him instantly that it was his own — he was on his own horse!

A lurid glare shot upward, brightened — a crimson tongue flared into the face of the wind.

"Fire!" a piercing shriek came from somewhere.

Then something struck Bannister on his right side, almost knocking him from the saddle. He struggled with it as his horse bolted. It was a piece of canvas. One of the horse's hoofs caught in it and they went down. Bannister held to the reins although he had been flung over the animal's head. He was up instantly, pulling at the canvas. A flash of lightning showed him something white darting overhead. The tents were going.

He freed his horse and swung back into the saddle just as the great cloud reservoir burst and the rain came down in one solid sheet like a cataract.

CHAPTER TWENTY-SEVEN

Bannister's horse was cavorting wildly. He drew a tight rein on the animal and started around the line of tents, guided by the continuous flashes of lightning that played incessantly through the downpour. The thunder crashed and rolled as the storm unleashed its fury. He finally reached the street, dazed and drenched. Tent ropes and wooden stakes and torn sheets of canvas were hurtling through the air on that roaring wind. The rain came heavier and heavier — a cloudburst.

The fires, deluged with water, were speedily put out. But the canvas had been ripped from board floors and sides of booths and was strewn about the street, which was a sea of mud and running water. The great brown tent that had housed the Dome Palace bars and gaming tables and layouts had been torn straight across the high ridge. The canvas was in tatters, whipping in the wind; men were lying close to the board side walls and behind the bars to avoid being struck. The framework of the roof had given way and sticks were being hurled in every direction.

All was chaos. Screams of women and children and hoarse shouts and curses of men mingled with the hideous uproar of the storm. The thunder closed in with terrific explosions, rocking the earth, leaving the ears numb. Vivid lightning flashes seared the utter blackness, blinding the terrified victims of this vicious onslaught of the angry elements. Horses broke their halter ropes in the corrals and dashed out, running madly about the plain. Some went into the ditches, there to be shot on the morrow with broken legs. Others plunged into the débris of tents and wooden framework to flounder, go down, and struggle until their breath and strength were gone. Seats were torn from wagons, buckboards overturned. And still the solid wall of water stood between earth and sky, lightning bolts shook the universe, and the wind shrieked its defiance and ridicule to any storm that had ever raged on the north range before.

Bannister raked his mount with the steel, driving the horse into the teeth of the stinging rain. "Florence!" he shouted futilely.

All the events of the day and night were forgotten in his overwhelming anxiety. He came to the hotel. There was light in the lobby but not upstairs. The frame building was swaying with the force of the blast. They had gone to see the fireworks, of course. Had they started back and been caught? Had they taken refuge under the stands? Bannister became frantic — panic-stricken. The stands might go.

The lightning showed him the wide space between the tents where the road led to the stadium. He turned into it, his horse shying and rearing and lunging as it plunged through the débris. Then the plain. The lightning showed hundreds of people lying flat on the ground. It was the only way they could protect themselves.

He rode on, his face whiter than the forked lightning that streaked everywhere. "Florence! Florence!" He shouted and screamed until he was hoarse and his agonized cries were merely croakings in his throat. Dead ahead were the stands. Even as he looked at the largest of them, there came a series of sharp ripping, tearing, splintering sounds, and the stand swung backward and collapsed. Shrieks and screams followed from those who had sought shelter under the flimsy structure.

Loose boards were ripped off and went sailing on the wind, glistening in the lightning flashes like demon arrows shot from the black bowstrings of the tempest.

"My God!" exclaimed Bannister with no thought of irreverence or blasphemy. He spurred his horse toward the scene, and the lightning flashes showed him to be the only horseman abroad in that turmoil. He could see men running about the fallen stand, starting rescue work. Then a cry came to his ears on the wind.

"Bannister!"

He jerked his horse to a stop, rising in the stirrups and staring northward with his face to the wind and the slanting downpour. He thought he heard the cry again. Then in a vivid flash of lightning he saw a hand being waved on the plain. He whirled his horse. It must be she. He had been conspicuous on his horse and she had recognized him. He reached the shadowy form on the ground and threw himself out of the saddle.

"Florence!" he shouted joyfully, and gathered her up in his arms. "Where are the others?" he shouted in her ear.

"With John Macy," she said as he bent over her. "They started back. I lost them in the crowd." She tried to say more but could not.

Bannister lifted her into the saddle and climbed up behind her. He held her with his left arm, her head on his shoulder, and turned south, riding easily with the wind. He veered off to the west toward town. They came to the wagons, passed along them. The lightning still played incessantly and the rain continued to fall in torrents. It was such a storm as Bannister had never experienced. Florence lay inert against him, her eyes closed. Bannister shielded her face as best he could. He was hatless, soaked through and through, as was the girl. There was a chill in the wind and rain now, too.

He reached the end of the wagons and saw implements ahead. Behind some huge dump wagons he descried a small shack that he took to be a tool house. The big wagons broke the force of the blast and prevented the shack from being blown over. It was an excellent refuge, but there was a ditch just ahead. Bannister hesitated a few seconds, then sank his steel, and the horse leaped ahead, straight for the ditch. Bannister tightened his hold on the girl in his arms, then the splendid black left the ground and soared gracefully over the menacing gash in the surface of the plain.

"Good boy!" affirmed Bannister, patting his mount's neck.

He rode to the shack, dismounted, and lifted Florence from the saddle. The wind howled past on either side, but they were sheltered here in the lee of the shack and wagons. Florence stood bravely in the downpour while Bannister ascertained that the door of the shack was padlocked. He cast about him and found a heavy bolt on the ground. With this he smashed the hasp and kicked open the door. He drew Florence inside. The lightning illuminated the place, showing a big assortment of tools and piles of empty cement sacks. He knocked over some sacks and Florence sat down upon them. Then he went out and tied his horse and took his slicker from the rear of the saddle. The man who had stolen his horse had emptied the pack that had been wrapped in the oiled slicker, but had tied the slicker back on the saddle. *Evidently took a fancy to my things,* Bannister thought to himself. And well any rustler might, for everything Bannister possessed was good. All this time, he had never stopped to think, until now, of the coincidence of his horse being behind the bank. The man who had stolen the animal was, of course, a member of the gang who had planned the bank robbery. He wondered how much they had gotten away with. Tommy had seen the man come for Bannister's horse, had secured his own mount, and followed him. He had seen Bannister alone in the street by chance, just as Florence had seen him as a lone rider in that fearful storm. After all, an element of luck had favored him, as against the attack of those other elements that made the night one of horror and madness.

He hurried inside with the slicker, shook it out, and, as it was dry inside, he wrapped it about the girl.

She grasped one of his hands in both of hers. "Bannister!" she cried above the tumult. "People have been killed tonight!"

He sat down beside her and her arms went about his neck. He held her close as she gave way to her emotions and wept on his shoulder. His hand caressed her hair. Then he remembered something and slipped his hand into the right pocket of the slicker. There he found a bandanna handkerchief, as he had expected, and it was dry. It had been protected by the oilskin.

He dried her face and hands and hair and put the handkerchief on his shoulder so her head would not lie on his wet coat. She snuggled up to him and lay, still and silent. His heart beat wildly. She was his girl. And because of that other — that mistake haunting the shadow of his past — was he to lose her? He wanted her — wanted all of her for his own, wanted her heart, her love, her respect. . . .

The wind shrieked and screamed overhead, the rain pounded upon the roof, the shack quivered to the deafening crashes of thunder, lightning played with the intensity of celestial fires rampant and uncontrolled. Sheltered from the storm's furies, save for the dreadful sound, Bannister and Florence sat in the tool shack. She opened the slicker and insisted that he draw it about them both, for the wind had become colder and they were soaking wet. Alone in their snug retreat, they seemed thousands of miles from other human beings — in another world. Bannister forgot everything save the warmth and sweetness of the girl in his arms. The specter of that thing that would thrust them apart was far, far away. He drew her face up to his and kissed her.

Then came the magic of the storm, as Bannister knew it would come, as it had always come before. The violence of the wind began to abate as suddenly as it had burst from the clouds. The rain eased off. The lightning ceased and the thunder rolled away with grumbling reverberations to southward. Lighter and lighter the rain fell until it merely beat a light tattoo upon the tin roof of the shack. Then wind and rain subsided altogether, and a great silence fell over the land.

Florence's arm tightened about Bannister's neck. She was the first to speak. "I feel so safe with you, Bob Bannister," she said softly — and raised her lips.

Bannister's supreme moments of joy and happiness were akin to pain. "Florence, girl, I love you," he said brokenly. "I love you better than life. I love you, and love you, and love you . . . oh, I can't tell you how much."

Her hands were on his cheeks, over his lips and eyes, in his hair. Tender, loving hands that thrilled him until he trembled as they gently conveyed their message.

"But it can't be," he said hopelessly. "It just can't be, sweetheart of mine."

"Why can't it be, Bob?" she asked in a whisper.

"Because . . . because. . . ." The words choked in his throat.

Her lips caressed his cheek. "Because you're The Maverick?" she said gently. "Oh, Bob, I know. And I don't care! I love you, and that's all I care about. They can't drive you away from the Half Diamond, Bobbie boy. They can't do that. And you're not afraid of them. You didn't lie to me and tell me you weren't The Maverick, dear. You just refused to answer when I asked you. And I love you for that. You know, Bob Bannister" — her voice softened until it barely reached his ear — "I need you."

It seemed to Bannister that the whole world was alive with light, a great, pure, white light that shone with sublime brilliancy. He would not have been surprised to see angels floating in the firmament. It was heaven there in that rough shack, with tools scattered about, with rusty shovels and picks with earth clinging to them leaning against the board walls, and chalky cement sacks beneath them.

"You don't understand, Florence girl," he said slowly. "I . . . I have given my word. I can't tell you now. But maybe . . . maybe, if it could be."

He clasped her tightly against him and kissed her fiercely — her lips, her eyes, her hair. And then he released her. "We must go," he said in a voice strangely stern.

They went out into the open air to find the miracle of the storm accomplished. The clouds had hurried on southward and the stars were out. The moon rode among them like a bright, new silver coin flung into the skies by some superhuman hand.

Crowds were moving on the plain and

lights were showing in the direction of the street. Florence and Bannister mounted and rode slowly along the ditch until they reached the crossing. They picked a way through débris and mud and water between two buildings and gained the street, where the scene of devastation caused them to catch their breath. They continued up the street — filled now with a bewildered, shivering crowd that knew not where to turn — and finally reached the hotel. The lobby, stairs, rooms, and halls were packed with people, as was every other building in town. They made their way upstairs, Bannister parting the jam, and found the others of the party in one of the three rooms that had been reserved for them. The others had started for the hotel as soon as the storm began to slacken.

Bannister did not stay to answer questions. He left that to Florence and hurried back downstairs to his horse. He rode a few doors up the street to the bank building. It was aglow with light. He dismounted and pounded heavily on the door, which was locked, wondering what the bandits had reaped in plunder. When the door was opened, he saw Sheriff Campbell before him. He entered quickly, noting that several other men, including Van Note, the deputy, were there.

"Grab him!" came a shrill voice. "He was with 'em! Don't let him get away. Grab him quick . . . he's tricky."

It was Cromer, his eyes snapping with vicious fire, his whole body trembling with excitement. Sheriff Campbell had locked the door. Now he stood, as did the others, staring keenly at Bannister, who appeared amused.

"Why don't you act, Sheriff?" Cromer demanded angrily. "He was with 'em, I tell you. When I ran back there, he was coming in. I shot at him but missed him. Then I slammed the door in his face. He was the ringleader and I know it!"

Bannister looked casually around at the sober faces about him. Then he walked close to Cromer and looked straight into his eyes. "Your bullet went through my hat," he said in a voice of ice, "and, if you hadn't slammed that door, you never would have touched a gun again except in the land of Kingdom Come."

CHAPTER TWENTY-EIGHT

For a brief space Cromer's eyes burned into Bannister's. Then he turned his gaze on Campbell. "You hear, Sheriff?" he said stridently. "He intended to kill me. Now what do you think?"

"I think you're pretty much excited," said Campbell with a trace of irritation. "Suppose you let me do the investigating." He turned to Bannister. "How did you come to be here at the time of the robbery?"

"I followed two men who tried to pick trouble with me over by the corrals, just at dark," Bannister replied. He had no intention of mentioning Tommy Gale, and was thinking rapidly about the best way in which to avoid it. "I knocked them down when they bumped into me and set their mouths loose. One of 'em pulled a gun and I shot him in the right arm. He dropped it. They went to the hospital, and then around to the back of the Dome Palace tent." He paused to flash a look at Cromer, who was standing behind him with a sneering expression on his face. "Two men joined them behind the tent, coming out of the Dome Palace. The four of them went to a room under the big stand over east and laid their plans for the robbery. The time was set for the moment the first rockets went up. I came back into town and looked around the street and in the Palace, but I didn't see anyone I wanted to see. Time had passed quicker than I thought, as I was slower getting back than the others. I was in the street when the first rockets went up, and the storm broke at the same time. I ran around to the rear of the bank."

He had looked at Cromer frequently during this slow recital and saw the sneer leave the man's face, to be followed by a gleam of frowning interest. At first he had thought that Cromer himself might be in on the deal, but now he changed his mind.

"I got there as a man ran out the rear door of the bank," he continued. "He shot at me and I dropped him. Did you find a wounded man out there?"

Campbell shook his head. "No, we found a dead one," he said.

"So much the better," observed Bannister coolly. "I thought there were more of them inside and started in just as Cromer came running to the door and fired in my face. In a way, he can thank me for his life. I could have got him when he reached for the door, but held my fire when I saw he didn't intend to shoot again. All this happened in a space of seconds. I leaped away from the door and a riderless horse came along. I caught it and swung into the saddle."

He stopped talking, as if he had said all that was necessary.

"Did you follow these men?" the sheriff asked sharply.

"I didn't," Bannister replied. "The cloudburst came down at that moment and a piece of a tent hit me. My horse got tangled in the canvas and went down. I went over his head, but kept the reins. When I got back in the saddle, it was too late to follow them in that storm, even if I had wanted to. I came into town with Miss Marble and her cousin from the Half Diamond. I was concerned about her safety. I started out to find her and by pure luck I did. I guided her to shelter, and, when the storm was over, I brought her into town and took her to the hotel. John Macy, his daughter, and some others had gone with her to see the fireworks, and they were already back when we got in. Then I came straight here."

There was a period of heavy silence when he had finished. Then: "Do you believe that?" Cromer exploded, addressing the sheriff.

"Well, yes . . . I do," said Campbell slowly. "Yes, I'm inclined to believe it. There was a man treated at the hospital tonight for a bullet wound in the right arm, although that in itself doesn't prove anything. It will be easy enough to substantiate the last part of Bannister's story through Miss Marble. You say he was the ringleader. If he had been the ringleader, don't you think he would have gone into the bank in the first place and not have attempted to enter *after* the robbery?"

"Rubbish!" snorted Cromer. "He might have been coming back for more. He probably wasn't satisfied with the few thousand they got and intended to try and make me open the vault. And he might have been there in the first place. They were masked when they came in."

"But why would he want to throw away his mask and come back without it and be recognized?" asked Campbell shrewdly.

"How the devil do I know?" cried Cromer angrily. "I haven't had any experience in robbing banks."

"Well, I've had to deal with men who have

305

had experience in robbing banks," the sheriff retorted, "and I don't think the dumbest of them would pull a fool stunt like that. And I can't see yet how that back door came to be unlocked." He looked searchingly at Cromer, who threw up his hands in genuine disgust.

"For the last time," he said harshly, "I'll tell you that I don't know, either. There were a few in here making deposits when the doors closed at ten. I had kept the back door locked and bolted all day. Somebody must have slipped back there and unlocked it and shot back the bolts. Again I tell you, I was in the rear of the cage and knew nothing until a gun was shoved in my face and three other masked men were holding the customers and cashier at bay and scooping up all the money in sight. There was a shot out there in the back that scared them away before they could make me open the vault. And according to this Bannister, he didn't fire a shot until he saw the men running out the door." The sneer was on his lips again.

"Did you hear a shot before you came to the door?" Campbell asked Bannister.

"I did," replied Bannister readily. "But I don't know who fired it, and I didn't have time to ponder over it, for bullets were whizzing in my direction right *pronto*."

"Well, we're getting nowhere here," said the sheriff with a puzzled frown. "It looks to me as though one of those late customers sneaked back there and unlocked that door. But nobody knows who the late customers were, save by the names they gave. Nobody seems to know anything except Bannister and I'm banking on what he's said being true."

"Does anyone know the man who was shot?" Bannister asked.

"No," said the sheriff. "Nobody knows anything."

"How much did they get?" Bannister inquired casually.

"About eight thousand, Cromer thinks," the sheriff answered sarcastically. "They don't even know that for sure."

"Well, *he* ought to know the exact amount," Cromer snapped.

Bannister whirled on him, his face set and stern, his eyes flashing. "Cromer," he said in a forbidding voice, "if you don't dry up your mouth so far as your remarks concern me, I'll knock every tooth in your head down your throat and make you spit 'em out, one by one."

Cromer, taken aback by the fierce look in Bannister's eyes, and convinced by his tone that he meant what he said, turned away muttering.

"And now we've got to see about the people who've been hurt and the damage done and get order restored," said the sheriff. "That's a danged lot more important than this robbery. Close up your bank, Cromer, and get out and help. You don't seem to give a continental damn about anybody but yourself, Cromer, but you're taking my orders tonight and tomorrow, and don't you forget it."

The official opened the door and the party filed out. On the short cement walk in front of the bank, Bannister touched the sheriff's arm and got his ear. "Just one thing before we start work and I get my orders," he said. "That horse I caught out back of the bank was my own . . . the one stolen from me in the river breaks the night I was trailing the supposed rustlers. I know Howard told you about my experience down there when I was shot. That shows the same gang pulled off this job up here that's working in the badlands. It's something we want to remember."

Sheriff Campbell was silent a few moments, digesting this information. "That makes it harder and easier," he said ambiguously. "We won't forget that. But now we'll get busy. You get together a bunch of riders. There are a lot of Half Diamond men in town and some from other ranches south. Get Macy to help you round 'em up. The horses have broken away and must be driven in so people can start home. That's your job. The rest of us will try to restore order here and look after those who were hurt over at the stands."

Bannister was off on his mission with the sheriff's last words. He rode to the hotel and made his way upstairs. There he explained what was wanted to John Macy and Howard, who both agreed at once to help. He told Florence and the other women there to remain in the room until morning. The three men started out to round up the riders and commandeer the first horses they came upon for emergency use. The first mounted man Bannister saw was Tommy Gale, and he enlisted his services immediately.

A glorious dawn found a semblance of order in the stricken town of Marble. Scores of horses had been driven in from the plain and men were identifying them, leading them to the corrals, where the saddles still straddled the rails, or to wagons and buckboards and stages to be hooked up. Already people were leaving — disheveled, weary, their clothing torn, such belongings as they had brought with them mostly lost.

Men were at work clearing the débris in the street. Owners of booths were salvaging what they could from the wreckage of their places of business on the night before. Hot coffee was being served free to all who wanted it from such board stands as remained. Cromer had ordered it in the hope that it might in some small way offset the disastrous effects of the storm. No one could tell what the result of the catastrophe would be and Cromer was almost in a frenzy. And always in the back of his head was that burning fire of hatred of Bannister. He was not sure that Bannister really had a part in the bank robbery, and that made him all the more angry. Then Bannister had rescued Florence Marble from the fury of the storm. He ground his teeth whenever he thought of it. Why couldn't he have had such luck himself, instead of staying in the bank counting his loss?

Five people had been killed in the collapse of the big stand. Scores had been hurt there and in the town proper. They had been taken to the board shacks of the engineers and other officials and cared for by the company doctor and Dr. Holmes, who was early on the scene from Prairie City. Two people had been killed by the bolt of lightning that had struck a smaller stand. Many had been knocked unconscious by the shock. The stand had taken fire, but the deluge of rain had quenched the flames.

Looting had begun to some extent by the time Sheriff Campbell had organized his force of special deputies. It had stopped with the word that the special deputies had orders to shoot to kill if they saw any plundering.

Engineers and laborers were strengthening the head gates of the big ditch against the roaring, gushing waters of the swollen river. Water was pouring like a cataract over the overflow of the dam. But the dam held, and even if it had given way, it would have released its waters eastward from the town. Meanwhile, as the sun swung up into the eastern sky, bathing the plain in its golden glory and shedding its warmth, every member of the Marble Dome Land and Irrigation Company organization was broadcasting the fact that never had such a storm been known in that country, and that it would not have wreaked so much havoc if there had been only buildings instead of tents, that it had not injured the land or the works of the project, and above all things that there would probably never be such a storm again. Thus, gradually, as the sun mounted higher and food was served gratis, prospective settlers regained their composure and confidence and complete order was restored.

By 10:00 A.M. celebrants from the ranches in the surrounding country were on their way home, the street was clear, the bank and company offices were open, stores, cafés, and resorts were doing business. But the celebration itself ended with the payment of the prizes won by contestants in the rodeo of the day before.

Bannister came upon Sheriff Campbell, who, despite the fact that he was tired and worn after his strenuous work during the night and morning, was nevertheless still on the job, master of the situation.

"What next, Sheriff?" asked Bannister cheerfully, his duty done.

"You better go home," said Campbell. "There's nothing else for you to do." He looked at the man before him quizzically. "You know, you did mighty good work last night, Bannister," he said soberly. "You helped me more than any other man in town. I'm thanking you for it here an' now. And I'm inclined to believe you know more than you told us about that bank affair." He raised his brows. "Not that I think you had anything to do with it," he added hastily.

"But . . . well, maybe you'll tell me more later. Anyway I think you've got something up your sleeve."

Bannister frowned in thought. He didn't want to tell the sheriff that he had seen Le Beck with the other men, and that he thought Hayes was implicated, also, for the reason that the sheriff might question them. He didn't want either of the men to suspect that they were under suspicion. "If I've got anything up my sleeve, Sheriff," he said slowly, "anything I'm not telling you, it's because I've got a good reason."

A look of understanding passed between them and the official turned away with a so long.

Bannister next went on a hunt for Tommy Gale and found him in a resort — the oldest in town and housed in a stout building — below the bank. He signaled him to go out the rear.

When he met him behind the resort, he came to the point at once. "Tommy, I want you to stay up here and keep an eye on Le Beck and Cromer and on Hayes, too, if he stays in town. If any of them leave, try and follow them or find out where they're going. But keep dark. The Half Diamond is the first ranch south of here, on the river, and you can't miss it if you want to get word to me about anything. You better pose as a wandering 'puncher who's made a stake gambling and is trying to plug it up some more. What say?"

"You're giving me orders," said Tommy loyally. "That's enough for me. My hearing ain't bad an' I got you straight."

"You're top-grade, Tommy." Bannister chuckled. "Did you see anything of those fellows at the bank when they beat it?"

"Lost 'em right off the bat," growled Tommy. "Who wouldn't in that storm."

"Right," said Bannister. "Didn't expect anything else. How much money have you got?"

"Got enough," was the dignified answer.

"You're a liar and you know it," said Bannister with mock severity. "You never had enough money one time in your life. Here, take this. It's expense money, and, if you don't make good, I'll take it out of your hide." He thrust a roll of bills in Tommy's hand and was off before the diminutive cowpuncher could frame what in his mind would be a suitable reply to the sally of his old friend.

Bannister went to the hotel and found Howard and Florence there. Howard had just come in, and upon his arrival John Macy, his daughter, and others from the ranches south of the river had secured their horses and gone home.

"Aren't you two going home?" Bannister asked, simulating surprise.

"We were waiting for you," said Florence.

"All right, we'll be on our way just as soon as I can buy a new hat," said Bannister, almost boisterously. "I've got the horses ready. We'll have to lead one . . . that is, I will, for I found my own last night."

Both Howard and Florence wanted the details, but Bannister said he would wait and tell them on the way back. "It's a peculiar story," he hinted.

As they were about to leave, Cromer appeared in the doorway.

"Oh, you're going?" he said. "I'm glad you're all right, Flo . . . er . . . Miss Marble. I was going to look for you, but assumed you were safe with Bannister and your cousin, and then I was going anyway, but saw the light in the windows up here."

Bannister coughed slightly, but his face was innocently composed as Cromer looked at him.

Cromer turned again to Florence. "I would like very much to see you for a few moments on a . . . *er* . . . little business matter before you go, Miss Marble," he said, glancing at Howard and Bannister significantly.

"I have neither the time nor the inclination, Mister Cromer," said Florence coldly as she pushed past him, followed by the two with her.

Cromer's face went dead white in the heat of his anger as Bannister's laugh floated up to him from the stairway. And in that moment Cromer's teeth clicked together in ominous decision.

Chapter Twenty-Nine

On the way back to the Half Diamond, Bannister told Florence and Howard about the bank robbery of the night before and the recovery of his horse. But even from them he kept secret the arrival of Tommy Gale. Nor did he mention his suspicions in connection with Le Beck and Hayes. He wanted time to think, for one thing, and this morning he was too tired to think. It seemed impossible to arrange his thought trends in logical sequences. And it was just as impossible — if not more so — to keep his mind off that delicious hour he had spent with Florence in the shack during the storm the night before.

She knew he was the man known as The Maverick. He was sure of that. How she had found out for certain, he did not know. He might never ask her. No, he wouldn't ask her. She would have to tell him of her own accord, if she so wished. She knew he was

The Maverick and she didn't care. She loved him. Every time he met her eyes a message seemed to flash between them. It thrilled him and he forgot his weariness. But his promise to Campbell. . . . A shadow seemed to drift over the sparkling gold of the clean-washed plain; the brilliant green of the trees along the creek faded to gray, and the blue sky turned to slate.

At noon it was fearfully hot — hotter, perhaps, than it had been before the storm. There lingered no doubts now but that it was going to be the driest season in years. The flood waters of the river were already subsiding. The river would be down to where it had been before the cloudburst in another forty-eight hours. The river was going to be low this year. Bannister remembered one casual remark John Macy had addressed to Cromer the day before when he thought no one was within earshot. "I'll be up to get that signed paper about our water protection the day after your directors' meeting," Macy had said. "That'll be the Sixteenth." And Cromer hadn't answered him.

They reached the ranch shortly after noon. Martha came fluttering out to meet them, relief glowing in her misty eyes. She hugged Florence, muttering: "I was so worried." She repeated it over and over. "The lightning struck in the cottonwoods by the river and shook the house. I thought the end of the world had come."

Bannister and Howard rode on to the barn with Florence's horse following them. Old Jeb came out to meet them and take the horses. Both Howard and Bannister stared at him and looked at each other. They had forgotten all about old Jeb in the excitement of the arrival in town and the subsequent events.

"I thought you was going to the big blowout," said Bannister.

"Wal, I got to thinkin' it over an' there wasn't any man left here at the ranch an' I decided it was up to me to stay," drawled Jeb. "So I stayed. An' it was a danged good thing I did, fer Miss Martha all but went plumb loco during the storm last night."

"Jeb, you're a brick," Bannister told him. "Just for that I'm going to buy you a new hat, and you'll wear it, or I'll rope and tie you and make you wear it. That thing you've got on looks like something a coyote had dragged in."

"This hat," said Jeb, taking off his dilapidated headgear and gazing at it fondly, "has seen 'em come an' go for ten years, an' I reckon you wasn't such a terror of a buckaroo that far back. An' Howard, there, was just learnin' how to sit in a saddle without being tied on."

He insisted on taking care of the horses and Bannister and Howard went to the wash bench. When they finished with the soap and water and comb, Martha called them to dinner. They were all too hungry to talk much during the meal. And after dinner they sought some sleep. Florence was the only one who dreamed.

That night Bannister made a trip to Dome range to see Manley. He learned that the men had all returned from town, each bringing a different and, if possible, more vividly colored account of what had taken place. Link hadn't gone, Manley told him, nor had he been away from the camp. Hayes hadn't been down that way, Manley said in response to a question from Bannister.

Then Bannister gave Manley an accurate account of what had happened in Marble before, during, and after the storm. He told him of the bank robbery and the recovery of his horse. As Manley already knew about Bannister's experience in the river breaks, this information started him thinking. He told him about Le Beck and Hayes and the Canadians, and next he told the Half Diamond manager of his suspicion of Hayes and Link as being implicated in the rustling operations and in the bank robbery as well.

"I'd watch Link," Bannister suggested. "I'd bet everything I've got that sooner or later he will sneak away. If we can learn where he goes, we'll learn a whole lot more."

After this, while Manley listened intently, Bannister had much to say about Cromer. He left the manager looking at the night sky, thinking hard.

Next day Bannister and Howard rode along the outer fringe of trees along the river breaks. The ground still was soft from its drenching and any tracks made upon it since the storm would show plainly. They found tracks on the wide trail leading to the main ford of the river, but these undoubtedly had been made by John Macy and those with him on their return from town the day before.

Bannister, convinced that the rustling operations and the bank robbery were linked together, decided to play a waiting game. Moreover, he looked forward anxiously to the meeting of the company board of directors and their action in the matter of providing the southern stockmen with water. In four more days John Macy would go to Cromer and demand that he keep his promise. This would be a crucial moment, and Bannister could not forget that Florence Marble's big investment was at stake. As a last resource he had a plan — a move that none of the stockholders' would have thought of at this time.

The river had gone down steadily. The heat was terrific. Its hot breath shimmered on the plain and raced across it in waves when there was a breeze. The oats were doing none too well. By the Sixteenth the river might be expected to be lower than in years. Old Jeb, who knew the signs, didn't hesitate to say so.

"It's the worst I've seen in more than twenty-five years," he declared. "An' if that fool Cromer keeps takin' the water out, the river will dry up sure as daylight."

Bannister respected the old-timer's knowledge, born of long experience in that country. But he said nothing to Florence. In fact, he avoided the girl as much as possible as he struggled with his problem. And, as there was no sign of Tommy Gale, he assumed everything in Marble was quiet. And that also disturbed him.

On the morning of the Sixteenth, the day John Macy was to go to town, Bannister was abroad before dawn. He took up his station by the trail leading to the main ford where the stockman would cross the river. He did not expect Macy to stop at the Half Diamond this day, and he meant to have a few words with him on his way to town. The sun had been up two hours when Macy hove in sight.

"Hallo," he greeted Bannister. "Down to look at the ford?"

"I've seen it," Bannister replied, catching the significance of the rancher's question at once.

"Then you know," said Macy with a heavy scowl. "It's lower than it's been almost since I can remember. This is hitting us fellows down below, I can tell you. We depend on the river . . . the river is everything in a season like this. Every spring and creek south of here is dry."

"Bad business," was Bannister's comment. "You're going in to see Cromer, I suppose?" Macy nodded, frowning. "Well, I'd like to hear what he had to say when you come back," he continued. "I reckon Miss Marble will want to know."

"I'll stop in," said Macy shortly. "I'll come back by way of the ranch an' tell you. If that girl will stick with us. . . ." He swore roundly.

"She's between two fires," said Bannister. "You know she's made a big investment up there."

"Yes, an' I'll bet her old dad is turning in his grave," Macy flared. "He was a cowman, not a confounded farmer. The girl's plumb crazy!" With that he was off on the Dome trail northward.

It lacked two hours of noon when Macy rode into Marble. He left his horse at the livery to be attended to and went straight to Cromer's office.

"He's over at the bank," the clerk told him.

When Macy walked into Cromer's private office at the rear of the cage in the bank, he suspected what was coming by the look on the man's face. His own eyes hardened, and for a space the two challenged each other in silence.

"Sit down, Macy," said Cromer finally. He frowned as the stockman put his hat on the desk, before taking a chair. "I suppose you've come in about . . . about. . . ."

"About the water," Macy finished for him. "I want that signed agreement as you promised, an' the association wants your head gates closed during this dry spell. We're up against it down there, or will be in another week or so, an' you've got more water stored up than you have any need for in that dam of yours."

Cromer waved a hand in a gesture intended to indicate his helplessness. "My hands are tied," he said slowly. "I have to keep the head gates open. Directors' orders. But we're only taking a small amount. This dry spell won't last, anyway."

Macy leaned far forward in his chair and looked at Cromer with a narrowed, burning gaze. It was impossible for Cromer to take his eyes from the other's, but he retained his cool composure and waited for the stockman's words. They came like the crackling of a whiplash.

"I've lived in this country forty years," said Macy. "I know these dry spells. This is going to last, do you hear me? Now I want to know if you're going to give me that signed paper and keep your word."

"I'm not authorized to do so," replied Cromer in a tone as sharp as Macy's. "I'm not the whole works."

"You talked like it down at the Half Diamond," Macy pointed out. "An' in this country, when a man gives his word, we expect him to keep it. We expect you to keep yours. We have no dealings with your dummy board of directors. We don't ask for anything we're not entitled to. Now . . . will you give me that paper and close your head gates?"

"I told you I couldn't do it," Cromer said angrily. "We're taking water from the dam for the hay over east. We're running it in the main ditch south to town, we're. . . ."

"Do you take me for a fool?" demanded Macy loudly. "The water's been running over your spillway ever since the big storm. Cromer, you're a liar. Your word isn't worth that!" He snapped a thumb and finger. "You're worse than a sneaking, yellow coyote. You're a skunk! Do you think it'll be wise for me to take such a message back south?"

Cromer's eyes were snapping fire, but he knew better than to make a move signifying that he might intend violence. He knew that much. But in the heat of his anger, he failed to read the ominous message in Macy's eyes. He was treading on ice as thin as a hair and failed to realize it. He tapped with his fingers on his desk and delivered his ultimatum. "You can carry any message back you wish," he said icily. "We've got as big an investment up here as all your damned ranches put together, and we've got the law behind us. When you get some sense and put in with us, the head gates will close. And not a fraction of a second before."

Macy had risen to his feet. "You want us to throw in with you, eh?" he said softly — so softly that Cromer misunderstood the portent of his words and manner. "You want us to buy stock, I suppose . . . put up money to help ruin ourselves. Cromer, we'll think that over."

He was out of the office and striding past the cage before Cromer could answer.

Later, when he arrived at the Half Diamond on a lathered horse, Bannister was out to meet him.

"You wanted to know," Macy said in a voice that Bannister could not misunderstand. "Well, I'll tell you. Cromer went back on his word. He told us to put in with them or go to the devil. That's the message I'm taking back, an' that's the message I'm leaving for Flo Marble. An' tell her I hope she's proud of the way she's betrayed her dad's old friends. If she is, she must be happy! And before Cromer gets his answer, she'll no longer be a member of the Cattlemen's Association an' entitled to our protection. Her dad had it one or two times when he needed it damned bad. Maybe she'll wish she had it yet."

He spurred his horse and dashed away through the trees.

Bannister stood still, his face pale. It was time he made his big move and played the card that would decide this dangerous game. But was it? Would he have to wait

327

until . . . ?

Within fifteen minutes of the time of John Macy's furious departure from Marble, Cromer was riding out of town behind a team of spanking grays. He was alone. But if he had looked back, he would have seen a thin spiral of dust following him. Tommy Gale was obeying orders.

CHAPTER THIRTY

When Macy had gone, Florence came out of the house to ask Bannister about the stockman's visit. She had seen him from her windows upstairs but had not expected him to leave so suddenly. "Whatever is the matter with him?" she asked petulantly. "He was here and gone like a house afire."

"It's the water," Bannister replied in a troubled voice. "The river is getting pretty low and they want Cromer to close his head gates and stop taking water."

"Won't he do it?" the girl asked.

"No," said Bannister. "He told 'em to kick in and help the project or he wouldn't close the head gates. It doesn't look any too good, but I'm banking on the cattle crowd to hold their heads." Not for the world would he have told Florence what Macy had said about her. And now, with the sun shining in her hair, and the troubled look in her eyes with a slight pouting of her lips, Florence looked more beautiful than ever.

"Trouble, trouble, trouble!" exclaimed the girl. "I wish Cromer had never come here with his scheme and begun all this. I don't know where it will all end. What do you think, Bob?"

"I'll tell you something, Florence," said Bannister seriously. "Cromer can't have this thing all his own way. I don't like to talk about a man behind his back, but I don't think he has the ability a lot of people give him credit for. I have an idea or two. Just let me tend to this business, Florence, and you forget it all and don't worry. I have a card up my sleeve, and, when the right time comes, I'm going to play it."

"Well, I have all the faith in the world in you," she said, giving Bannister a look that brought the thrill again. "So I won't worry. I'm through. Tend to the business and play your card. And tonight we'll go riding."

"I'm going out east tonight, Florence," said Bannister, striving to control his voice. "I'm keeping watch out there, you know. If I miss a night, something might happen and my work would all be for nothing. We'll have to put it off."

She looked at him curiously. "That isn't the whole reason," she said finally. "Bob Bannister, in some ways you're a coward."

With that she flounced back into the house.

Bannister walked slowly toward the cool, dark interior of the barn. He was biting his lip savagely. Florence Marble was right. He was a coward! He was afraid to ride out with her — afraid of himself. Where was his vaunted willpower? Why didn't he tell her everything and put himself in his proper place? Why did he stay when he might be of service to her almost as well if he worked independently? He could even confess he was The Maverick — kill Le Beck, and Hayes, too, for that matter — send a chill into Cromer's heart and play his trump card. But no, he wanted to be near her. He told himself that he had his own selfish interests at heart. He was no good. He decided to keep away from her as much as possible. Hereafter he would eat with old Jeb in the bunkhouse kitchen. Dreams. Why, he was not only a moral coward, he was a fool.

Bannister had supper with Jeb, telling Howard he wanted to please the old man. He was rather cool toward Howard, and the boy wondered at this. He had wondered considerably lately at the demeanor of both Bannister and Florence. Something seemed to be going on right before his eyes that he couldn't fathom. Florence had been moody;

that afternoon she had been cross and irritated. Now Bannister had spoken to him almost as if he were a stranger. The ramifications of his suspicion reached out everywhere except in the right direction.

And Florence, too, was wondering. Was Bannister becoming impatient to go back on the trail as The Maverick? Was he just what Cromer hinted he was, and nothing more? Did he really love her or was it a part of the strange game that appeared to be his life? Was she a brainless young fool? That night in the storm — it had been their situation, perhaps. She had been terrified at first; he had been excited. The raging elements had found response in his wild nature. Now he was cool, calm, considering, seeking to control himself. Did he love her? If he did, why, why . . . ? There was no answer to her unasked question.

With the deepening of the twilight, Bannister rode alone up the road above the cottonwoods. A breath of air was stirring the heat that still lay upon the land. The far-flung sea of gold that was the plain grasped at the purple veil of dusk, and Marble Dome glowed with the soft rose tints of the sunset's dying reflection. It was a peaceful scene, this great, silent world that whispered of eternity. But the effect upon

Bannister was not peaceful. In his soul was a tumult of rebellion.

He spurred his horse and shook his head savagely. Since he couldn't have the chance he wanted, someone would have to pay. The thought took hold of his mind and fairly shook his whole being. Yes — someone would have to pay. And now what was this? A shadow was coming toward him at racing speed, coming along the road from Prairie City with its trailing plume of dust. A rider — and no poor rider, either. Bannister veered southward directly in the horseman's path. He recognized the man in the saddle while he was still a good distance away, checked his horse, and waited.

"Well, Tommy, you sure seem to be in a powerful hurry," he said as the rider brought up beside him on his sweating mount. "You act like a bearer of tidings. Let's have it."

"Lucky I caught you out here," said Tommy Gale in great excitement. "Didn't know just how I was goin' to get you at the ranch without everybody gettin' wise. Pure luck. Listen." He nodded his head and tapped his saddle horn with a forefinger. "Our friend Cromer is in the know . . . he's wise to you. Anyway, that's the way I see it. He left town an' I followed him. He steered clear of Prairie City, went down an' got on the train, an' hit for Big Falls. I rode with him. Who do you think he went to see down there? Nobody but the sheriff, Bob. That's all."

To Tommy's surprise Bannister merely laughed. It wasn't a pleasant laugh, to be sure, but it conveyed the impression that Bannister welcomed the news.

"You needn't take this as a joke," said Tommy, feeling that he was being ridiculed in some way. "I did a little detective work down there an' followed Cromer to Wills's office. Of course he doesn't know me from Adam, as I've kept out of his way. But he went in there with one of those Reward notices that are out about you, an' I'd bet my trigger finger they'll be up after you tomorrow."

Bannister had sobered. "You're probably right," he said calmly. "Cromer has had a bee in his bonnet for some little time. This is his last play. Then will come my turn." His words were coming sharper and colder. "Here's what you do," he continued. "You ride on to the ranch. Follow this road and you can't miss it. Go to the bunkhouse and there you'll find an old fellow by the name of Jeb White. I trust him. Tell him you're looking for a job, if anybody is around. He'll put you up for the night. If he's alone, or when you two are alone, tell him frankly that you're a friend of mine, but that I don't want anyone else to know it. He'll understand. You hang around there in the trees by the river tomorrow, and, if Cromer and Wills should come to the ranch, you slope for Prairie City. They may cut across to the ranch, you see? When you get there, tell Sheriff Campbell and no one else. You won't see me. If they don't come by tomorrow night, you ride into town anyway and keep within roping distance of the hotel. Now, you know what to do?"

"I'm starting to do it this minute," said Tommy. "You ridin' tonight?"

"Yes." Bannister's tone startled his friend. "Yes, Tommy, I'm riding. So long."

They separated. Tommy went on along the road to the ranch, and Bannister rode fast into the west toward Prairie City, his face set, his eyes gleaming with a light as cold as that of the low-hanging stars.

He was in town well before midnight and put his horse up at the livery, telling the liveryman the animal might be there a few days and to take good care of it and his saddle and bridle. He made sure of this by pressing a gold piece into the man's palm. Then he went to the jail, where he was lucky enough to find Sheriff Gus Campbell in his office, just preparing to go home.

The sheriff and the turnkey both looked at him in surprise.

"Sit down, Sheriff," said Bannister, business-like, signaling him to send the turnkey out. When the man had left the office, Bannister tossed his gun on the table. "Arrest me," he said curtly.

"What for?" asked the astonished official. "You figure you're through out there?"

"No." Bannister shook his head. "I'm just beginning. I want you to arrest me on the charge of shooting Link that time in Marble. As a matter of fact, I did shoot him."

"Huh? He was shooting at you, wasn't he?" snorted Campbell.

"Maybe so, maybe not, anyway that's the charge," said Bannister. "It'll do as well as any. Also you have certain suspicions you're not disclosing to anybody, see? That ties it up better. And you won't let me go. You propose to keep me in jail just as long as it suits you and you won't deliver me to any other sheriff, either. Now do you begin to see the point?"

"No, unless it's that somebody is after you." The sheriff scowled.

"You've rung the bell." Bannister smiled. "Cromer went down to Big Falls to see Wills. His calling card was a Reward notice for my scalp. I look for 'em to come up here to get me. They may go to the ranch first, but I expect them to come here. Well, you'll refuse to give me up. And you better say I'm suspected of being implicated in the bank robbery up there . . . you have Cromer's own argument to use. Anyway, you don't let me out. And you see that the word is spread around that I'm grabbed. See that it gets to Marble if you have to send Van Note up there to holler the news in the street. From now on, Sheriff Campbell, you and I work together."

"Just so," said Campbell dubiously, "and what's going to be the big result of all this?"

"A clean-up," Bannister declared. "Now I'm going to tell you something. No more secrets. Le Beck was with the men who robbed the bank. And he and Hayes were with the two Canadians I had trouble with just before the storm. I think Hayes was mixed up in it, too. Then the man who stole my horse in the badlands was there. That connects the bank robbery with the rustlers, I believe. And I think Hayes is engineering the cattle thefts. His pal, Link, came back to his old job. I asked Miss Marble to give it to him so we could watch him, for I believe he is the one who helps sneak the cattle out of the Half Diamond herds from the inside. If that bunch hears I'm in jail, they'll get busy. But I'll get out of jail and they won't know it. That'll be between you and me. Later you can say I escaped, or something like that, if you want to. I don't think it'll be necessary. And after Cromer and Wills have been unsuccessful in getting me out of here, and Hayes and the others think I'm here, I'll be down there in the river breaks with a friend of mine who blew into Marble for the celebration, watching. And I'd bet my last white chip that I'll get 'em all."

The sheriff's interest had become more and more apparent as Bannister talked. Now he asked questions, and they began to plan on an elaborate scale. It was long after midnight, in the wee hours of the morning, when Sheriff Campbell locked Bannister in a cell and went home with a look of satisfaction on his face.

Sheriff John Wills and Cromer arrived in Prairie City on the stage at noon. They proceeded directly to Sheriff Campbell's office. Campbell was there, expecting them.

"Hallo," he said heartily, rising from his chair. "How are you, Wills? Cromer, I believe you had the right hunch about that fellow Bannister."

"I knew I did," said Cromer, his eyes light-

338

ing. "He's a gunman and an outlaw. I knew it from the first. Sheriff Wills knows it, too, and he's up here to get him."

"That won't be necessary," said Campbell, smiling. "I've already got him."

Sheriff Wills appeared to sigh with relief. "That saves me a lot of trouble," he said. "You got him locked up?"

"Sure have," said Campbell. "Hard an' fast, with the turnkey watching him like a hawk. Got three charges against him . . . shooting that fellow from the Half Diamond named Link, taking part in the bank robbery, and general suspicion."

"I suppose you know who he is," drawled Wills.

"Calls himself Bannister," said Campbell, "but that probably isn't his right name. I don't care what his right name is. I reckon I've got the goods on him just the same."

"His name may be Bannister," said Wills with a scowl, "but he is called The Maverick. I suppose you've heard of that outlaw."

"Yes, I have," said Campbell smoothly, "and I'm suspicious of this fellow as being that same party."

"Well, he is," said Wills sharply. "I've been after him a long time. I want him bad an' I'm much obliged to you for getting him. I'll be taking him down to Big Falls this afternoon."

"Well, now" — Campbell frowned — "you can't very well do that. I have charges against him up here, as Cromer knows. When we're through with him, you can have him, I suppose."

"Oh, I waive my charges," said Cromer quickly. "Wills can have him. And I know Link won't bother about that shooting, so. . . ."

"How do you know?" Campbell interrupted sharply.

"Well . . . *er* . . . it doesn't stand to reason that . . . *er* . . . Link would prefer charges when he knows who this man is and what he's wanted for," Cromer stuttered.

"You mean to tell me you'd interfere with my office?" Campbell demanded harshly. "After you whined and begged me to arrest him the night of the robbery?"

"It'd be better to let Sheriff Wills have him," said Cromer. "He's got more serious charges against him, anyway."

"That's right, Campbell," said Wills. "You can see that, I'm sure."

"Well, I don't see it," said Campbell, scowling. "I don't see any such thing. I've got charges against him an' that's enough for me. I'm the sheriff of this county, Wills, an' here he stays."

"Can I take a look at him?" asked Wills, who was becoming angry.

"Sure," said Campbell. "C'mon." He led them inside the jail proper to Bannister's cell.

"That's him!" cried Wills in great excitemcnt. "How are you, Maverick?"

Bannister swore. But instead of looking at Wills, he glared at Cromer.

"Do you know this man?" Campbell asked him sternly, pointing to Wills.

"No," Bannister growled. "But I know the white-livered, stinking rat that's with him."

Cromer laughed, a mean, sneering laugh. "They've got you where you belong," he said, mouthing his words. He turned to Wills. "The fool told me he might take my irrigation project away from me," he jeered. "He thinks he can steal anything . . . even land and water. Next he'll be wanting to steal the sky."

When they were again in the office, Wills spoke sternly.

"Sheriff Campbell, I demand the custody of The Maverick. I have a prior right to him. You'll be entitled to the rewards, of course, and I'll see you get 'em. I want to take him back this afternoon."

"Maverick or no Maverick, he's my prisoner and here he stays!" thundered Camp-

341

bell, bringing his fist down on his desk with a terrific blow.

"I'll go to the governor!" shouted Wills.

"Go to the governor an' be damned!" Campbell retorted hotly. "An' tell him, if he sends you up here for that prisoner, he'll have to send the whole state militia with you!"

"We'll see," said Wills, his face dark with anger. He shook a forefinger at Campbell. "We'll see," he repeated. "You're not running this state."

"But I'm running this county!" cried Campbell. "An' you or no other sheriff is coming in from the outside an' tell me what to do."

Wills spluttered and fumed and swore. He glared at Campbell, started to say something, swore again, and stamped furiously out of the office, with Cromer following.

Sheriff Campbell went in to see his prisoner and thrust a fat cigar through the bars.

Bannister was smiling and his eyes were sparkling. "Campbell," he said in his richest drawl, "it wouldn't be hard to take you on for a friend."

CHAPTER THIRTY-ONE

Bannister smoked and read in the cell during the afternoon, while Sheriff Campbell had a confidential talk with his deputies and the turnkey. The word was sent out that Bannister had been arrested and would be held for the grand jury, after which he would, of course, be tried. It was whispered, too, through the enterprise of Cromer, and because of Sheriff Wills's presence in town, that Bannister was indeed the notorious Maverick. The news created a tremendous sensation and was speedily carried to Marble by the stage drivers and travelers. Someone took the news to the Half Diamond outfit north of the Dome, and Manley rode posthaste to the house and told Florence Marble.

The girl received the news calmly, although she turned white, and informed Manley that she had been aware of Bannister's true identity for some time. She suggested that he go back to his cows and not bother himself in the matter.

"But, Miss Florence," he protested, "don't you know what they'll say? They'll say you hired him as a gunman, that's what they'll say. You mustn't admit that you knew it, don't you see? Did he tell you himself?"

"I don't care what they say," Florence retorted irritably, "and I'm not answering any questions. Maybe I know a thing or two that you don't. Just keep your hands and tongue off, Manley. Those are orders."

Manley rode back to the outfit puzzled, nettled, and grumbling to himself.

When she was alone, Florence dropped weakly into a chair. So it was all over. She felt like crying, screaming, or laughing. Her composure was so shaken that she couldn't keep still. She rose, and fell to pacing the room. It was incredible that they had taken Bannister without a fight. He was not the kind to give up tamely. There must be some kind of a trick to it, she decided. Meanwhile, the best thing to do was to obtain more detailed information.

She sent for Howard and quickly told him what had happened. "Go to Prairie City and see him," she ordered. "Don't do any talking to anybody, but keep your ears open. And ask Sheriff Campbell if he can't be released on bail. Tell Bannister I want to know . . . that I'm entitled to know all about it. And, Howard, don't you whisper a word of anything he says to you to a living soul."

"I guess I know enough for that," said the boy scornfully. "They've framed him, that's what they've done. He'll talk to me, you see if he don't. And it's up to us to get him out of there. This is Cromer's work, Florence, and don't you forget it."

Florence made no comment on this, for she was of the same opinion. Howard started for town just before dusk.

It was noted that Sheriff Wills spent the afternoon in the Prairie City office of the Marble Dome Land and Irrigation Company. This was considered significant as it had got about that Bannister had been one of the bank robbers at Marble. The town — both towns, for that matter — seethed with excitement. Then, just before the 6:00 P.M. stage started south, Wills again visited Sheriff Campbell. He had cooled down and realized that Campbell could hold Bannister if he so wished. Whether or not Wills could get Bannister away from Campbell would be a matter to be decided by the courts. He so informed Campbell, and the latter curtly informed him to go to it.

Shortly afterward, Wills left on the southbound stage, and Cromer drove out of town on the Marble road behind his fast grays. Wills was satisfied, for he expected to get Bannister in his custody in a few weeks, and Cromer was jubilant because Bannister was jailed. The sheriff would, of course, come to see him at Marble when he learned he had left town, and he would cement a case against Bannister to keep him jailed while Wills made his legal moves.

Such was the situation when Howard rode into town an hour and a half after nightfall, with Tommy Gale arriving a half hour later. Howard went directly to the jail after putting up his horse. Tommy went to the hotel for something to eat, and then sat in the little lobby, picking his teeth and waiting. He expected a message or a messenger. He was not to be disappointed.

When Bannister was told by Sheriff Campbell that Howard was there, he scowled and paced the cell in deep thought. Should he tell the youth? In all probability he would need Howard. He finally decided the thing to do was to have Howard get his horse, on the presumption that the boy was going to take it back to the ranch. He would be instructed to wait among the trees below town. It wouldn't be necessary to tell him how he would be gotten out of jail. And

Howard could be sworn to secrecy. Sheriff Campbell himself could see Tommy Gale and have him waiting near the place where Howard was to take the horse. Tommy had been faithfully described to the official, who couldn't fail to recognize him. Bannister could introduce Tommy to Howard and tell him just as much as was absolutely necessary. This seemed the best way. Campbell could hardly get into trouble if the whole scheme was revealed later, as he had Bannister's word to report to him and give up his gun when his work was finished. Bannister intended to keep his word, and Campbell knew it. And Campbell could fix it with the county attorney.

He announced his decision and outlined his plan to the sheriff, and Campbell readily agreed. Howard was shown in. The boy was excited, angry, puzzled — in an almost irresponsible frame of mind. But Bannister steadied him as he talked to him slowly, distinctly, and reassuringly. "There is just one thing," he finished. "You must not ask questions. You'll know everything later. And you mustn't breathe a word of this to anyone. Don't answer questions yourself. Just mutter and scowl and keep away from people and look worried. They'll understand and leave you alone. Now remember the time. Two in the morning. Those who see you going away with my horse, if anybody does see you, will think you're taking it back to the ranch, which is what the liveryman will think and tell people."

So Howard went away, gratified because Bannister was in some manner to get out of jail, and feeling important because he was playing an important part in the coup.

Shortly after Howard had left, Sheriff Campbell strolled over to the hotel, looking casually up and down the street and toward the livery barn. Then he entered the hotel lobby and he and Tommy recognized each other instantly. The sheriff signaled Tommy to follow him and went out the back way. Tommy joined him in the shadow of the rear wall of the building a minute or so later.

"You're Gale, are you not?" Campbell asked.

"The same," Tommy replied. "An' I know you."

"All right," Campbell grunted. "I've got some instructions for you. Listen hard and go quick. And you aren't to publish this anywhere." He told the cowpuncher what to do in short, terse sentences delivered in an undertone. A minute later Tommy was getting his horse.

By midnight the streets and resorts of

Prairie City were clearing. Stores and other places of business were closed, save for an all-night café. Small groups of roisterers broke up and dispersed. Echoing hoof beats died away on the night air as visitors from nearby ranches galloped homeward. By 1:00 every place in town was closed, except The Three Feathers. This resort never closed.

An hour passed and the street was silent, with not even a straggler abroad. The stars and moon shone brightly and a cooling breeze was stirring. Howard and Tommy Gale had some time since taking up their station. A dim light burned in the main office of the jail, but Sheriff Campbell's office was dark.

At 2:00 the turnkey looked out the jail entrance. A minute later the light went out and a swift-moving shadow merged with the deeper shadow along the wall of the building. The lamp glowed again in another minute and the turnkey reposed on an old hair sofa. The jail was empty save for his presence.

Bannister stole between darkened houses and shacks and reached the trees along the creek. He followed them to the east end of the town. A horse whinnied and a voice spoke cautiously. It was Howard with their mounts, and Bannister was soon in the saddle. At the point where the trees met the plain, they were joined by Tommy Gale. Then they put the spurs to their horses and rode at racing pace through the early hours of the morning until they reached the river at the southwest corner of the Half Diamond. They rode around the bend and then east on the south side of the river. They passed the main Dome trail leading to the river ford and entered the badlands at a point below it. The river was so low they could ford it anywhere. The only danger would be quicksand. Howard was now acting as guide. It was because he needed him for this purpose that Bannister had decided he would have to be in on the scheme. Soon they arrived near the little cabin below the leaning cottonwood, where Bannister had been left a prisoner and where Howard had found him next day.

Bannister himself reconnoitered and found the cabin empty. They dismounted. Bannister now introduced Tommy Gale to Howard as a friend of his from the south range who had come up for the celebration. "Don't mention the fact that he's here to anybody," he admonished the boy. "He's all right and he's helping us."

"That's enough for me," said Howard, offering his hand to Tommy. "But I've got to get back to the ranch and tell Florence something. Bet she's been up all night, waiting for me. She sent me up to find out all about it and, well . . . what'll I say?"

"Tell her the truth," said Bannister. "Tell her I'm out of jail and you don't know how I got out, which you don't. And tell her to keep still about it. If it gets out that I'm not in jail, all my plans will be spoiled. Understand?"

"Yes, I guess so," said Howard doubtfully. "But she's going to ask a powerful lot of questions."

"Tell her I said everything is all right," said Bannister impatiently. "And then slope back here with something to eat for the rest of the day. You've got to use your head, Howard. And I'm going to need you for a guide, most likely. You better start, for it's getting pretty light."

After Howard had left, Bannister and Tommy decided it would be best to stay in the timber lest somebody should come to the cabin. The rustlers had used it before and they might take a notion to use it again. Never for an instant did Bannister doubt but that the men who had attacked him and shot him that night in the breaks were rustlers.

They found a small, grassy knoll that afforded them a view of the meadow about the cabin by peering through the foliage, and there took up their station. Bannister told Tommy what had taken place in town and how he had come to give himself up and then get out of jail. And Tommy had praise for both the sheriff and old Jeb. For Jeb had taken care of him and no one had seen him.

In a few hours Howard was back with food and milk and they made a meal. All day they stayed on the knoll and until after nightfall. Then they made their way cautiously to the edge of the plain near the leaning cottonwood. For the first time, Bannister was assailed by misgivings. It was not at all certain, or even probable, that a rustling attempt would be made this night, or that a rider would appear to lead them to the rendezvous of the cattle thieves. It might be days before rustling activities were resumed. He had banked on the rustlers working fast when they heard he was jailed, because Hayes, if he were the ringleader, would be wanting to get out of the country after the bank robbery as soon as he could. Bannister was certain he had had a hand in that. Well, they could watch for a while and then they could begin a systematic search of the breaks with Howard as guide. There would hardly be any waylaying three of them the way he had been waylaid alone. But before midnight their vigil was rewarded — and from a quarter that they had least expected.

Hoof beats of many horses came from across the river. They drew back well within the shadow of the trees. Next came the splashing of the horses in the water as the riders crossed the river. When they came plunging out of the shadows on the main trail, Bannister gave a low whistle of surprise. He had seen the face of the leader in the clear light of the moon. It was John Macy. The cattlemen were riding north!

There must have been more than two score of riders in the cavalcade that swung off into the northeast. The pounding hoof beats became fainter and fainter — died away.

"It's the association outfit," said Bannister in excitement. "They're making for the project. Now something is up. They're circling around the cow camp north of the Dome to ride into the project from the east. I reckon we better drift up there and see what's doing."

The two others, realizing the seriousness of this new move, were eager to go. So they took the trail of the stockmen and rode out

353

under the star-filled sky. Because of the brightness of stars and moon it was not hard to follow the trail left by the riders ahead. It led them far east of the cattle range and then swung in the opposite direction for the project.

They rode faster, Bannister trying to think of any possible way he could prevent Macy and the men with him from doing violence. Were they going after Cromer? Did they intend to do him bodily harm? They came in sight of the first lone shacks of the project. There were no lights to be seen. Then, some distance ahead, there were shadows — horses and riders standing motionlessly. The trio stopped. Bannister was in a frenzy as to what to do. It was an angle to the business he hadn't had time to consider. He put the problem up to Tommy, but Tommy was likewise unable to solve it. Then suddenly there were flashes ahead, the riders were moving, the reports of guns broke upon the still night air.

Instinctively Bannister drove in his spurs and dashed ahead. His two companions followed. Before they had gone two rods there was a burst of fire — another and another. Then came a tremendous detonation and the earth rocked with the terrific force of the explosion. Dirt and small pieces of rock and cement rained down even that far out, and their horses shied and plunged and reared.

The swift realization of what had happened caused Bannister to rise in his stirrups, holding his horse with an iron hand — speechless. He finally found his tongue.

"They've blown up the dam!" he shouted hoarsely.

Then they streaked after the fleeing cattlemen, who were riding madly southward.

CHAPTER THIRTY-TWO

At the outset of the dash into the south it became apparent that, while the cattlemen did not wish to be seen on the way up to town, they had no intention of taking a roundabout course on the way back, but would depend upon speed to escape identification. They rode furiously and recklessly, and they were mounted on the best horses the various ranches they represented could boast.

Bannister realized that in following them to the project he had accomplished nothing, nor could he afford to be recognized. Already there were horsemen on their trail. Surely Cromer would have watchmen abroad. He thought of turning east toward the cow camp, but immediately rejected the plan. He couldn't afford to be seen there, either. Meanwhile they were racing southward some little distance behind the men who had blown up the dam.

The thought of that explosion struck a chill to Bannister's heart. He looked back and saw that for some distance east of the dam was the silver gleam of water. Undoubtedly the dam had been shattered. Now the water in the lake was rushing away across the plain. It would be necessary to build a new dam. And to build a new dam the water in the big ditch would have to be shut off — the head gates would have to be closed. This would send all the water in the river downstream. By blowing up the dam the cattlemen had succeeded in getting the water they wanted. And it would cripple the project, endanger its chance for success, detract from the value of the plots and the stock. Bannister ground his teeth as he thought of Florence Marble's investment.

And now a new factor entered into the nefarious business. The Half Diamond men had heard the explosion and the alarm had been spread. They came racing from the east in an effort to cut the cattlemen off. They had taken in the situation at a glance and knew that whatever had happened in the north was the work of these riders. Flashes of flame burst against the shadows of the trees along the creek and the reports of guns punctured the stillness of the night. The riders ahead answered the fire and spurred their horses. It became a race for the river.

Bannister saw that, while the cattlemen might make it, he and his two companions could not expect to do so, unless they shot their way through. He shouted and spurted off to the west, with Howard and Tommy following. To the left of them the battle raged and the race began to show a wide gap between the cattlemen and their pursuers. As the Half Diamond men were mounted on average cow ponies, they could not be expected to overtake the splendid horses the others rode. The trio behind kept toward the west and soon was riding through scattered cattle. In a short time they were out of sight of the two factions to eastward and eased their pace to save their horses. Of his next move, Bannister was not sure, except that he and Tommy couldn't be seen and would have to go to the cabin in the clearing below the leaning cottonwood. He changed their course now to due south and soon the sounds from eastward had died away.

They rode on at a fast pace until finally they came to the fields and pastures east of the house. Here they swept southeast, avoiding the fences, and came to the trees along the river. Bannister reined in his horse, and, as they halted, he spoke to Howard.

"You better go home," he advised. "And don't tell anyone there what has happened, or you'll have to explain how you knew about it so soon. The news will get there fast enough. Manley will send a man in or go himself. Come down to the cabin tomorrow."

"You want to watch out," said Howard. "They'll be down there from the project in no time. And there's liable to be some of our outfit hanging around. You better get some place where you can keep an eye out."

"We'll watch out, don't worry," said Bannister in a tone of aggravation. "But you want to get home as soon as you can, since this thing has happened. I reckon you savvy that."

"I'll be down tomorrow," said Howard as he rode off.

When he had gone, Bannister swore softly. "Tommy, that play of Macy's has knocked my plans into a cocked hat," he said with a note of bitterness in his voice. "That is, so far as getting Hayes and this bunch I believe is working on the cattle." He shook out his reins impatiently. "But we'll have to mosey along and keep dark. I've still got a trump card to play and then I'm through."

The way Bannister said this puzzled

Tommy. Somehow he could think of nothing to say. Nor did Bannister give him a chance for speech. They started east along the trees, riding until they came to the Dome trail to the river ford. Here they paused and listened. No one was in sight, but the air vibrated faintly. Horses were coming from some direction. They drew farther into the shadows of the trees. In a short time it was plain that the riders were approaching from the south.

The hoof beats became stronger and stronger, until finally the splashing of the horses crossing the ford could be heard. Then the riders swept past them. As they galloped out upon the plain, a rider in the rear of the cavalcade darted aside into the shadows across the trail. But in the moment of turning, the moon had shown a small figure that Bannister recognized. "Link," he whispered tremulously. "Now what . . . ?"

The other horsemen, members of the Half Diamond outfit undoubtedly, since Link had been with them, disappeared on the plain below the Dome. Tommy also had seen the rider slip into the trees and had caught the name Bannister had whispered. As Bannister had previously told him everything, he knew who Link was and all about him. He was about to whisper to Bannister, when Link rode out of the shadow and back along the trail to the ford. They listened for the splash of water at the ford but no such sound came. They kept listening for what seemed an eternity and then Bannister spoke in a low tone.

"Listen, Tommy, we're in luck after all. That was Link . . . you remember what I told you about him, of course. He didn't cross at the ford, and that means, I believe, that he has taken the river trail east, the same trail near which I was attacked and shot. He is going to report this night's business to someone, perhaps Hayes. Now don't forget where your gun is hanging and we'll trail this ornery cuss to the hornets' nest."

They rode slowly along the trail to the ford, crossed it, and climbed the slight rise to the river trail about halfway. There, Bannister dismounted and examined the ground. Sure enough, there were fresh tracks of a horse. He signaled Tommy and they went on. When they reached the intersection of the trail Bannister had been on the night he was shot, they stopped again. Once more Bannister made his examination. The tracks led on eastward. They again pushed on.

It was the dark hour before dawn. They proceeded slowly, both keeping watch for any opening in the trees or any slope of the riverbank where Link might have taken another trail or gone into the stream. There was a faint, ghostly glimmer in the east when they came to a slope that led down to the water's edge. There also was a narrow trail on the left.

Bannister halted here, puzzled. The spot was somehow familiar. He looked down at the shallow waters of the river and then he had it. This was the place where Howard and he had turned west on the river trail that day when they had first gone into the badlands. He remembered Howard had said the trail below led back under the hanging banks. He dismounted and ascertained that the tracks of Link's horse led down this gentle slope.

"Now we're getting close," he said to Tommy in an undertone. "There's a trail down there leading in under the banks. That's where Link has gone. If I'm not mistaken, and if there aren't too many of them, we're going to have action soon."

"Suits me," grunted Tommy, "an' about time. I'm plumb fed up on monotony."

They went down the slope and found the trail, as Bannister had expected, led downstream under the banks. Many horses had passed this way and here and there a cow

362

track could be seen along the edges of the trail. It was rapidly growing light. Ahead was a projection of rocks and earth, like an elbow thrust into the stream. When they rounded this, they pulled up their horses in surprise.

To the left was a large open space walled in by high cutbanks. Some cattle were grazing there, and a few horses — they counted only seven. And in the foreground was a shack. Smoke trailed from the stovepipe above the roof. At the lower side of this cup in the riverbank there was a narrow strip of ground leading downstream. The two men surmised this was another entrance to the rendezvous, if it should prove to be such. They were not kept long in doubt.

Men rushed out through the door of the cabin. Hardly knowing they did so, Bannister and Tommy counted five. Then the guns began to bark. Bannister drove in his steel, and, as his horse leaped to the spur, the long, blue barrel of his six-shooter flashed in the cold light of the dawn.

"Let's take 'em!" he yelled as his gun roared.

A man went down. Tommy was riding well to the left and his gun was popping. Another man stumbled and fell on his face. A bullet ripped leather from his saddle horn, and then they were behind the cabin, with only three antagonists left. The red light of battle flashed from Bannister's eyes. Tommy's lips were drawn back against his teeth as he reloaded his gun, Bannister following his example.

"C'mon, let's go around!" cried Tommy, and he started.

Bannister chose the opposite corner and they dashed to the front where the door was. Two shots greeted them. Tommy's gun roared its answer and the man who had fired at him staggered back, dropped his weapon, and fell in a sitting position. But Tommy slumped in the saddle, and then slid to the ground as the cabin door slammed shut.

"We've got 'em in a rattrap!" he called, his face white.

Bannister was at his side in a few moments. "Where you hit, Tommy?" He saw the little cowpuncher's left arm hanging loosely and Tommy's gun barrel came up to his left collar bone. "Just a shock," he said. "All right in a minute."

Bannister caught sight of a short log lying on the ground. He picked it up and drove it as a battering ram against the door of the cabin. The door shook with the impact. Again he smashed the log against the door at the edge where the bolt should be. Something cracked. With the next blow the door broke loose and was hurled open, its fastenings splintered.

Bannister's gun spoke before he could see inside. There was no answering shot. All was still in the cabin. Then he saw an open window at the right side. At the same moment there came a cry from Tommy and the little cowpuncher's six-shooter barked sharply. Bannister whirled. Dashing past them at some distance, headed straight for the river, was a small figure on a big horse. Bullets were streaking from the rider's gun, whistling past Bannister's head. Bannister leaped aside as he recognized this enemy. It was Le Beck. He had left the cabin through the window. He was riding bareback. With one shot left in his gun, he deliberately turned the weapon on Bannister's horse and fired. The animal leaped in the air, stumbled to its knees, and stayed there.

Next Le Beck was splashing across the shallow river, while Bannister ran foolishly after him with an empty gun, cursing horribly.

A shot came from the cabin doorway at this moment. It tore through the handkerchief about Bannister's neck on the left side. As he whirled, Tommy's gun split the echoes and a big figure sank in a heap in the doorway. Bannister recognized Hayes's form even before he saw his face. And a terrible face it was — contorted by pain and fear.

"He got me in the stomach," Hayes croaked. "If it had been any place but there. . . ."

"I reckon you deserve it," Bannister snapped, as he dragged the big man inside, with Tommy following. With almost super-human strength he lifted Hayes and put him on a bunk. Then he hurried out.

The stricken horse was lying on its side, its head on the ground. Bannister knelt and took the head in his arms, muttering: "Good bye, old-timer." Then he put a handkerchief over the glassy eyes. He ran to the cabin. "You'll have to stay here, Tommy," he said quickly. "I'll send help down from the outfit. I'm going after Le Beck. He shot my horse, thinking he could slow me up on the trail, but he didn't know how fast yours is. I'm off."

He hurried to Tommy's mount, length-ened the stirrups, and swung into the saddle. Then he galloped upstream toward the river trail.

CHAPTER THIRTY-THREE

Marble was in a turmoil. Scores of rumors were rife, but gradually the word got around that the wrecking of the dam had been the work of the cattlemen along Indian River in the south. The office of the company was jammed and the street outside crowded with settlers who had already taken up their residence upon their plots. They were in a frenzy. They had been lied to and cheated. Where was the water now that had been promised? They demanded to know what the company proposed to do and the company representatives could not answer. The crazed land buyers became almost hysterical and were on the verge of riot.

Cromer sat in his office, his face white and his eyes cold and hard. Something had to be done; a move had to be made and at once. The settlers must be quieted. Already he had withdrawn most of the men from their labors about the project and brought them into town as guards to try to preserve order. The riders who had taken after the cattlemen — Cromer knew in his heart who had done this thing — had returned. The fleeing horsemen had made fools of them, outdistanced them, and left them behind in half an hour or less. And the worst of it was that not a single one of the men who had engineered or taken part in this stroke against the project had been killed or captured. None had been recognized. What was he to prove?

He had sent a messenger to Prairie City with word of the disaster for Sheriff Campbell. Little good that would do, he thought bitterly. Was his bubble about to burst? His eyes blazed and he brought his fist down on his desk with a blow that hurt. It couldn't be. It wouldn't be! He flung open the door of his private office and confronted the raging crowd, holding up a hand. A great shout arose. The throng pressed against the front counter till it gave way and was thrust backward against the wall. Clerks climbed upon it to avoid being crushed. And Cromer mounted it himself, waving his arms for silence. Gradually the shouts and cries subsided.

"There is no reason for this," he said in a harsh, ringing voice. "The damage to our property this morning was due to the jealousy of a group of disgruntled stockmen south of here who are opposed to farming. They don't want the land to bloom. They don't want the soil to grow wheat and oats and alfalfa and other crops that will mean prosperity for the farmers. They have in mind only their own selfish interests. But they are only a few, with their cows, which are feeding on government land that is open to homestead entry. They are too narrow to see that the lands they do own are far more valuable for farming purposes. We expected this opposition, but we did not expect they would resort to violence. We are a big company. We have practically unlimited resources. Every buyer of a plot of land in our project will be protected!"

He paused and wiped his forehead with a white handkerchief as a feeble cheer swelled to a roar of approval. He was winning them over. Satisfaction and confidence glowed in his face. He swept a hand before him and smiled at the throng that again was ready to listen.

"Go home, my good people," he said. "It is not your part to worry. Let the company do the worrying. Now that we see what attitude these blackguards in the south have taken, we know how to deal with them. We

369

have the law and the state behind us, and
you have the law and state behind you. The
damage to the works will be speedily repaired. Only a small section in the middle
of the dam was blown out by those raiders.
It will be repaired as soon as all the water is
out of the dam. And the men who perpe-
trated this vile deed will be punished.
Remember, you are pioneers . . . all of you.
Pioneers have always had to withstand hardships. But this will not be a hardship for
you. Again I say, do not worry . . . for the
company is responsible. We are depending
upon you, and the others to come, to make
this a garden spot in the West. Every resource at our disposal is at your command.
In the name of the Marble Dome Land and
Irrigation Company, its officers, directors,
and stockholders, I pledge and promise and
give my own personal word that you will be
protected."

Cheers that shook the little building followed this life's effort on the part of Sydney
Cromer. The crowd fought its way out of
the office into the street. The word was
passed from mouth to mouth; Cromer's
remarks were exaggerated; the hysteria of
fear changed to one of joyous excitement —
the crisis passed.

"That was a great speech, chief," said the

clerk in admiration as Cromer jumped
down from the counter at the door to his
private office.

"Put that counter back where it belongs
and see that everyone wears a smile today,"
snapped Cromer viciously as he shut his
door. He knew he had lied to the settlers.

As he started for his desk, he stopped suddenly, his eyes narrowing. Le Beck was
standing near the rear door. As the gunman
started to speak, Cromer's hot words fairly
struck him in the face.

"Where were you?" Cromer demanded.

"Where was I?" Le Beck's face darkened
with anger. "Don't get cultus with me! D'ye
hear?" The small, beady, black eyes flashed
evilly. "I wasn't supposed to guard the dam.
I was down to see Hayes. What do you care
where I was anyway? You're not so smart
yourself. You thought that Bannister was still
in jail, didn't you? I guess you think he's
there yet. Well, if you want to know, I'd be
willing to bet he's on his way to Marble this
very minute."

"What're you talking about?" shouted
Cromer.

"Oh, you're interested," sneered Le Beck.
"Well, listen. Bannister isn't in jail any more
than you are, or any more than I am. If I
know anything about his type of critter at

all, he's on his way here on a slow horse right this instant. He an' some other of his stamp raided the place in the river breaks this mornin' . . . d'ye hear? Shot down three of the gang. Pretty near got me. Link was over at the spring an' sneaked away. I shot Bannister's horse to slow him up on the trail. I 'spect they got Hayes. I had to leave him behind. They'll see the worked brand in the few cattle that are in there an' put two an' two together, an'. . . ."

"Shut up!" Cromer roared. "You say Bannister is out and on his way here? Then, get him! Get him, do you hear? Get him and I'll lay ten thousand cold in your lap!"

Le Beck's eyes gleamed. "How do I know that?" he asked.

"Because I tell you so," flared Cromer. "Don't you think it'll be worth it to me to have that meddler knocked out of the picture? You'll have to take my word for it, but if you know anything at all about men, you can see I mean every word I say."

"All right," said Le Beck. "I'll get him. An' if you don't come through, I'll get you, too." He started for the door.

"By the way," said Cromer, "if that fool Link should show up in town . . . which he's liable to do . . . tell him I want to see him. I want to find out where the protection was that I'm paying for and why they didn't stop that raid. Great snakes. Is everybody in this country a double-crosser? Go ahead. Your work's cut out for you."

As Le Beck slipped out the door, Cromer stood motionlessly. Did Le Beck know for sure that Bannister was The Maverick? If he did, he would take no chances. He wouldn't wait for a face to face draw. He'd shoot on sight. Well, they could claim that Bannister was one of the raiders. People would believe anything about him now. And wasn't he an escaped prisoner? There was a hint of a smile on his face as he thought of the possible effect upon Florence Marble.

When Manley brought the news of what had happened on the project in the early hours of the morning, Florence had dropped limply into a chair. She stared with drawn features at Manley. She could not shake off the feeling that she was in some way responsible. If she had sided with the association, would Cromer have dared to keep the head gates open? She felt in her heart that, if she had yielded a point, she could have prevented this thing that had struck at the heart of the project and jeopardized her investment. To her, Cromer now became a monster for having lured her into the thing. She was a fool. Nothing else. She might have known she couldn't run this great ranch and attend to her finances without the expert advice of some honest and experienced banker. Yet she hadn't made any attempt to secure such advice. She made up her mind suddenly.

"Call Howard and get the horses ready," she said crisply to Manley. "We're going up to Marble."

She didn't know what she could do, but she intended to see Cromer and find out if there wasn't some way to put an end to the trouble.

Bannister had followed the river trail at as fast a pace as the trail would permit. The horse he was riding was a good horse, but it could not compare with his own mount, lying dead back there in the rendezvous from Le Beck's bullet. His face was the color of ashes, his lips pressed tightly into a thin, white line, his eyes narrowed and burning with a light that would have struck fear to the heart of any gunman who looked into them. In every slightest movement, in the steel-blue fire of his darting gaze, in the nervous twitching of the fingers of that deadly right hand, here was the super gunfighter — the killer.

Bannister knew as well as if Le Beck had shouted the information back at him that the man was headed for Marble. He wouldn't leave until he had told Cromer what had happened and had bulldozed a bunch of money out of him. Le Beck was not one to get nothing out of a deal like this. It was not his fault that he hadn't killed Bannister. The moves had been made too swiftly, and Le Beck was a ground fighter, not much good on a horse as at the last when he had had his best chance. If Bannister could only catch up with him, or see him in town, he would have his chance.

When he came out of the Dome trail to the plain, Bannister urged his horse to its best pace. This was better than Le Beck might have suspected. But Le Beck had a start and he had a faster horse. And Bannister had to stop at the cow camp. When he reached the camp, he found only the cook there; the men were out with the herd and Manley had gone in to the house. Bannister had to ride out and find one of the men who would convey his message to the others, so they could go to the rendezvous in the river breaks and bring back the dead and wounded. It took him a little time to attend to this, and then he again was streaking across the plain in the direction of

Marble. He saw three riders to the west of him but he paid no attention to them. Le Beck would be riding alone.

He rode into town less than an hour after Le Beck's arrival. He tied his horse behind a building midway the length of the short street. Then he hurried to the bank, where he strode past the cage and opened the door of the private office unceremoniously. There was no one there. He walked back to the astonished cashier.

"Where's Cromer?" he demanded.

"I . . . I don't know," faltered the cashier, frightened by the look in Bannister's eyes. "I. . . ."

Bannister's gun came up as if by magic. It was leveled at the cashier's heart. "Where's Cromer?" The words cracked like pistol shots in the cashier's ears. "In . . . his office at the company," came the faint reply.

Bannister hurried out and across to the company office. The crowds were dispersing, discussing Cromer's speech. He stamped through the outer office and opened the door in the rear. Cromer leaped from his desk as Bannister entered, his face going white. The fire of Bannister's passion seemed to burn in the very air of the room. Cromer cowered before him. Here, as he knew, was — not the man Bannister he had known, but The Maverick.

"Is Le Beck back in town?" asked his visitor.

Cromer licked his dry lips with a dry tongue. He tried to speak but his vocal organs would not obey his will. Now came the gun. Steady at The Maverick's hip as if it had been held in a vice. The sweat broke out on Cromer's forehead as he realized he was looking straight in the face of death.

"Is Le Beck in town?"

There it was again — the question he must answer. He could not lie; he knew it. But he couldn't talk. Terror gripped him until he shook like a leaf in its grasp. He nodded his head — nodded and nodded. As his visitor strode out, he sank into his chair.

Florence, Howard, and Manley were riding up the street. Suddenly there was a commotion. A group in front of a building were hurled aside and Bannister was in the street ahead of them. They checked their horses in wonder. Florence felt a chill grip her heart as she caught a fleeting glimpse of Bannister's eyes and face. It was a different man, one who she didn't know. This wasn't Bannister, she realized with a sinking feeling of horror and awe. The man out there was The Maverick. Now words, biting cold and clear, broke upon the silence that had fallen over the crowd.

"Le Beck . . . come here!"

For the first time, Florence saw the small, spider-like figure of the gunman in the street at the edge of the crowd. He was leaning forward, his right hand poised for the swoop to his gun. He took a step — another.

"Take one more step and go for your gun," came the words of The Maverick. "If you don't, I'll kill you where you stand."

Le Beck didn't step — he leaped. The air was split by the sharp report of a six-shooter. He staggered back two steps; his gun was in his hand. The Maverick had permitted him to start his draw first. And now The Maverick stood, a curl of smoke above his hip. For a space that seemed an eternity, Le Beck wavered, trying to raise his weapon, then he plunged forward on his face in the dust.

Another moment and Bannister had started for the building behind which he had left his horse. Two shots rang out behind him. He whirled as his left arm whipped backward, pierced by a bullet.

"You, too?" he called.

Then he literally ran into the face of a stream of bullets from Link's gun. The man, seeing he had missed a vital mark, shot at random, shaken, terrorized. Bannister's gun spoke once. There were two crumpled forms in the street as he ran for his horse.

Manley was just able to catch Florence Marble before she could fall from her saddle.

CHAPTER THIRTY-FOUR

The scene following the shootings was one of riotous confusion. People milled about the street, leaving an open space about the bodies of the two dead men. Cromer, when he appeared on the scene with men to take charge, was nearly mobbed. He had difficulty in fighting his way out of the crowd, and finally reached the company office surrounded by his own men, his clothing disarranged and torn, a frightened look in his eyes.

Howard and Manley got Florence Marble to the hotel, where she lay down in a room upstairs. She no longer wanted to see Cromer. She begged them to leave her alone. It wasn't so much the shock of the gun play she had witnessed as it was the look on Bannister's face as she had seen it before his gun spat its message of death. The Maverick! He would never be anything else! She sobbed quietly when she was alone in the room.

Meanwhile Sheriff Campbell had ridden into town with Deputy Van Note and another officer. He learned at once what had happened and went to Cromer's office. He found the irrigation head slumped in the chair behind his desk, pale, dishevcled, frightened.

"So you sent Le Beck after Bannister, eh?" said Campbell, jumping at once to the right conclusion.

Cromer's eyes opened wide and Campbell saw he was right in his conjecture. Then Cromer straightened in his chair and spoke harshly. "I told you this Bannister was The Maverick, and Sheriff Wills told you the same thing. But you were too bull-headed to believe it. You acted like you wanted to make a pet out of him, or something." A sneer came to Cromer's lips. "Now you can see for yourself. This is what you get for letting him out of jail. Oh, don't tell me he escaped or anything like that. I can see two and two before my eyes. He came here and broke loosc this morning, just as I knew he would do, sooner or later. And now two men are dead and he's gone. He's gone, you understand? Try and catch him. He's made fools out of better sheriffs than you could ever hope to be."

"Maybe so," said Campbell with a trace of anger. "But so far as I'm concerned in this you keep your mouth shut. I let him out of jail and make no bones about it. You'll find out soon enough why I let him out. I don't have to try and catch him. He'll walk into my office sooner or later and lay down his gun. You can sneer . . . go ahead. But you can lay to it that I'm telling you straight. As for the men he killed, if ever a pair needed killing bad, it was those two."

"Stick up for him," Cromer jeered. "Maybe the state authorities will have something to say about it."

"Maybe they will." Campbell nodded. "Now tell me what you know about this explosion at the dam."

"Lot of good it'll do," snarled Cromer. "Macy and his crowd down there have had a couple of men working with our bunch, as I see it. They had most of the dynamite planted, that's what. Then they came up here after midnight and held off our men while they attached the fuses and caps, or I suppose that was it. Maybe they brought more dynamite with them. After the explosion they rode south, back to their ranches. That's all. What you going to do about it?"

"I'm going to send for Macy," said Campbell. "And I've heard a heap about this business, Cromer. You've acted like a plain damn' fool. You should have played the game straight with those stockmen instead of trying to ride them. You don't seem to understand the old-timers in this country. They're all men from the soles of their boots to the crowns of their hats. And they're all square."

"Oh, you'll all stick together," said Cromer with a wave of his hand. "I expected that. But we'll put up a fight."

Campbell turned away with a look of disgust on his face and went out to superintend the task of getting the crowds in hand.

The killings had undone what Cromer had accomplished by his inspired speech. The land buyers were again assailed by doubts. This was too wild a country for the mild occupation of farming. The dam had been blown up. If the stockmen didn't hesitate to do a thing like that, what would they hesitate at? And now a notorious gunman and killer had come into their midst and shot down two men before their very eyes. What would be next?

It was a long time before they became quieted and then the calmness that descended upon them seemed ominous in itself. They gathered in little groups and talked in low tones. Then they went out and gathered at each other's shacks and the conferences continued.

In the afternoon John Macy arrived. He sought out Sheriff Campbell, and, at Campbell's suggestion, the two of them went at once to Cromer's office. Cromer received them calmly.

"I wanted you to hear this conversation, Cromer," Campbell began.

"That's all it'll amount to," Cromer snapped out.

"Then all the more reason why you should hear it," said Campbell sharply. He turned to Macy, who had taken a chair and was lighting a long, black cigar. "Macy, who blew up that dam?"

"Representatives of the Cattlemen's Association blew up that dam to protect its members for water for their stock and fields," replied Macy calmly.

Cromer started up in his chair. "You hear!" he cried to Campbell. "You hear? He acknowledges it . . . he confesses. Now you've got to do your duty. It's up to you to. . . ."

"Shut up!" Campbell interrupted angrily. "If you don't keep a check rein on your mouth, Cromer, I'll gag you. Now, Macy, who were these men?"

"We're not telling that," said Macy, flicking the ashes from his cigar. "No individual is responsible. The association is taking the responsibility upon itself. If you want to make charges against anyone, you will have to prefer charges against the entire membership of our organization. And then you'll have to prove them." There was a glitter of triumph in John Macy's eyes.

Sheriff Campbell saw through the play and turned away from Cromer so the man could not see the smile upon his lips. Then Macy spoke again.

"You an' I are old-timers in this country, Gus Campbell, an' you understand," he said in a stern voice. "We have always been men of our word in this country. We have never been forced to call upon the law to make a man keep a promise. We've never had to ask the law to punish a man for not keeping a promise. Cromer gave us his word that he would let us have our water. He broke it. We busted his dam. Now we're ready to compromise and to make certain reparations. This is all I have to say about the matter an' all I will say. It's up to Cromer to say if he wants peace or war."

Cromer's face darkened. He looked at Campbell, who, in turn, was looking at him, his brows elevated. Slowly the sneer that came to Cromer's lips died and the lines of his face set. "I see through it," he said. "If you're going to keep your hands off, Campbell, and let this thing go on, then we'll fight them with their own weapons. So far as we're concerned, it's war."

"I'll give you twenty-four hours to think that over," said Campbell. Then he and John Macy went out.

The wounded men, Tommy Gale and Hayes, had been brought to the hospital. Hayes died on the operating table, but before he died he told Sheriff Campbell that there had been an understanding whereby the members of the Half Diamond outfit who had been hired by him were to prevent an attack by the southern cattlemen. This had been in line with Cromer's idea to keep Florence Marble allied with the interests of the irrigation company. He confessed that he had been the leader of the rustling band, and, when he learned that both Le Beck and Link had been killed by Bannister, he told Campbell they had all been connected with the bank robbery, together with the Canadians who had been killed in the rendezvous. The cup in the riverbank had been used as a place to change the brands of the cattle. Later they were driven eastward and up into Canada, where they were sold.

Tommy Gale had nothing to say. He refused to talk. His collar bone had been shattered by a bullet, but the doctor said he would recover. Sheriff Campbell did not press him for details.

That night all was quiet in Marble. Manley took Florence home, but Howard stayed to await developments and learn such news as he could. His faith in Bannister was not shaken, although Florence had said that she never wanted to see him again.

But, though the town was quiet enough, matters were coming to a crisis on the project. The land buyers had had several meetings in different shacks and had come to the conclusion that they had made a mistake. Their confidence in Cromer and the company was shaken. They were prepared to act.

Next day brought another scene of turmoil and confusion in the town of Marble. But, unlike the day before, it had a sinister aspect in its early quietness. Settlers began to draw their deposits from the bank. This went on in unostentatious fashion during the morning until the employees of the company learned of it. Then began a run on the bank. All who had made deposits, who were on the project, started to withdraw them. In vain Cromer tried to reassure them. And at 1:00 P.M. the bank closed its doors, refusing to pay out more.

This brought the climax. Scores of land buyers, hundreds of laborers, and people of the town thronged the street. Stones were hurled through the windows of the company office and the bank. Sheriff Campbell, gun in hand, with his deputies and such men as he could gather in the emergency, kept the crowd at bay before these places. Howard rode madly to the Dome camp and Manley came with almost the entire Half Diamond outfit to help in the efforts to preserve order.

Such was the state of affairs when Bannister rode into town behind a fast team in the late afternoon. Sitting beside him on the seat of the buckboard was a stranger. A great cry went up. The killer was back. The crowds broke up and fled as the pair drove down the street. Sheriff Campbell, sensing some dramatic and effectual move on the part of the man he trusted, made way for them to the hotel. As they went in, the crowd massed in the street.

After a few moments Bannister, Sheriff Campbell, and the stranger appeared upon the single balcony above the hotel entrance. The talking below ceased and the crowd became still. There was something magnetic about Bannister's manner, something electrical in the flashing gaze he turned on the throng that filled the street. Even Cromer, on the outskirts of the crowd, was impressed; also, he was beset with misgivings.

Then Bannister began to speak in a clear, ringing voice. The mighty audience listened, hung on every word — more interested than they had been on the occasion of Cromer's oration of the day before.

"My friends," said Bannister, "you have heard me called The Maverick. You have heard me described as everything that was bad. I have no alibi and nothing to deny. It is not for myself that I speak but for you. This project has been mismanaged by a man who did not understand, and who now does not understand, the principles and temper of real Westerners. You have been led to believe by this man that the stockmen are your enemies. They are not. What has happened here was due to the fact that this manager failed to play square and keep his word with these stockmen who he would have you believe are against you."

As Bannister paused, the silence was so intense that a pin could have been heard if dropped in the street. Cromer's face had turned a sickly green.

"Now, people," Bannister continued, "you have come here to make your homes, many of you, and you have invested money. There are many others who live in this state who have invested in the stock of this company. I represent a prominent stockholder at the present moment. After I have finished, I will represent no one. I have something to say to you, and a man to introduce to you . . . and your worries and troubles will be over. This project is not merely a company affair or a state affair. There is a government in these United States."

As he paused a second time to let the force of his words sink in, Bannister looked tired and worn. The crowd noted this and strained their ears to catch what he might say next.

"You can think what you wish," he went on, slowly, "but I am your friend. From now on the Marble Dome Land and Irrigation Company project will be under the supervision of the federal government. Everyone who needs water will have it. The work will be completed under the direction of capable engineers, many of whom must be here now, and there will be no more trouble. Now I am through, and I introduce to you Frank Browning of the Department of the Interior, with headquarters at Helena, who is taking charge."

The stranger stepped forth. The crowd held its breath as it gazed at the strong face, the kindly eyes, the erect bearing of the representative of the government. Then suddenly, like a mighty explosion, the cheering broke forth. The very earth underneath seemed to shake with the roar of sound. Hats were thrown in the air and men threw their arms about each other. They cheered and cheered and cheered. Then they looked for Bannister. But Bannister had disappeared. He had played his trump card.

Chapter Thirty-Five

As Bannister left the balcony, he found Howard Marble in the hall. His look of pain, of resignation, of weariness after his long ride and train journey to get the government official and lay the facts before him, commingled with a gleam of triumph, caused the boy to hold his words.

Bannister took his hand. "Listen, Howard," he said in a low voice, "I want you to say good bye for me to Florence. Don't tell her what I'm about to say, whatever you do. But I am telling you, so you will understand, that anything I've done was done because I thought it was in her best interests. If I never see you again . . . so long."

He left the youth staring after him with respect in his eyes.

Sheriff Campbell remained in Marble the rest of the day and that night. He saw Browning take charge of the affairs of the company, which were in a chaotic state. It was this fact, as Bannister had explained and Browning had suspected, that made it possible for the government to step in. The land buyers were jubilant. Where there had been hisses and doubts, there were cheers and confidence. John Macy, speaking for the cattlemen, said they would co-operate under the new conditions. The investments of all were safeguarded.

On the afternoon of the second day, Sheriff Campbell sat in his office. Deputy Van Note had just returned from a hurried trip to the state capital and Campbell was musing over the news he had brought. He had had a visitor that day who was now in the hotel. Florence Marble had learned everything from Howard. She had sent Manley to Prairie City to learn more. Then she had come herself.

The sheriff chewed his unlighted cigar in contented satisfaction. He was awaiting another visitor. He did not know if he would come this day or the next or the next, but he expected him sooner or later. He was not kept in this anticipatory frame of mind long. Bannister entered the office and nodded to him.

The official nodded in turn.

"Nice day," drawled Bannister. "Want a

light for that piece of rope?"

The sheriff removed his cigar and examined it critically. "No," he said. "If I wanted it lit, I'd light it. You here on business or just dropped in for a personal call?"

"Both," said Bannister. He took his gun from its holster and placed it on the desk before the sheriff. "It isn't loaded," he said quietly.

Campbell called to Van Note. "Go get that party at the hotel," he ordered when the deputy came in.

"I'm glad I'm going to get an early start," said Bannister. "And before I go down there, I want to say to you, Campbell, that you're not so bad and I don't hold anything against you. Savvy?"

"If I thought you held anything against me, I'd crack you with your own gun," said Campbell with a heavy frown. "Here, take it, before I do it anyway." He pushed the weapon toward Bannister.

Bannister looked at the gun, and then at the sheriff with wide, puzzled eyes. "Are you crazy?" he asked.

"Sometimes I think I am," said Campbell whimsically. "I've been sheriff of this county a good many years . . . more than is good for me, I reckon. Yes, I suppose I'm crazy. Oh! Here we are."

Bannister followed his gaze to the door and started.

There was Florence Marble. She looked at him with a soft, glad light in her eyes — a glow of pride.

"Hello, Bob Bannister," she greeted.

But Bannister could only nod foolishly. What was this? What . . . ?

"Bannister" — it was the sheriff speaking — "I've gone into your record down south there and there's more in your favor than against you, as I've told Miss Marble. We haven't known you by the moniker they hung on you. We know you only as Bob Bannister. I sent Van Note to Helena to see the governor and I don't think it will be necessary for you to take a trip south. I'm releasing you in the custody of Miss Florence Marble. Now take your gun and get out of here . . . I've got business to attend to and can't be bothered."

For some time Bannister looked into Florence Marble's eyes. The world suddenly blossomed again with that wonderful light he had seen the morning of the storm. He turned to the sheriff and took his gun from the desk. Then he held out his hand.

"Sheriff," he said, in a tone meant to convey a fierce meaning, "you're an old fraud. I expected this very thing."

The room glowed with the sunshine of his smile.

Bannister and Florence rode back to the Half Diamond in the gathering shades of the twilight. They spoke seldom. Florence appeared shy, and Bannister, too, had little to say. He learned that Tommy Gale had been hired to work on the ranch. He found out that Howard — the young devil! — hadn't kept a thing to himself. The future appeared rosy both for farmers and stock-raisers.

Old Jeb took their horses, his grin extending from eat to ear. "I reckon we've got a new steady hand," he said boisterously as Bannister scowled at him fiercely.

Howard was there, too, to greet them. He winked outrageously and also received a scowl.

Then Bannister and Florence were alone on the porch of the ranch house. The dusk had fallen and the stars were out. A breeze murmured in the branches of the trees and willows.

"Florence, did you believe all the things you heard about me?" Bannister asked.

"Not once," was the low reply.

"I said it couldn't be," Bannister whispered as he took her in his arms. "But now. . . ." She stopped his speech with her lips and for a long time stood there. Then Martha, happy and flustered, called them to supper. They entered their home, hand in hand.

ACKNOWLEDGMENTS

"Marble Range" first appeared under the title "The Maverick of Marble Range" as a seven-part serial in Street and Smith's *Western Story Magazine* (12/10/27–1/21/28). Copyright © 1927, 1928 by Street & Smith Publications, Inc. Copyright © renewed 1955, 1956 by Street & Smith Publications, Inc. Acknowledgment is made to Condé Nast Publications, Inc., for their cooperation. Copyright © 2010 by Golden West Literary Agency for restored material.

ABOUT THE AUTHOR

Robert J. Horton was born in Coudersport, Pennsylvania in 1889. As a very young man he traveled extensively in the American West, working for newspapers. For several years he was sports editor for the *Great Falls Tribune* in Great Falls, Montana. He began writing Western fiction for *Munsey's All-Story Weekly* magazine before becoming a regular contributor to Street & Smith's *Western Story Magazine.* By the mid-1920s Horton was one of three authors to whom Street & Smith paid 5¢ a word — the other two being Frederick Faust, perhaps better known as Max Brand, and Robert Ormond Case. Many of Horton's serials for Street & Smith's *Western Story Magazine* were subsequently brought out as books by Chelsea House, Street & Smith's book publishing company. Although all of Horton's stories appeared under his byline in the magazine, for their book editions Chelsea House published them either as by Robert J. Horton or by James Roberts. Sometimes, as was the case with *Rovin' Redden* (Chelsea House, 1925) by James Roberts, a book would consist of three short novels that were editorially joined to form a "novel". Other times the stories were magazine serials published in book form, such as *Whispering Cañon* (Chelsea House, 1925) by James Roberts or *The Prairie Shrine* (Chelsea House, 1924) by Robert J. Horton. It may be obvious that Chelsea House, doing a number of books a year by the same author, thought it a prudent marketing strategy to give the author more than one name. Horton's Western stories are concerned most of all with character, and it is the characters that drive the plots rather than the other way around. Attended by his personal physician, he died of bronchial pneumonia in his Manhattan hotel room in 1934 at the relatively early age of forty-four. Several of his novels, after Street & Smith abandoned Chelsea House, were published only in British editions, and Robert J. Horton was not to appear at all in paperback books until quite recently.

The employees of Thorndike Press hope you have enjoyed this Large Print book. All our Thorndike, Wheeler, and Kennebec Large Print titles are designed for easy reading, and all our books are made to last. Other Thorndike Press Large Print books are available at your library, through selected bookstores, or directly from us.

For information about titles, please call:
(800) 223-1244

or visit our Web site at:
http://gale.cengage.com/thorndike

To share your comments, please write:
Publisher
Thorndike Press
10 Water St., Suite 310
Waterville, ME 04901